S0-BYZ-528

Absentminded?

It was more like this professor had mislaid his brain permanently, Stacy decided. She paced the hotel lobby, worriedly regretting her decision to let him go up to his room unaccompanied. If she hadn't taken that cab ride with him, who knew what kind of mishap the man might have wandered into?

How had he even found Belize, she wondered, let alone a supposedly priceless Mayan tomb? She had a grim foreboding that her social life in general was about to go down the tubes, since making this exhibit marketable was bound to be an overtime job.

There was no sign of the professor yet. Stacy strolled through the plush lobby, eyeing the Palm Court lounge from a distance. He was, after all, the classic out-of-towner—or maybe he was in a class by himself. All the way over here he'd been rubbernecking the city sights. At one point he'd leaned so far out the open cab window that she'd had to literally yank him back in as their oblivious cabbie took a corner at perilous speed.

When they'd arrived at the Plaza, he'd gotten so mesmerized by a horse and carriage parked in front that she'd actually had to take his arm and steer him toward the hotel entrance.

Professor Brody was one for the books, all right.

ABOUT THE AUTHOR

Leigh Anne Williams calls New York City
home. She lives in picturesque Greenwich
Village, and since she likes to write about
places that she knows well she chose New
York as the setting for this novel. In addition
to writing romances, Leigh Anne is a
lyricist and scriptwriter.

Books by Leigh Anne Williams

HARLEQUIN AMERICAN ROMANCE

*The Taylor House subseries

Don't miss any of our special offers. Write to us at the
following address for information on our newest releases.

Harlequin Reader Service
901 Fuhrmann Blvd., P.O. Box 1397, Buffalo, NY 14240
Canadian address: P.O. Box 603,
Fort Erie, Ont. L2A 5X3

Love Me
Like a Rock
Leigh Anne Williams

Harlequin Books

TORONTO • NEW YORK • LONDON
AMSTERDAM • PARIS • SYDNEY • HAMBURG
STOCKHOLM • ATHENS • TOKYO • MILAN

Published June 1989

First printing April 1989

ISBN 0-373-16300-2

Copyright © 1989 by Leigh Anne Williams. All rights reserved.
Except for use in any review, the reproduction or utilization
of this work in whole or in part in any form by any electronic,
mechanical or other means, now known or hereafter invented,
including xerography, photocopying and recording,
or in any information storage or retrieval system, is forbidden without
the permission of the publisher, Harlequin Enterprises Limited,
225 Duncan Mill Road, Don Mills, Ontario, Canada M3B 3K9.

All the characters in this book have no existence outside the
imagination of the author and have no relation whatsoever to
anyone bearing the same name or names. They are not even
distantly inspired by any individual known or unknown to the
author, and all incidents are pure invention.

® are Trademarks registered in the United States Patent and
Trademark Office and in other countries.

Printed in U.S.A.

Chapter One

"What *is* this?" Stacy peered at the slide, holding it up against the light. But no amount of squinting gave her any further clue as to what she was looking at.

Behind her, Russell flipped through the sheaf of Xerox papers. "What've you got?"

"Slide 73B."

"Ah." He rustled more papers. Stacy turned the sheet of transparencies upside down, her already sinking spirits descending another notch. The whole sheet was made up of photos very similar to this one.

"Let's see. Here we go." He cleared his throat. "Well, it's a ... rectangular hammer-dressed block with striations of lime mortar."

Stacy put the sheet down. "It's a rock."

"In a manner of speaking, yeah," said Russell. "What you got there is a dozen photographs of a rock."

"Another rock, Russell."

He nodded. "But a very *old* rock, Stacy."

Stacy gravely regarded her assistant for a moment. "I think you should cover your ears, Russell. I'm going to scream."

"No, you don't want to do that," he said.

"Yes, I do," she assured him. "And then I want to take this whole godforsaken box of worthless slides and heave them out the window, before or after I devise a means of killing Richard."

"Let me argue against all of these things," Russell said nervously. "First of all, the acoustics in this basement are really going to make a scream carry."

Stacy looked around the long, cavernous room they were in. It did indeed have very high ceilings, and as it was filled only with crates and boxes, sound would certainly reverberate. "That only makes the idea of screaming more attractive," she mused.

"Secondly, even though you may not like what you've been seeing on those slides..."

"Like?" Her voice rose an octave in incredulity. "I loathe every inane—"

"...the nearest window is a little high for a good heave," he continued calmly. "And besides, they don't belong to us."

"True," she said. "They belong to the second person I'd like to murder, after Richard: Professor Brody."

"Thirdly," Russell hurried on. "Killing your boss and mine, although it would certainly give me satisfaction, especially if you let me watch, will not solve the problem at hand."

"Oh, I don't know," she said, surveying the collection of crates around her. They probably contained ancient artifacts that looked about as interesting as the bit of limestone she'd just been studying. "If I'm in prison, I won't have to do the promotional campaign for this ... rock collection."

"Don't forget the jewels," Russell said hopefully.

"Yes, the jewels, thank God," Stacy said. "But I think what we're dealing with here is a ten to one ratio of rock to jewel. I'm going to get a migraine," she added. "I've never had one before in my life, but I guess this is about as good a time as any for the first. Wouldn't you say?"

"I'd say you need another cup of coffee," Russell said. "That's the ticket, right? Maybe with one of those nice whole wheat doughnuts they have at the staff caf. I'll go get you one. And then you'll feel like a happy unit again."

"'Staff caf,'" she echoed. "I'm going to be working in a place that has a staff caf. For an entire month. I'm never going to feel like a happy unit again."

"You just sit there," Russell said. "Try to relax. Let those creative juices flow. I'll be back with your caffeine fix in a minute."

Stacy stifled a sigh. "Thank you, Russell," she said, and watched him trundle off through the labyrinth of crates. The curly-haired, stocky young man was the only saving grace of her current predicament. At least if she had to mastermind a promotional campaign for a bunch of old rocks, she didn't have to do it entirely single-handed. At least Richard had let her take Russell out of the office.

Richard, Richard Powell. He was the *P* in P and W, one of the more successful advertising companies in Manhattan. Her firm. Once there had been a time when the very thought that she'd been lucky enough to land a job working for Richard Powell had filled her with exhilaration. Now, a scant two years later, she was filled with another sort of feeling. Richard was a tyrant—suave, charming and a genius at his work, but a tyrant, nonetheless.

And he was a Machiavellian manipulator. Once again, like the scene of an accident one can't help replaying in one's mind, despite the horror of the details, she remembered the meeting in Richard's office that had led to her being here, buried in the basement of the Museum of Natural History on a beautiful spring day, a day when her P and W co-workers were at least stuck in an air-conditioned skyscraper with nice views of the park.

When she arrived, Richard had been suspiciously cheery, always a bad sign. He had on his trademark cashmere cardigan and no shoes, leaning back in his Italian designer's leather chair, rubbing his already unkempt silver hair into further disarray as he motioned her to take a seat. "This is the big one," he said.

Stacy's heart had quickened. Maybe he was going to get her involved in the AT&T "Arts on TV" project, one of their major new accounts. Then she noticed the brochure from last year's film festival on his desk, and her pulse went into overdrive.

That prestigious New York institution had undergone a change in management, and word was out around the office that P and W had been approached to handle its publicity for the upcoming fall. P and W was a good choice, since the firm specialized in promoting the principal events of New York's cultural institutions. They'd done wonders with the image of the Metropolitan Museum last year, and were currently convincing jaded New Yorkers to take the First International Exposition of the Arts seriously.

And Stacy, as she'd let it be known in myriad subtle ways, was the best choice to handle the film festival. Movies had been her first love. She'd gotten a film school B.F.A., had started out as a film publicist and knew her cinema cold, from Antonioni to Zeffirelli. Promoting the festival was a dream gig, and for the duration of that moment in Richard's office she'd thought that the dream was about to come true.

Not quite. "What do you know about Mayan tombs?" Richard asked her.

"Nothing," she admitted, confused.

"Heard of Professor Ethan Brody?"

"No," she said.

Richard nodded, as if immensely satisfied with this response. "Even though the professor's discovery of a Mayan tomb was on the front page of the *New York Times* last fall," he said.

"Oh!" Stacy colored slightly, wondering why she was being given this test. "Yes, I remember reading something about that. It was a big deal, right? Intact skeleton or something."

"Intact everything," Richard said. "Some rare and precious jewelry, lots of important artifacts. Not King Tut, mind you, but a major find. Major enough to warrant an exhibition."

"Here?" she ventured, light dawning.

"Yes," he said. "But obviously the general public is going to need their minds refreshed. And their appetites whetted."

Stacy nodded and did her best to muster an enthusiastic attitude. "We're working with the Met again?"

"No. The Natural History Museum."

Stacy blinked. It was sounding grimmer by the minute. The Natural History Museum was not exactly Manhattan's hotbed of hip cultural activity. And there could only be one reason Richard was telling her about this.

"You need some help," she ventured, praying he'd already given the account to Jeanette or even Christopher, and only needed some extra brainstorming from her.

"I want you to do it," he said. "The whole campaign. From top to bottom."

Stacy tried not to sag in her seat. This was cruel and unusual punishment, and as far as she knew, totally unjustified. Hadn't she just done a fantastic job on the Met's new wing? Wasn't she on tap for that vice presidency at the end of the year, if slimy Christopher didn't weasel his way to it first? If anything, shouldn't he be inviting her to join the AT&T account's team? She couldn't keep a tiny bit of edge out of her voice. "Why me?"

Richard looked surprised. "The Met people loved you," he said mildly. "I think you've got a knack for handling the museum sensibility."

"I appreciate the compliment," she said carefully. "But it sounds like a . . . problematic promotion."

Richard shrugged. "Well," he said, and absently played with the film festival brochure, gazing into space for a moment. "I could ask Christopher."

This was quintessential Richard, and Stacy suddenly got the whole picture. The tyrant knew it was a bum assignment, but he also knew *she* knew she'd have to take it. Because he was dangling the festival in front of her like a diamond carrot, and he was blackmailing her with Christopher. Richard's implicit equation was, whoever makes good on the Mayan tomb gets the film festival account, and looks even better for the V.P. promotion.

So she'd taken it. And here she was, surrounded by artifacts, swathed in the museum's dead air and a little cloud of desperation. Her clipboard's pad was covered with useless notes. Because try as she might, she didn't have an idea in her head about how to sell a handful of jewelry, one mummy and countless mounds of shells, stones and potsherds to Mr. and Mrs. Big Apple.

Stacy got to her feet again, trying to shake off the imagined migraine and a real mounting panic. Feeling sorry for herself was both an unfamiliar and a foreign activity. She prided herself on being someone who could out-create anybody. Was she not the youngest female account executive at P and W? Was she not due for a healthy bonus in the upcoming salary period? Wasn't this supposed to be hard, the horrific Richard's last ordeal-by-fire test before he deigned to give her the position she truly deserved?

Thoughts of imminent coffee cheered her. Stacy took out her compact. The ritual of makeup check was always conducive to meditation. She peered into the little mirror at her slightly pouty, full red lips, her slightly hooded blue-gray eyes with their naturally long lashes. She wrinkled her straight and slender nose, then sucked in her cheeks a bit to bring out a hint of bone structure. Oh, to possess prominent cheekbones!

But no, she was stuck with a soft roundness in her cheeks that had once prompted Stanford to facetiously call her "Chipmunk." Chipmunk? She was better off without that man. Stacy ran a hand through her shoulder-length, straight light blond hair and bared her teeth in the semblance of a smile. No, not the happiest of faces, but not unhappy. Just a trifle . . . stressed, she decided.

Stacy squared her shoulders, straightening the left shoulder pad in the man-tailored black jacket she was wearing over a cream silk blouse. Fatigue came with the territory, she thought, but you never let them see you sweat. Wasn't that what they said in one of those dumb career-woman deodorant commercials? Well, it was true.

Stacy smoothed her slim black matching skirt. Here came Russell bearing coffee, doughnuts and, as it turned out, possible good news. Professor Brody, who had been missing from the action all morning, had been found.

"He's upstairs now talking to Caroline," Russell told her. Caroline Pratt was the curator of this upcoming exhibit, a corpulent and officious woman who had only been of minimal help since Stacy's arrival that morning. She hadn't been able to do much more than show Stacy around, point at various cartons and deliver the slides. Because the absent—and apparently absentminded—professor was the only one who knew where and what everything was.

Stacy gulped a welcome sip of coffee. "Is he coming down here?" she asked.

Russell nodded. "If he can find us," he said, then grinned at Stacy's questioning glance. "The reason he was late? The poor sap got on the wrong bus and nearly ended up on 125th Street.''

"Oh, great.'' She tried the doughnut. Not bad for staff caf food. "What've we got here? Four-inch-thick glasses and a beard down to his knees?''

"No beard,'' Russell said. "But he is a little...'' He put up his palms, at a loss for the proper word.

"Out of it?'' she suggested. "I wouldn't be surprised. Hasn't he been digging his way through the jungles of Central America for about eight or nine years? Well, let's just hope he can help us organize this chaos.''

She had yet to meet the infamous Ethan Brody. What she'd heard of him from Tony, Richard's right hand at P and W, wasn't encouraging. The man was rumored to be publicity-shy and suffering from a bad case of culture shock. He'd never been to New York City in his life, having been raised by archaeologist parents at various sites all over the less-than-civilized world, and schooled in obscure universities in Mexico and the Southwest. He was such a rube that, as Tony had crowed, the first thing he'd done after checking into his hotel the day before was to visit the top of the Empire State Building.

As soon-to-be collaborators went, this man didn't exactly possess the optimum character profile. She needed a great deal of input from Professor Brody. She could only hope that, being an academic, he'd be reasonably intelligent about the organization of this massive project.

But she doubted she'd be able to call upon him for any creative ideas. The main challenge with promoting Brody's show was in finding an angle that read Entertainment, not Dry-as-dust Academia. A man who, as Tony reported, had eluded reporters upon his initial arrival from Belize last fall and rushed off to Kalamazoo for a symposium on ancient burial mounds before retreating to the jungle again, was not likely to be savvy about what would appeal to a general audience.

"Well, I might as well go meet the man responsible for this," she said. "I don't suppose we could convince him to take his rock collection to L.A. instead?"

"Look at it as the challenge of your PR career," Russell said.

"Or the end of it," she said dryly. "Now, where did I put that—? Damn!" She'd been looking for her notepad and in reaching for it, upended her coffee cup. Enough hot coffee splashed onto the sleeve of her jacket to instantly create a dry-cleaning problem.

"Not my day," she muttered, waving off Russell's proffered napkin. The cream silk blouse she was wearing was clingy and sheer, and wasn't intended to be worn without the jacket's discreet covering. Stacy mentally cursed herself for having worn a bra today that was almost as see-through. But she didn't have any choice but to take off the wet jacket.

She draped it over her arm, blotted the coffee spill on her pad—the top page of notes now illegible in running ink, which was par for the course—and headed for the elevator with Russell, who attempted to cheer her up with mummy jokes that were painfully bad. She appreciated his effort but was glad they only had a few floors to ascend.

Caroline Pratt was there to greet them in the hall, but alone. "Where's the professor?" Stacy asked.

"He was just here," the gray-haired woman said, apologetic. "But he stepped outside when the fire engine came by. He seemed quite excited by it," she said at Stacy's startled expression.

Stacy and Russell exchanged a look. From without the building she could hear the fading strains of a siren. "Well, why don't we join the professor outside, Russell?" she suggested. "That is, if he hasn't decided to become a volunteer."

"Actually, I've got to get back to the office," Russell announced as they emerged into the bright sunlight. "Richard phoned when I went up, and he wants—"

"No!" she cried. "He is *not* going to snatch you away from me. I'm telling you, if he tries—"

"Stacy, Stacy, relax," Russell beseeched her. "I'll be back in an hour or so. It's just some paperwork I forgot to clear up before I started with you on this."

"One hour," she said darkly. "Don't you dare let him seduce you into doing anything else in that sweatshop we call an office. All right? Now, where's our fire engine chaser?"

Russell shaded his eyes with a hand and surveyed the sidewalk beyond the back lawn of the museum. "Over there," he said, and pointed toward the corner.

Stacy looked. "Where?" The only man in the vicinity was a tall guy in khaki pants and boots.

"That's him. Brody," Russell said.

Stacy looked again, surprised. She'd been picturing a stoop-shouldered, long-haired creature—certainly someone a great deal older. This man was young, tanned and healthy. And although his wire-rimmed glasses gleaming in the sun and the manila folder he clutched to his chest gave him a certain air of studiousness, she couldn't help noticing that he was what certain women's magazines would have called a hunk.

"Do you want me to introduce you?" Russell asked.

"No, that's okay," she said. "You hurry up and take care of your errand. He knows who I am?"

"Yeah, I told him I was bringing you upstairs to meet him."

"Fine," she said. "Russell, take a cab and have Richard reimburse you. I'm serious, one hour!"

He nodded affably and strode off. Stacy turned back to assess Ethan Brody. He was standing in the middle of the sidewalk, gazing off in the direction of the dying siren with an air of absolute fascination. Stacy shook her head. "We've got a live one here," she murmured, and began walking across the lawn.

He hadn't seen her yet, so she had a chance to size the man up as she approached. She hadn't realized, though she should have, she knew now, that a man who literally did a lot of digging for a living would be in good physical shape.

From the distance she registered broad shoulders, with a little thatch of sexily curled chest hair peeking from the open collar of his light blue work shirt. Quite tall but not too lean. His tanned arms, revealed below rolled-up sleeves, were muscular, and the slightly baggy khaki pants he wore accentuated the strong lines of his hips and long legs.

When he turned in her direction, she glimpsed clear blue eyes peering out from a deeply tanned face beneath a tousle of light brown hair. In the inquisitive gaze of those bright eyes, the tilt of his aquiline nose and the thrust of his strong chin, she could see an attitude that was at once profoundly masculine and childlike.

He was either a hopeless hick or a true original with idiosyncrasies that might prove problematic. Any man who ran out into the street after a fire truck wasn't likely to be particularly dependable. As he drew closer, the cynical Manhattanite in her was searching for the proper wisecrack. But before she could formulate one, a gust of wind blew open the folder he was holding, and the air was suddenly filled with flying white sheets of paper.

FOR THE PAST FEW DAYS Ethan Brody had been trying, with little success, to comprehend Manhattan. He still didn't know what to make of it.

Ever since he'd stepped off the familiar tarmac at the tiny Belizean airfield and onto the plane that had begun this roller-coasterlike trip, everything seemed to have changed dramatically. And he wasn't sure if that change was for better or worse.

The initial barrage of publicity that had greeted his discovery when he returned to the States had so overloaded his senses as to send him reeling. He'd been so hounded by the media and the academic community, everyone vying for what one journalist had termed "a piece of the action," that his first impulse had been to flee right back into the jungle. But even that hadn't worked. As soon as the location of the site became public knowledge, whatever peace he'd ever had in Belize had been permanently disrupted.

You'd think he and his crew had been the only people in the world to ever hack and dig their way into an untouched Mayan tomb. Well, they were the only ones in the past few decades, he had to admit with a touch of pride. But even though he'd understood in academic terms the magnitude of what they'd found in that stretch of swamp outside Belmopan, he'd seriously underestimated what the American media were going to try to do with it and him.

So when Lloyd and the others had arranged for this exhibit in New York, he'd grudgingly agreed that he'd have to handle it. After seeing himself misquoted in print and the finds they'd made hopelessly exaggerated, he no longer trusted anyone else to oversee the inevitable exploitation of what was, after all, his baby. And so, a few months later, here he was, in civilization at its most civilized. Or was it?

Ever since his arrival here he'd felt he might as well be in a dream, in Disneyland, or in an outer ring of Dante's inferno. He'd always prided himself on being immune to the charms of big-city life, and he wasn't about to be intimidated by the place. No, not after having survived encounters with tarantulas, scorpions, snakes, small landslides and near-burial alive in the heart of a heat-wave-crazy jungle.

But the city kept surprising him, nonetheless, keeping him just far enough off balance to be uncomfortable. Everything about it was surreal. People rushed around, hurrying into glittering boutiques as if their lives were at stake, jostling him to beat traffic lights while cars seemingly tried to run them down.

They appeared to take so much for granted, like those fire engines he'd come out to see. In his American hometown, a fire would have been a major event. Here, pedestrians absently stuck fingers into their ears and gave the speeding red behemoths barely a passing glance. They ignored both towering skyscrapers and dilapidated hovels, taking in stride the strange juxtaposition of wealth and poverty that surrounded them.

But to Ethan, the electricity in the air, the noise, the slightly sooty smell of it—nothing was familiar, everything was somehow foreign. It wasn't as if he'd never been to a big city before. Mexico City was no slouch in terms of size and population, and he'd visited cities like Morocco and Buenos Aires. But he'd spent most of his time during the past eight years in places where any building over three stories high seemed gargantuan, and any more than a few dozen people congregated in one street constituted a riot. Manhattan was quite an adjustment, to say the least.

Such were the meditations that had been preoccupying him when the wind had yanked the folder from under his arm. But now he was galvanized into action, because his notes for the exhibition catalog were in danger of blowing away.

Ethan ran for the lawn, grabbing sheets of paper as he went. His eyes scanned all directions as he moved, registering—one sheet by the curb, one against that black car, two blowing underneath it.

He sprinted for the street. A chauffeur was holding open the door of the long black automobile for a woman with two small poodles on leashes. Ethan dashed past her for the sheet of paper that the wind had just whisked into the back seat. The woman shrieked, her dogs barking, and the chauffeur shouted. But the paper was in his hand.

Unfortunately he'd also gotten a foot caught in one of the leashes, and the next thing he knew, he was sprawled on the pavement. The chauffeur, standing over him, was belligerently demanding an explanation, the woman babbling and the poodles nipping at his leg. Ethan got up as gracefully as he could, repeating the word "Sorry," like a litany. He didn't have time for more than that. Where were the rest of the papers?

There was one, by the curb, and another lay on the edge of the lawn. And—

"Here," said a voice.

Ethan turned. He found himself staring at a remarkably attractive woman. She was smiling at him, and holding a few of the stray sheets in her hand. For a moment he was too distracted by the beauty of her upturned face in the bright sun and the graceful lines of her bare shoulders to say a word. "Oh," he managed. "Thanks."

He took the papers from her, noting her red fingernails, and, as he couldn't help his eyes from straying, her rather voluptuous figure. That blouse she was wearing! It was practically transparent, and the ample view it allowed him of her...femininity was enough to make his blood race.

"Behind you," she was saying.

"What? Oh!" He turned to see a man in tattered clothes picking up another sheet of paper from the sidewalk. The guy looked as if he lived right there, and for all Ethan knew, he probably did. He was reading the notes with a perplexed look as Ethan hurried to his side.

"Excuse me," he said.

The man looked up at Ethan with bloodshot eyes. "Man, what is this craziness? Is this English?"

"Yes," Ethan said, reaching out to take the sheet from him. But the man pulled back.

"How much you want for it?" he asked. "I mean, I'm the guy who fetched it for you. I see you getting all messed up with poodles, but I'm on the case, right?"

Ethan sighed. He'd been accosted by a constant stream of beggars of all shapes and sizes ever since he'd arrived. At the moment he wasn't in a charitable mood, but he also didn't feel like arguing. He dug a quarter out of his pocket.

"Thanks, bro," the man said. "That's some wild stuff you got there. I bet some of those six-syllable words'd be worth twenty bucks apiece, huh?"

"Uh-huh," Ethan muttered, taking the papers from him and moving off before the man tried to hit him for a higher fee. That seemed like all of them. Ethan started counting sheets.

"I'm Stacy Morrison."

Ethan looked up, surprised that the woman was still there. What did she want? One thing he'd learned quickly enough about New York—anyone who stopped you on the street was bound to want something from you. It was getting to be annoying.

"Ethan Brody," he muttered, his attention on the papers. Wait a second. What had he done? They were all there, thankfully, but it was the wrong folder! These weren't the catalog notes. They were notes for a paper he was due to deliver in Detroit.

The woman was saying something about the museum, but he hadn't heard a word of it. He looked up again, frowning, irked at his own stupidity. He'd have to go back to the hotel. "I'm sorry," he said. "But these aren't the right papers."

She gave him a quizzical look. "No?"

"No," he said. "I've forgotten my catalog notes. I have to go back to my hotel. So, thanks, but if you'll excuse me—"

"Wait." The woman glanced at her watch. "Why don't I come with you?"

Ethan stared at her, startled. "Why?"

"Well, we could have quite a long afternoon ahead of us," she said. "We might as well get acquainted now."

She was smiling again, and in spite of his confusion, he was aware that there was something about the way her hair gleamed golden in the sun and the shine in her eyes seemed to increase the sunlight's wattage that was working an unsettling, subtle voodoo on his solar plexus.

"Get acquainted?" he echoed vaguely, perplexed.

"Where are you staying?" she asked.

"The Plaza," he told her, still befuddled by her oddly aggressive behavior. Who had she said she was, anyway? Someone who worked at the museum?

"Well, then, let's go." She said this as if it was the most natural thing in the world.

Ethan blinked, stymied. "Look, I appreciate your interest, but I don't—"

"I'll get us a cab." She was already striding to the curb. Once again he couldn't help but take in her appearance, the hip-hugging skirt, the very revealing blouse, the shapely legs in black stockings. An unsettling thought suddenly occurred to him. She wasn't . . . was she?

As she scanned the street for a cab, Ethan tried to convince himself that he shouldn't jump to conclusions. But why was this total stranger inviting herself to his hotel? "You're not . . . busy?" he asked.

"I'm extremely busy," she said. "But like I said, why waste time? We might as well dive right in, don't you think? We can get to know each other on the way over."

Ethan cleared his throat, caught between bewilderment and suspicion. This kind of friendliness was unusual, unless ... He knew he was far out of the swing of things, but was his inexperience with the denizens of New York making him completely misinterpret what kind of a woman she was? "I ... wouldn't want to keep you from your work," he said uneasily.

Now she looked at him as if *he* was the one acting odd. "This *is* my work."

Streetwalking? Ethan stared at her, in spite of himself both aroused and disappointed. Initially she'd struck him as a nice, helpful and very pretty stranger. Now he could only view her as yet another of these predatory New York types he'd been meeting every day and night.

For one crazy moment, though, he was actually tempted. Are you mad? he admonished himself. The long polished fingernails were a definite tip-off. Hadn't he long ago decided—after Lucille Bender, to be exact—that any woman who didn't work with her hands should be avoided at all costs?

Maybe that was a narrow-minded supposition, but once bitten, he was definitely twice shy. And after the kind of isolated bachelorhood he'd just emerged from, he was certainly feeling twice or three times as shy where any women were concerned. The only females he'd had any contact with while he'd been down there were the occasional archaeological students and the local mestizo women.

That was why he felt completely vulnerable to the attentions of almost any attractive American female. It was annoying. He'd hoped that his self-imposed exile after the troubles with Lucille would have strengthened him, that he'd be way past being swayed by a pretty face.

But he was being swayed now, and it was entirely inappropriate. Good Lord, didn't he have work to do, arguably the most important work of his career? "I think you've got the wrong man," he told the woman, apologetic.

The woman laughed. "As far as I'm concerned, you're the only man," she said. "Come on, let's get going. I want you to give me everything you've got, and that may take some time."

Ethan wasn't prone to blushes. But if he could have blushed, he would have. He knew that New Yorkers had a reputation for being straightforward, but this kind of forwardness was downright embarrassing.

"Look," he said. "Honestly, I . . . I don't need you to come along." He searched for an excuse that wouldn't be insulting. "You know, this isn't the kind of thing I usually—that I've ever done."

She nodded, apparently unfazed. "If it's inexperience you're worried about," she said, "well, you can leave everything to me. I'd be happy to show you exactly how something like this is done."

She was smiling, the demure innocence in her expression completely at odds with what she was saying. Ethan had never encountered this particular combination in a woman before. New York City was full of surprises, all right.

He decided he'd better find his way out of this by getting down to brass tacks, and quickly. But how to do it without really hurting her feelings? Even if he didn't approve of her chosen profession, he still couldn't help liking her. She was a likable sort.

"Listen, don't take this personally, okay? But I have a feeling I wouldn't be able to afford you."

She looked puzzled. "Afford me? It's a little late to worry about that now. Hasn't it all been worked out already?"

"What?" Now he was entirely out of his depth. "Listen, Miss—I'm sorry, what did you say—?"

"Stacy."

"Stacy, the thing is, I have an appointment here at the museum that I have to get back to, and first I have to get the proper papers from my hotel—"

"Professor Brody," she interrupted impatiently. "We can do it there."

Do it? He didn't want to "do it," even if she was the most attractive and sophisticated-looking hooker he'd ever laid eyes on. But even as he prepared to brush her off for good, a little warning bell went off in his head. Professor Brody? How had she known to call him "Professor," unless . . . ?

"We don't have to work at the museum," she was saying. "If the catalog papers are at your hotel, we should go get them together. We can start discussing the entire project over a lunch there. Now, doesn't that sound like a fine idea?"

She was talking to him as if he were a child, or worse, an adult of retarded mental capacity. But then why shouldn't she? Obviously he'd just made a gargantuan mistake in simple perception. Ethan suddenly felt like sinking through the sidewalk.

"You're Miss Morrison," he murmured. "From P and W."

Her eyes widened slightly. Now as she spoke, it was with the careful cadences people sometimes used when dealing with the clinically insane. "Yes, and you're Ethan Brody," she said. "And this is a taxicab," she added, as one pulled up beside them in response to her waving arm. "Why don't we both get into it, now?"

Ethan kept his mouth shut; it seemed the wisest course. His working relationship with the woman responsible for handling the highlight of his career was certainly off to a very promising start.

Chapter Two

Absentminded? It was more likely that this professor had mislaid his brain permanently, Stacy decided. She paced the hotel lobby, worriedly regretting her decision to let him go up to his room unaccompanied. If she hadn't taken that cab ride with him, who knows what kind of mishap the man might have wandered into?

How had he even found Belize, she wondered, let alone a supposedly priceless Mayan tomb? And she'd been banking on this man's assistance to make her promotion a successful one! Sighing, Stacy checked her watch and then glanced at the elevator bank. According to the dial there, Ethan Brody had at least gotten off at the proper floor.

Time to make a quick phone call, she decided, and strode over to an empty booth opposite the elevators. She needed to cancel that date. She had a grim foreboding that her social life in general was about to go down the tubes. Making this exhibit marketable was bound to be an overtime job, but she wasn't in the mood for Phil, regardless.

Phil was nice, really, but that was precisely the problem. Nice was all he was. And although she'd tentatively agreed to have dinner with him tomorrow night, then attend a book signing party at the Tango, a new club somewhere downtown, she'd already decided she'd rather use the time to stay home and *read* a book, a luxury she could rarely afford herself these days.

Phil, when he answered, was gracious, understanding and so nice about it that Stacy found herself compromising. If not dinner, all right, she would drop in at the Tango Club for at least a drink. When she hung up, she shook her head at her own guilt-induced niceness.

There was no sign of the professor yet. Stacy strolled through the plush lobby, eyeing the Palm Court lounge from a distance. Now that wasn't a bad idea. If she had to suffer through a business lunch with Ethan Brody, why not do it in style? Though with her luck, he'd probably opt for the more touristy Trader Vic's next door.

He was, after all, the classic out-of-towner, or maybe in a class by himself. All the way over here he'd been rubber-necking at the city sights. At one point he'd leaned so far out of the open cab window that she'd had to literally yank him back in as their oblivious cabbie took a corner at perilous speed. She'd had to dissuade him from making the cabbie take them through the park, which made no sense, since they were already at Columbus Circle by then.

When they'd arrived at the Plaza, he'd gotten so mesmerized by a horse and carriage parked in front of it that she'd actually had to take his arm and steer him toward the hotel entrance.

Professor Brody was one for the books, all right. And here he was now, a briefcase clutched in his hand. That was a good sign. Mission accomplished. As she watched him move across the lobby, she reflected again that he was unusually good-looking for such a yo-yo. Her movie-oriented mind played a familiar game. Who would've played him, in what picture?

She was five feet ten inches herself, but he was definitely over six feet. She contemplated the tousled hair, the boots, the earthiness his aura suggested that made him seem about as natural to the Plaza lobby as an oil rigger might be. Gary Cooper, she decided, in a Frank Capra movie, at a loss for a more contemporary comparison. Besides, she couldn't think of any current actor who wore wire-rimmed glasses.

"Everything's fine now," he said, patting his briefcase.

Somehow his statement didn't entirely inspire confidence. "Good," she said. "Maybe we could have lunch at the Palm."

Ethan Brody frowned. "They're pretty snooty here," he said. "I'm thinking of changing hotels. You know what they charge for a soda in this place?"

She might've known. Visions of a cool cocktail in the refined Palm Court evaporating, she followed Ethan out onto the street again. He wanted to walk down Fifth and "find someplace." Stacy reminded herself that being out in the sun was preferable to being stuck in the museum's basement, and buttoned her lip.

Ethan, unlike most other reasonable people on the street who were aware that they had places to go, had a habit of walking slowly and not watching his step. He seemed to avoid collisions both automotive and pedestrian only through some instinctual sixth sense. In its way, Stacy found this impressive but also unnerving. They had gone only a few blocks when Ethan stopped in his tracks altogether, gazing up at the building beside them with a look of frank incredulity. "What is *that*?" he inquired.

"The Trump Tower."

Ethan's mouth was slightly agape. "What, they've still got their Christmas decorations up?" He was referring, she saw, to the little evergreen bushes that topped each ascending tier of the building's facade.

"No," she said dryly. "It's part of the aesthetic statement." The Tower, erected by a billionaire mogul in the middle of Fifth Avenue, had obviously struck some chord in Ethan Brody.

"Can you eat in there?"

"There is a small restaurant, yes." Stacy had never dined within this infamous den of luxury. She'd never wanted to. Who would? Only someone like . . .

"I've got to see this," he murmured.

"Why?"

He turned to her with a look of innocent awe. "Because it's amazing, isn't it? I mean, isn't this one of the ugliest places you've ever seen in your life?"

Score one for Professor Brody, she mused, as she walked up to the entrance with him. Apparently he wasn't entirely the gullible, starry-eyed tourist. They paused as Ethan surveyed the doorman. He was dressed, for reasons only understood by Mr. Trump, like a cross between an English palace guard and a "Nutcracker Suite" soldier, with a headdress that rose about two feet above his hairline.

"I'd like to meet his tailor," Ethan murmured, and they went through the revolving door.

They were past the prime-time lunch hour, so getting a table at the glitzy little plaza below the main floor wasn't any problem. Ethan settled back in his chair, briefcase in his lap, and gazed around him with an amused expression. He seemed just as out of place here among the marbled walls, frothy fountains and gold and silver bric-a-brac that vied for one's attention, every exotic palm and gilded statuette silently shrieking "Money." But then, where was his place? Behind a lectern or up a tropical tree, she supposed.

"Lunch is on the firm, Professor Brody," she told him, as he glanced at the menu a silent waiter was proffering him.

"Ethan," he said. "Thanks."

"Ethan," she repeated. "Why don't we order fairly quickly, so we can get to work?" At last, she nearly added, but she was trying not to be cranky. The two of them did have to work together for a while.

"Fine," he said. "Hey, c'mon back!" He was waving at their departing waiter with a friendly smile. Stacy cringed inwardly as a few heads turned in their direction. The man apparently had the social graces of a large chimp. But then again, he was nodding at her expectantly, waiting for her to order first.

"I'll just have the spinach salad and a white wine spritzer, please." The waiter nodded, writing.

"Burger and fries," said Ethan.

Stacy and the waiter looked at him simultaneously. The waiter cleared his throat. "Yes," the waiter said. "The charbroiled chopped sirloin steak, with fried potato slices."

"Whatever you call it," Ethan said magnanimously. "Rare, please. And a Coke with lots of lemon in it."

"Maybe we could look over your papers now," Stacy suggested, after the waiter had left. Ethan nodded, opened his briefcase and started searching. In a moment, their table was covered with half a dozen manila folders and a variety of other things, including a camera, a map of Detroit, a *Times* crossword, a pencil sharpener in the shape of the Empire State Building and a banana.

He offered her the banana when he saw her staring at it, but Stacy declined. Instead she turned her concentration to the sheaf of papers he handed her, which were, to her immense relief, the right notes, and neatly typed. Stacy studied them as their drinks arrived.

"To our successful collaboration," he said.

Stacy looked up, and raised her glass in a casual toast. "These are very helpful," she said, tapping the notes. "The only thing is, you refer to a number of objects I haven't seen yet, at least not in the museum slides. This Mayan wall carving, for example—''

But Ethan wasn't listening. He was staring fixedly over her shoulder. Stacy turned and saw only the wall.

"That waterfall," he said.

"What about it?" she asked, annoyed.

"It's running backward," he announced.

Stacy looked again. Defying gravity, the cascades of water were definitely shooting up, not down, controlled by jets below, so that they could arc over an artificial rock formation and reach the next water plateau in the Byzantine arrangement along the wall.

"That's interesting," she allowed. "Now about the Mayan carvings..."

Ethan was smiling, shaking his head. "Can you believe this place?"

"It's unbelievable, yes," she said. "Could we please talk about your catalog?"

"Right. Sorry," he said, and adjusted his glasses, looking like a schoolboy caught playing hooky.

"Let me explain what I'll be trying to do here," she said. "Normally we wouldn't be involved with the actual nuts and bolts of the exhibit and how it's being mounted, but this is a special case. We're trying to sell the exhibit and the museum to a public that's been apathetic to natural history in the past, so I'm here to find a fresh, commercial angle."

"Have you always had those?"

"What?" She glanced down. He was pointing at her fingernails.

"Since birth," she told him, with an edge in her voice.

"I mean, worn long," he said.

Stacy sighed. She supposed she should give up trying to follow the logic of this man's thought processes. "For a while now, yes. Ethan, really, we have a lot of material to go over, so do you think—?''

"You're looking for a fresh, commercial angle," he said.

"Yes. Now, the slides I saw this morning seem to concentrate almost exclusively on the...ah, potsherds and smaller stones, along with the jewels and gold pieces. But you're listing large wall pieces here, and they sound interesting. You see, what we want to highlight if possible are the articles any man or woman off the street would be impressed by.''

He nodded. Encouraged, Stacy hurried on. "The museum people don't really understand this very well. They seem content to mount an exhibit that's typical of their more scholarly approach, and that's at odds with the new image we want to create."

"They're pompous," he said.

"Well, maybe, yes," she said uncertainly.

"No, up there," he said, pointing over her head. "Not pompous. *Pampas*. Pampas grass, also known as *Cortaderia selloana*."

She stared at him, not understanding, momentarily distracted by the ease with which the Latin words had rolled off his tongue.

"Up there." He was pointing behind them. Stacy turned to follow his gaze up the marble wall behind the bank of escalators. "You see those green plants, with the long silky white plumes? Pampas grass. Grows wild in South America.''

"Oh." She looked at the plants in question, which lined the marble shelf above the waterfall, intermixed with similar, fernlike plants bearing smaller pink plumes. Then she looked at the notes in her hand and her watch.

Stacy made a decision. When in Rome... She put down the notes. Clearly they were getting nowhere fast here.

Maybe if she just went *with* this nut case and followed his lead, instead of trying to get him onto her track, she'd have better success. Ethan was still staring upward.

"Are they rare?" she asked.

"Not really," he said. "But you seldom see them checkerboarded with Chinese pennisetum, and indoors, besides. In spring, no less. Somebody around here has either a truly bizarre and eclectic taste in greenery, or just picked a bunch of stuff blindfold from an international plant catalog. But either way, it's kind of offensive."

To Stacy, the plants were perhaps the least objectionable of the many gauche touches in the Trump Tower's interior, but she was willing to take his word for it. "Well, this whole place is kind of offensive," she said. "Are you a botanist, too?"

He shook his head. "Nope. Just a hobby." He looked from the wall back to her again with an apologetic air. "Don't get me wrong," he said. "I'm not climbing up on any high horse. But do you know what it must've cost to import those grasses, along with all the other ferns and vines they've got all over this joint?"

"I can imagine it wasn't cheap."

"Why, those pennisetums won't last the month," he said. "And they'll probably put in something just as exotic to replace 'em. You could support a whole family in Chetumal for a year on what they lay out for greenery every couple of months."

"I'll bet," she said, wondering where Chetumal was. "For that matter, you could probably support a whole family in Harlem."

"Besides, the whole thing's cockeyed," he went on. "There's not a natural thing inside these walls."

"Like waterfalls that run backward."

"Right," he said, and smiled at her.

It was here that a subtle but extraordinary thing happened. Stacy smiled back. She hadn't meant to, but there was a genuine friendliness in his expression that took her by surprise. It was the kind of smile you almost couldn't help smiling back at.

Come to think of it, that was her first smile of the day, she reflected. It was also the first time she hadn't been concentrating on this terrible job and fending off a headache. Maybe it was only the wine spritzer and the expectation of a nice salad, but she felt this lunch might not turn out to be a total fiasco, after all.

It was at this point that the waiter arrived with their food, and Ethan, in the process of trying to hurriedly clear the contents of his briefcase from the table, spilled the rest of the spritzer into her lap.

Actually it was her knee that got wet, and the edge of her skirt. "Boy, I'm sorry," he was saying. He'd been muttering apologies continually during the cleanup of their table, which was efficiently managed by their waiter plus another.

"It's all right," she told him, beyond being either startled or upset by now. Clearly time spent with Ethan Brody was spent at the risk of one's own well-being. "The matching jacket has to go to the cleaners, anyway. I spilled coffee on it this morning."

"Oh," he said. "*Oh*. You mean you . . . usually wear a jacket?"

"With this blouse, yes," she said, self-consciously crossing her arms.

He was nodding with a mysterious satisfaction, as if she'd said something profound. She wouldn't hazard a guess as to why. "Thank you," Stacy told the waiter, accepting a second spritzer. "Here's another toast," she said, holding up the glass. "Here's to . . . Take Two."

"Hmm?"

"As in Take Number Two," she said. "You know, let's do the same scene over from the top."

"Oh. Fine. Yes, let's," he said, and clinked glasses.

Stacy sipped her wine, by now feeling almost a trifle giggly. It was funny, the whole thing, she had to look at it that way. Working for Richard she had to have a sense of humor, and especially on this assignment. Otherwise she might go mad.

"Well, I'm glad we came here," Ethan was saying. "It's really a sight to see."

"Is it the pompous pampas or the fake fountains you're most taken by?" she asked wryly.

"The total effect," he said, looking around him. Ethan shook his head. "What a waste of resources. You'd think in a place like New York City they'd have better sense...." He paused. "But then, not much about this city seems to make much sense."

Stacy instinctively felt protective about her much-maligned home ground. *We're allowed to knock it, buddy, but don't you start.* She gave her hair a toss. "As cities go, this one works okay."

"I guess you'd know better."

His affable tone made her regret her own obviously patronizing remark. "There's a lot to get used to," she allowed.

"I'd never get used to this," he said, indicating their surroundings.

Stacy shrugged. "It's not one of our finest landmarks."

Ethan nodded. "You know, the funny thing is, you and I might think this place is in bad taste, but to a fisherman from the Yucatán peninsula, well... If you brought him in here right now, he'd think he'd died and gone to heaven."

"I suppose," she said. "I mean, never having met one."

"Hmm?"

"A fisherman from the Yucatán peninsula."

"Oh. Well, most of them are fairly poor. Really poor by New York standards. What I'm saying is, the things you and I might take for granted would put his head in a spin." He gestured toward the restaurant tables. "Getting served a glass of cold water with ice in it when you sit down, for example. That would make your average Belmopan man think he'd found the promised land, all right."

"I see." She nodded, seeing an opportunity to steer the conversation back to the work they had to do. "Belmopan. That's the area where you did your excavation?"

"I don't suppose you've ever been to Central America," he said.

"Not yet," she said. "My work tends to keep me closer to home."

"You were born here, weren't you?"

So much for getting back to the Mayan tomb catalog. "I'm a native New Yorker, yes," she admitted. "Why, is it that obvious?"

His gaze had strayed to her black-stockinged legs and lingered a moment before he remembered himself and quickly met her eyes again. The hint of embarrassment she saw in his look was charming, in a way. "No. I mean, I guess. That is..." He stopped, running a hand through his hair with a self-conscious air. "You'll have to forgive me," he said sheepishly. "I've been out of circulation for a while."

"In Belmopan," she prompted him.

"For about eight years, on and off."

"Eight years," she murmured. She hadn't meant that to sound as incredulous as it did, but it was an honest reaction. Although Stacy had done her share of traveling, she couldn't say she'd ever left the island of Manhattan for more than two months at a time. The idea of being off in a remote country like Belize, which, if she remembered correctly, was somewhere near Nicaragua and Honduras, for such a long stretch...

Where did you get your dry cleaning done? It made her vaguely anxious just to think about it.

"You make it sound like a prison sentence," he said, amused.

"No, no, I just..."

"Can't imagine," he suggested.

"Right."

"Well, this is pretty hard to imagine, if you want to know the truth," Ethan said, indicating the atrium. "I think I prefer the real jungle, myself."

That didn't surprise her. As they began to eat, the philosophical comparisons between the Third World and this one were momentarily suspended. Another glance at her watch convinced Stacy that it really was time to settle down to the business at hand.

"Look, let's start at the beginning with this," she suggested, waving her first forkful of spinach. "You be the professor and I'll be the student. For the next twenty minutes, you fill me in on what you did down there and what you found, exactly. But stick to the most important things, okay?"

"Important?" He paused before biting into his burger.

"The highlights. Meaning, what would impress a lay person like me. I don't need to know about every potsherd you uncovered, or the difference between a—" she glanced at the still-open notepad by her elbow "—terminal classic artifact and a postclassic one. Just give me a sense of what you want to highlight in this exhibit and why."

Ethan's brow furrowed. "That could take hours."

"The short form," she said.

He shrugged. "I'll do my best." She nodded encouragingly. "Well, what do you know about the Mayans?"

"Nada," she said promptly.

"Great." He chuckled ruefully. "All right, I'd better give you a little Anthropology 101."

"By all means," she said. "Fire away."

And so, in between bites of salad and sips of wine, Stacy slowly but surely set about familiarizing herself with the basic vocabulary of Ethan's field. Besides being able to communicate with Ethan, she needed to begin compiling some key phrases and buzzwords for her own promotional copy.

In this, at least, the professor was perfectly amenable to staying on the subject, and a good teacher. By the time their desserts arrived, she had a rudimentary understanding of the significance of Ethan's find.

She also got her first inkling of an insight into Professor Ethan Brody. When he talked about his work, he no longer seemed the somewhat bumbling, distracted innocent. His voice was a husky baritone, a kind of warm rumble that tickled her inner ear, and his enthusiasm as he related tales of the Belizean jungle was compelling.

Looking at Ethan now, it wasn't hard to imagine him with the stereotypical pith helmet atop his wavy hair, a pickax or a shovel in his hand. Her only images of working archaeologists came from the movies, she realized, but he did fit the type, if it wasn't for the glasses. But wait, hadn't Harrison Ford worn glasses in one of his non-Indiana Jones films?

That was movies, she reminded herself, surprised that her mind was wandering down un-work-related paths. She concentrated again on what Ethan was explaining to her about the nature of his expedition.

The main thing, as she understood it, was that Ethan and his partner had found a Mayan tomb undisturbed, so that everything in it was in reasonably good condition. Most known tombs and other ancient dwellings throughout Central and South America had been pillaged to the point of uselessness. It wasn't so much that the deceased Mayan prince himself was of great historical stature, like the famous King Tut, but that everything buried with him was relatively intact, therefore worthy of scholarly examination and display.

"But not to the general public," she interjected, as they dawdled over coffee. "You've got tons of artifacts, it seems, but only a dozen that are really... well, valuable. I mean, to our way of thinking."

Ethan nodded. "Civilization's a crazy concept," he mused. "The range of human values and how they change from epoch to epoch, it never ceases to amaze me."

Stacy watched Ethan as he surveyed his surroundings again. His face was almost hawklike in profile, and filtered sunlight from the atrium's roof gleaming on his dark skin seemed to imbue him with a glow of animal intensity.

"I've dug up pieces of stone that could fit in the palm of your hand," he went on, "dusty old chipped things at first glance. But they were the prize possessions of kings once. Chiseled by master jewelers, handcrafted. A single one of them is more beautiful, more valuable to me than six of these skyscraper towers."

"To you, yes," she said gently. "My job is figuring out how to get the general public as enthused about them as you are."

He turned to look back at her with a look of faint chagrin. "Sorry if I went on too long," he said. "But you did ask."

"No, that's okay," she assured him. "You've given me some ideas to mull over."

"Really?"

"Mmm-hmm." She signaled for the check. Ideas were all she had at the moment, and fairly vague ones. She was still lacking a solid angle.

It was ironic when she thought about it. What was attractive and exciting about Ethan's tomb was the finding of it. The real values in his expedition were more conceptual than concrete. The anecdotes he was telling her about the site and its discovery, the subsequent excavation—now, that was all good stuff. You could market that as a book or a documentary. But all she had to work with was the rocks and precious stones. They alone weren't going to impress a jaded public that had already seen the Tut treasures and more.

"It is going to be a tough sell, though," she muttered.

"I thought you New Yorkers were well educated and sophisticated," he said. "Why shouldn't they be interested in something like this?"

"Everything in the world gets thrown at them," she said. "That's why. We get Russian ballet, Chinese opera, New Orleans jazz, Japanese art.... If they miss an exhibit on the treasures of Belize, they won't lose sleep," she said wryly.

Ethan shrugged. "Their loss."

Or mine, she thought grimly. Unless she could make this a cultural event that attracted a good-sized crowd, Richard might take his dangling carrot of the film festival job over to Christopher's desk. Sure, he'd implied it was hers, merely for doing the museum job, but you never knew with Richard.

Ethan was looking at her frowning face with some concern. "Don't get me wrong," he said. "I don't mean to knock your city."

He'd misinterpreted her dark look. Stacy smiled. "Believe me, my city can take it."

"I believe you," he said.

"Where do you hail from?" she asked. "Pre-Belize."

"Hambone, Arizona," he said.

Stacy stared at him. She'd taken him for a small-towner, true, but this was ridiculous. "Seriously?"

"Would I make something like that up? It's a teensy town just across the Nevada border from Boulder City. I was born in Bali, actually, when my folks were on a dig there. Got some schooling in New Zealand and New Guinea, went to college in Mexico City. But Arizona's where my grandparents lived, and we used to use it as an occasional home base."

Stacy glanced up from writing out the credit card slip. "Boy, you really have gotten around, haven't you?"

"Keeps things interesting," he said.

Stacy shrugged. Really, talk about opposites. What did she have in common with a man who'd grown up in the backwoods of the world, who dug up ancient rocks to make a living? Who was willing to spend eight years practically *under* a rock in the jungles of Belize? Remembering his odd comment about her fingernails, she reflected that men like Ethan Brody weren't apt to find a cosmopolitan woman like Stacy their cup of tea, either.

But they were getting along decently enough. So far. "Shall we?"

They got up from the table. "I should give Wally a call when we get back to the museum," Ethan said.

"Wally?"

"Professor Canfield, my partner. He's still got some materials we were thinking of using. Maybe there's some stuff you'd want to know about."

Stacy nodded. "Was he with you the whole time down there?"

"Pretty much. We thought up this particular expedition together. It was Wally's expertise with grant proposals that got us our Fulbright." He glanced at her as they approached the revolving doors. "You must've seen him in the pictures. The guy with the beard."

Stacy shook her head. "I'm not sure. I was mostly looking at slides of stones."

"He's a funny guy," Ethan said. "A real joker. There's some stuff on the videotape. . . ." He shook his head.

"Videotape?"

"Yeah, we have some footage of the site, you know, before-and-after stuff. There's stills, too. Didn't Caroline Pratt give you the—?"

"Hold it, hold it," Stacy interrupted impatiently. She squinted at Ethan in the bright sunlight outside the Tower. "You have a videotape of the excavation? Like, shots of you guys going into the tomb?"

Ethan nodded. "It's not high-quality stuff, you know. Just for our archives."

"But it shows you and what's-his-name—"

"Wally."

"—actually going into this thing? For the first time?"

"Sure."

Stacy stared at him. "Why didn't you say so before?"

"Well, I . . . It's listed in the notes somewhere." He scratched his head. "In the documentation section. Why?"

There it was. The little hairs on the back of her neck were tingling. Suddenly she could feel it—the light breaking, the dawning of not just an idea, but The Idea. "You're in it?"

"In the tomb? On the tape? Yes."

"Do me a favor," she said. "Take off your glasses."

"Excuse me?" He looked at her, blinking.

"I'd like to see you without your glasses on. If you don't mind."

His expression indicated that he thought she'd taken leave of her senses, but he obliged, gingerly removing the curved ends of his wire-rims from around his ears. Stacy stepped back and looked him over with a critical eye.

Not Harrison Ford exactly, but not that far off. "You look good," she noted. "You talk well, in fact, you have a very good speaking voice. I think this'll work."

"What will?" he said, peering at her with a look that indicated she was entirely out of focus to him right now, both literally and figuratively.

"I've figured out what's missing from this exhibit," she said.

"What?"

"You," she told him. "Professor, I know you probably didn't plan on this, but I'm going to do my best to make you a star."

Chapter Three

"How do you know?"

"How?" Stacy removed the receiver from her ear and shook it in impatience, imagining it to be Richard's neck. Then she put it back to her ear and attempted a detached tone of voice. "Richard, I just do, that's all."

"But he's never done any public speaking. He's never been in front of a camera."

"That's where you're wrong." Phone cradled between shoulder and ear, Stacy moved over to her coffee table, where the four glossy eight-by-tens she'd had blown up from Ethan's contact sheets were spread out side by side. "Look at these shots," she said. "They're pure gold."

"Since we're still living in the prevideophone era," Richard drawled laconically, "perhaps you'd like to describe one of them."

"All right. Picture this hunky kind of guy in khakis and a work shirt, good tan, and he's standing in front of this sort of lean-to surrounded by jungle greenery, with heaps of dirt at his feet, with a shovel stuck in one, even. And he's surrounded by these smiling mestizo children, and—"

"Mest-what?"

"Local kids, Richard. And the best part is, on his shoulder, he's got a parrot or a cockatoo or something, I don't know, very colorful, and in his hand, which he is holding out toward the camera—" she paused "—an amulet of gold."

Richard "hmphed." This was good. A "hmph" from Richard signified his grudging acceptance of the fact that one of his employees had formulated a reasonable idea.

"I've got more," she went on. "Ethan, his partner and a friendly iguana at the door to the burial mound tomb. Ethan, machete in one hand, ancient Mayan cutting tool in the other. Ethan's parrot sitting on a reconstructed classic period polychrome plate."

"You've seen the videotape?" he asked.

"It's in California. His partner's Fed-Exing it in the morning. But if it's anything like these photos—look, the quality doesn't matter. It's history. You go into the tomb, Richard!"

"Air-conditioned?"

"Very funny." Stacy paced past the coffee table, gazing out her window at the streetlight and wondering if taking Richard's phone call at home had been the best idea. But when he'd returned her earlier call there, to "check in on the museum status," she'd decided to plunge ahead with her pitch instead of waiting for an office meeting.

"Look," she said. "I'm following one of your very own PR precepts—when in doubt, find a face. You remember how that blown-up reproduction of the dancer's profile worked like gangbusters on the International Exposition brochure? Well, this is even stronger. We've got a face, and a personality to work with. Ethan Brody will make good copy."

"He sounds like a stiff."

"He is *not* a stiff," she said indignantly. "Okay, he's fairly oblivious to anything that hasn't been around longer than a couple of centuries, he's inexperienced with this stuff, but that's the whole point! He's the real thing. He's eccentric. He's out of it, uncorrupted, like Jimmy Stewart playing Mr. Smith or something. He even looks a little like Gary Cooper. The media'll eat him up with a spoon.''

"Is he willing to get this involved?"

"I'm working on him," she said, flopping onto her couch again. "He's shy. But he wants the exhibit to be a success. I've already talked him into the audiotape idea."

"What about the museum people? Caroline? Arthur?"

"They were toying with the idea of an audiotape tour, anyway. They just hadn't thought to have Ethan himself be the narrator. But he'll be perfect. Good, deep voice. Tells a good story."

Richard was silent a moment. "Well, I'd say it sounds like you've got something, maybe."

This was high praise. "I have a natural instinct for these things. Isn't that one of the reasons you hired me?"

"Hmph. You sound unusually enthusiastic," he noted.

"I have a feeling about him."

"Hmm. You mean, like a fluttery kind of feeling in your heart? Bells ringing in your head?"

"Don't make me laugh," she said. "No, I mean like a dollars-and-cents kind of feeling in my bones. Like we'll generate a lot of business with him as our front man."

"Fraternizing with clients is a punishable offense, you know," he said.

"Get off it, Richard," Stacy told him. "My interest in Professor Brody is purely professional. And just for the record, I've had enough of relationships with the opposite sex. I'm perfectly happy concentrating on my work, thanks."

"Especially when it's over six feet tall and looks like Gary Cooper," he teased.

"Can we consider this meeting at an end?" she asked.

Once off the phone, Stacy surveyed the clutter of her almost-lived-in but not-quite-homey apartment. Now that her mission—getting Richard's okay on her basic concept—had been accomplished, her mind naturally turned to the other most pressing business in her life. To move or not to move?

Ever since the possibility of buying that co-op had come up, she'd been trying to assess the real value of this place to herself, with little success. She'd moved in here when she was first dating Stan, and in those days she'd viewed it as an in-between place. The plan, at that point embryonic, but still seemingly inevitable, was that she and Stan would be moving into a place of their own before too long. Well, that hadn't happened, and here she was, with some furniture that she liked and some she didn't, some space taken care of properly and other areas unattended to.

The available co-op, in terms of someone who wasn't a confirmed Manhattanite, wasn't the best of deals. The initial asking price, even through Cousin Ceil the realtor, who'd found it for her and had gotten a deal almost as good as an insider's, was so big that she didn't like to think about it. The apartment was actually smaller than this one.

And it was across the street.

Eva had had a good laugh over that. The idea of moving, after looking all over the city for a year or so, into a smaller place on exactly the same block, had struck her best friend as the height of absurdity. All right, it was absurd, but it was a co-op, in a good building and it would be *hers*. Any New Yorker, even Eva, could understand the attraction.

Stacy walked to the window. She couldn't see the building in question from here, but it was out there. How important was owning a co-op? But then how important were any of the many things people took so seriously in this city?

Every now and then, when she took a moment to really look at the way she was living, she felt a nagging uneasi-

ness. In New York terms, she was just where she should be:
pulling in a very good salary, doing work she generally
enjoyed. There were available men to date if one wanted to,
a ready social scene to slip in and out of at will, and the
extra status perk of contact with a stream of celebrities
through her P and W work.

Why, then, after eating a delicious gourmet diet meal of
her own devising, with her coffee maker merrily burbling
on the counter in counterpoint to the nice Vivaldi strings
wafting from her state-of-the-art sound system, did she feel
that something was missing, feel it with a sudden tiny ache
of indefinable longing?

It wasn't Stan she missed. She'd actually gotten so used
to spending time alone that she'd grown to like it. The
thought that a man, any man, would be necessary to make
a woman feel "whole" was exasperating to her. Hadn't
women gotten anywhere over the past few decades? Wasn't
she living proof that you could live your own independent
life and be happy in it, with no need for a man to complete the picture?

She was supposed to be happy, anyway. Stacy turned off
the coffee maker, opting instead for a glass of white wine.
Why was she feeling a little blue now? Things were going
all right. There'd be the film festival in the fall—knock on
wood—and possibly a new apartment of her very own....

Maybe it was her encounter with Ethan Brody. But it
wasn't him exactly, she mused. No, it was that talk of jungles and digs and faraway places. She'd gotten a glimpse
of a whole other world beyond this tight little island she
lived on, and that, if anything, was responsible for her
deepening sense of disquiet. She'd moved into this apartment as an in-between, in preparation for a certain life that
hadn't materialized. Now she was still here, and even if she
bought that co-op, was she destined to live on the same
square block of concrete...forever?

Such thoughts were pointless. Keep moving, she told herself. Things will work out.

She glanced at the phone, wondering if Ethan might finally get back to her this evening. After trying unsuccessfully to reach him at his hotel all afternoon, she'd left her home phone number with the desk. She wanted to get his decision about the exhibit promotion as soon as possible. Because if he was going to be the face and the voice of this thing, Lord, did she ever have her work cut out for her!

TRY AS HE MIGHT, Ethan couldn't quite get his mind around the idea. So as he usually did when his brain was stalling, he'd set his body in motion, and was traversing the sidewalk on the south side of Central Park, enjoying the cool night air—as much as he could enjoy an air that seemed to be three-fifths carbon monoxide.

He'd listened to Stacy this afternoon in half disbelief as she'd outlined what she had in mind. Having him narrate the exhibit tape, okay, he could see that. He could even understand wanting to use the photos from the dig and possibly the videotape as part of the exhibition. But have his face plastered on posters? Have him doing television interviews? It all sounded farfetched and fantastical. Was she sure she had the right guy?

That was the main question he was going to ask her, when he called her back. He didn't want to call her back, though. In fact, he didn't want to have anything to do with any of this. What he wanted to do was take a plane back to Belize and stay there. Because Ethan was having a problem.

Its name was Stacy Morrison.

Try as he might, he hadn't been able to get that woman's face out of his head all night. He kept replaying little things she'd said, little gestures she'd made, over and over in his mind's eye. It was ridiculous, unbecoming, entirely unprofessional and a total embarrassment, but there was no way he could deny it. Ethan had developed a major infatuation with the woman, and in record time.

Why? What kind of an idiot was he? First he'd thought she was a prostitute, then the kind of aggressive businesswoman that usually put his teeth on edge. But by the end of his first hour with Stacy, he'd been smitten. There was something in her eyes, a softness that shone out sometimes, and a nice easy laugh she had....

Fool. Ethan tromped onward into the park itself, following a path that seemed parallel to the street. Forget about phoning her. After all, she was only interested in using him as a...a product, wasn't she? It wasn't as if she had any of the kinds of feelings he'd suddenly developed for her, not that he wanted them.

But he still wasn't sure. When it came to the opposite sex, his reflexes were far from sharp at the moment. He didn't know whether she'd been making fun of him the whole time, uninterested, flirtatious, or what. He also didn't know why it should make such a difference to him, damn it.

Ethan frowned. They called this a park? It was all sidewalk and roadways, even in here. Absently he fingered the slip of paper with her number on it. Maybe the best course would be having Wally fly in and take over things. Unless he could get over this ridiculous—crush, he guessed you'd call it.

Again, why her? Because she'd listened to him talk with genuine interest. Because she didn't seem to mind having a wine spritzer dropped in her lap. Because she was smart and funny and...well, she did have the prettiest face and nicest figure he'd set eyes on since...

He thought briefly of Lucille, then pushed that image out of his head. Or maybe he shouldn't. Maybe he should remember what had happened the last time he'd gotten involved with a "career woman," remember every hurtful detail. But then, why worry about "getting involved"?

Even if for some odd reason Stacy Morrison reciprocated a little bit of his interest, it was a hopeless situation. Beyond the obvious fact that she was practically from a world other than the one he'd been inhabiting, what would be the point? He was due to leave New York within a month, anyway, and it looked as though most of his time would be taken up with work.

Work. That was the other disorienting aspect of being out of the real jungle and suddenly plunked down in the middle of this artificial one. Down in Belize, his work was clear-cut, straight ahead. Here his job was about to turn strangely abstract and complex, if Stacy went ahead with this plan.

He scowled, thinking about how he and Wally had had to dodge so many opportunistic sharks and entrepreneurs who wanted a piece of what they'd done, when they first came back. Ironically, one of the things he'd found refreshing about Stacy Morrison was that she'd been working *with* him, not *on* him. For nearly the first time since his arrival in the States, he'd been able to talk to someone who didn't want something from him. He'd liked how that felt. But then with this crazy publicity scheme she'd turned it all around....

He was not going to call her back tonight. It was that simple. Except that his path through the park had already emerged onto the sidewalk again, and he was looking at a phone booth.

All right, he'd tell her no, then. He found a quarter in his pocket, took out the wrinkled slip of paper and dialed. She picked up on the second ring.

"Hello?"

The voice. He liked her voice. Grimacing at his own folly, he plunged ahead. "Stacy Morrison?"

"Ethan!"

"Yes, it's Ethan Brody." Idiot. Did she know a lot of Ethans? He took solace in the fact that she seemed genuinely pleased to hear from him. "I hope I'm not calling too late."

"Oh! No, I'm glad you called. What have you been doing?"

"Doing?" He tried to remember. Walking, and thinking about her. Not a suitable answer. "Well, a colleague of mine invited me to a party somewhere, but I wasn't in the mood," he told her, since it was true. "What's the Palladium?"

"It's a club," she said. "A large disco."

"Fun?"

"Depends on your mood," Stacy conjectured. "It can be."

"I suppose I should be getting a taste of the New York nightlife, but—" He paused to yawn, then laughed, self-conscious. "You see the problem." Actually he tended to yawn when he was nervous, which he was. But fine, if he sounded tired.

"You're not missing much," she assured him. "It's like all the other clubs, really, only bigger."

"Ah." He paused. "And what are the other clubs like?"

"Sorry, I keep forgetting."

"That's okay." He paused again. He couldn't think of anything witty or charming to say, something he imagined that Stacy Morrison might want to hear, but then, when had he ever been witty or charming? Ethan leaned his head against the phone booth glass. You sap.

"The main reason I called," she was saying, "I remembered you said you had to go to that symposium at Columbia tomorrow, so we wouldn't be getting together, and I wanted to know if I could go ahead with our plans."

Our plans. He both liked and disliked the sound of that, for precisely opposite reasons. "If you mean using me as part of the exhibit..."

"Using you? I wouldn't put it that way," she said. "It's more a case of you utilizing your own natural skills to help foster a greater public awareness of your work."

She certainly had a way with words. "Well, when you put it that way, it sounds..."

"Ethan, there's simply no one else who can do it," she said. "And nobody better for helping you do it than me. So if you have any doubts about any part of this, put them aside. I'll be with you every step of the way, and you can trust me."

Ethan was remembering the glow of her upturned face when the sunlight sparkled in her turquoise eyes. He sure liked looking at her, that much was certain. And he liked the genuine quality of caring he was hearing in her words. But he couldn't let himself be carried away. Was he going to like being made into some kind of walking ad campaign?

"I've never done any promotional talks," he told her.

"It doesn't matter. You have a nice voice, and you've obviously got a real love for what you do. You see, it's that kind of enthusiasm that really attracts an audience. Come on! This'll be fun."

"Fun?"

"Sure, it's a chance to get out into the civilized world, Professor. Unless you'd rather retreat for the rest of your days into one of those huts from the photos. I mean, I could understand that, I suppose," she went on, and he could hear the hint of a tease in her tone.

She was swaying him, even as he did feel a pang of longing for that little hut and site in Selmatena, where a tree was a tree and a person was a person, and you didn't have to think any farther than that. "No, it's just—"

"Maybe you're right," she said suddenly. "I'm asking too much of you. Maybe we should go back to the drawing board."

"I wouldn't say that," he interjected, thrown off by this change of tack. "It sounds like a feasible approach. I'm only wondering—"

"Then you'll do it!" she exclaimed. "I knew you would."

Ethan smiled in spite of himself. Stacy Morrison was a funny one. Her energy reminded him of the Land Rover he'd been using in Belize, the one with the souped-up engine. She came barreling right at you in third gear, abruptly shifted into reverse, turned on a dime, idled in first and then zipped back at you again, smooth as can be.

Ethan sighed. "I suppose," he said.

"Great," she said. "Then we've got to get together again as soon as possible. Tomorrow's no good, but—I know! You wanted to get a taste of Manhattan nightlife, right?"

Things *were* happening awfully fast here. "Well, yeah."

"Okay," she said. "Then you can meet me at the Tango Club. We can have a drink there and start generating some specific approaches. Jot down this address...."

He walked out of the phone booth with his head spinning. Hadn't he just done precisely what he'd decided not to do?

Ethan started back into the park, checking his location from force of habit, even though getting lost in this bucolic chunk of urban greenery wasn't highly likely. The hope of walking on a surface other than concrete cheered him. He wanted to get his boots firmly on the ground again.

The thought of being photographed and talking to the press had absolutely no appeal to him, but he imagined there were worse ways to publicize the finds he and Wally had made.

Ethan shook his head, knowing his own mind too well. You're just interested in seeing Stacy Morrison smile at you again, you poor sucker. But who could blame him? That smile was heady stuff.

THE TANGO CLUB PARTY was in full gear by nine, as Stacy and Eva maneuvered their way from the bar to the sidelines of the dance floor, drinks in hand. Phil and Eva's date, a screenwriter named Andy, were talking to Martin Chaswick, the author whose just-published book was being celebrated this evening. Since the men were embroiled in a deep discussion, as deep as any conversation could be with mega-decibel rock music blasting all around them, Eva and Stacy grabbed a seat on the nearest Leatherette couch, surveying the crowd.

"I'm remembering why I don't like coming to these things," Stacy told Eva, practically yelling to be heard, even though she was only a few feet away.

Eva nodded, absently twirling a lock of her jet-black hair around one ear. She was wearing the kind of perfect little black dress that Stacy had considered putting on, but had thought twice about. It hugged Eva's small trim body in all the right ways and places, Stacy noted, and maybe that was why she had yet to brave such attire. She'd put on a few pounds après Stanford that she still hadn't entirely lost, so she'd chosen a looser, unbelted blue sweater dress for tonight that was fashionably short in length but left a lot more to the imagination elsewhere.

"We're not staying long," Eva yelled back.

Stacy nodded, watching the figures gyrating beneath the constantly shifting lights on the dance floor. The Tango, in the tradition of such New York late-night spots, had an aesthetic that had nothing to do with its name. No one danced tangos here or dressed as if they might. Up-to-the-minute rock music and attire set the tone, and whatever downtown artist had done the decor that month decided the visual scheme.

This month's motif seemed some odd amalgam of Mexican folk art and Lower East Side punk, with strange dancing skeletons in neon colors adorning the walls. Looking around her, Stacy tried to imagine what Ethan Brody would make of it all. Maybe having him meet her here hadn't been the best idea.

Phil, nice as always, hadn't seemed miffed by her inviting Ethan to join them. But she wondered if Ethan would have a good time. Stacy glanced at her watch. It was already twenty after nine. Some sixth sense told her that it might be a good idea to check the club's entrance. She'd left Ethan's name with the doorman, but you never knew.

When she worked her way through the crowd and up from the club's subterranean level, she was glad she had. As she approached the doorway she could see Ethan outside, and immediately sensed trouble in the air. Unfortunately a bottleneck in the crowd milling around the entrance kept her from reaching him immediately.

"You're not on the list," the doorman was saying.

"I'm meeting a friend inside," Ethan insisted.

"Yeah, yeah, they all are," the stocky doorman said, jerking a thumb at the crowd of people jostling behind the velvet rope. "So why don't you just get back in line?"

Ethan glanced at the others who were frantically vying for a way to get in, some clearly bearing the frustration of a too-long wait, then turned back to the doorman with a perplexed expression. "Why don't you just let some of us in now?"

"Nobody's getting in," the doorman said, and as he said it, gave a nod to a man with a clipboard at his side, who deftly unclipped the velvet rope to usher inside a couple that had alighted from a nearby limousine.

Ethan's expression shifted from vague befuddlement to a focused anger that looked scary even from a few yards away. She could see as she hurried over that he'd reached the limits of his patience. It was a good thing he *wasn't* really Indiana Jones. If she hadn't known him better, she'd half expect to see him whip off his wire-rims and prepare to use his fists.

"Ethan!" she called.

His eyes flicked briefly in her direction as he grasped the rope with one hand. She saw a little flash of silver, then Ethan stepped forward, suddenly seeming to tower over the doorman. "Hey," the man said. "Get back behind the rope! I told you, nobody's getting—"

"What rope?" Ethan inquired evenly, his other hand already replacing something in the sheath on his belt. The doorman looked down, startled, and Stacy followed his gaze to the neatly severed velvet cord that was now dangling from its pole. "I'm nobody," Ethan said. "So I'm getting in."

The few people directly behind Ethan at the head of the line let out whoops of delight as she hurried to his side, grabbing his hand to lead him away from the outraged doorman. "It's okay," she called nervously. "He's a guest of Mr. Chaswick's!"

Fortunately the doorman had too much to deal with as a surge of people, emboldened by Ethan's move, surrounded him in the entranceway. Grateful for the distraction, Stacy dragged Ethan off through the milling crowd.

"You carry a *knife*?" she gasped into his ear.

Ethan was smiling now, his expression as benign as a choirboy's. "Comes in handy now and then," he murmured.

Her heart didn't stop beating in double time until she had led Ethan downstairs. Personally she detested the abusive doormen who reigned at these clubs, but even as a part of her cheered Ethan's audacity, an inner voice was asking her, tremulously: Who *is* this guy?

She checked him out uneasily as they made their descent. Who'd have thought the professor carried a knife? But then, how well did she know him, anyway? Maybe she was planning to build a publicity campaign around a certifiable nut case.

Still, Stacy couldn't help being impressed by his command of the situation. And Ethan was already enjoying himself, if his expression of slightly bemused pleasure as she led him around the dance floor was any indication. His head kept swiveling in all directions as they walked, while nodding absently to the booming beat of the music.

"You come here often?" he yelled near her ear.

Stacy smiled ruefully at the clichéd line, then realized his question had been half in earnest. "No," she yelled back. "At least, I try not to. I mean," she added at his quizzical look, "I used to go to clubs like this a lot more a few years back. But I think I've gotten kind of 'clubbed out.'"

"Oh." He nodded. "Buy you a drink?"

Stacy glanced over at the crowded bar, where getting a bartender's attention often demanded a serious investment of energy and patience. She decided it might be better if she handled this round, since she'd just learned there was no telling what Ethan Brody might do if provoked.

"I'll buy you one," she called. "You're the client."

Eva, Andy and Phil were within hailing distance. She guided Ethan over and made introductions, then excused herself to take care of the drinks as Martin Chaswick appeared with a lanky man in black leather wearing an ear-ring below his peroxide-yellow-and-green-tinted hair. Stacy scoped Ethan out. He was shaking hands with the two men, apparently unfazed. She went to the bar.

Eva joined her there a few minutes later. "Your new friend is making quite an impression," she said.

"What do you mean?" Stacy asked nervously, looking over her shoulder. But she couldn't see Ethan or the group from here.

"Martin's friend asked him what he thought of the place," Eva said, with a little giggle. "Ethan said he thought it was a lot of fun, only he couldn't figure out what those inaccurately executed imitation Mexican death's-head fetishes were doing on the walls. You know, the skull things?"

"So?"

"Martin's friend *made* the Mexican skulls," Eva said. "He's Pedro Maartens."

"Oh, dear," Stacy murmured. So that was why the man with the peroxided hair had looked familiar—Pedro Maartens, one of the latest in a stream of successful young artists from SoHo, was on his way to making millions at the age of twenty-nine. "Maybe I'd better get back there, quick."

"He's *cute*," Eva said. "Where did you meet him?"

"Tell you later," she said, handing the bartender her money. She jostled her way through the crowd, drinks in hand, craning her neck for a glimpse of Ethan. He wasn't hard to spot, actually, his khaki pants and simple blue work shirt standing out amidst the wilder, outré fashions that were endemic to this arty crowd.

At first she thought her worst fears were being confirmed. Ethan and Pedro had squared off opposite each other, their faces reddened and seemingly hostile. Then she realized they were both on their knees with a small table between them, ringed by a crowd of laughing and cheering onlookers—arm wrestling.

"Quite a character."

Stacy started at the sound of a familiar and not too welcome voice. Christopher White was not one of her favorite people. And though they traveled in the same circles, worked in the same office and made the same polite noises at each other, she knew full well that the feeling was mutual.

She turned and smiled. His slick blond hair, always immaculately combed, shone in the club lights, along with his superwhite teeth. She'd always wondered if they were real or capped. "Hello, Christopher."

Christopher had seen her as direct competition from the moment she'd joined P and W, only months after he had. He'd immediately set about making things difficult for her in many subtle ways. Stacy had little choice but to go on the defensive, and she'd been in that position ever since.

"Is that your professor?" he asked.

Ethan and Pedro were on their feet, laughing, making a toast to some obscure city in Mexico, apparently now the best of friends. Stacy, relieved, turned back to face Christopher again. "Yes, that's Ethan Brody," she said, wondering how much about her promotional ideas he'd already ferreted out from office gossip.

"You've certainly got a colorful personality there."

"So it seems," she said warily.

"Richard is intrigued," he said. "We all are. If there's anything I can do to help..."

He'd probably like to help find a good place on her back to slide a knife into, she thought. "Thank you," she said promptly. "But I think I've got a handle on the situation."

No sooner had she said this than she was nearly knocked off her feet and had to grab the dance floor railing to keep her balance. "Sorry!" Ethan exclaimed. "It's a little crowded."

He'd been reaching out to get her attention, she realized, and been jostled into her by the nearby dancers. "That's okay," she said, flushed. Christopher was looking on, smiling. She supposed she'd have to introduce Ethan.

But Pedro and Eva had other ideas, grabbing Ethan's arm and motioning Stacy to join the dancers. "No," she mimed.

"Come on!" Eva called.

"I don't really feel like—"

But again, the club crowd had its own agenda. Even as she protested, laughing, she was caught up in the movement of people around her. When she turned back to where she'd been, Christopher was gone. The next thing she knew, she was facing Ethan on the dance floor.

The expression on his face was priceless. People were gyrating to the left and right of him, and he clearly had little idea of what he was expected to do. "Hi," he yelled.

"Hi," she yelled back.

"I guess this beats working at the museum."

Stacy laughed. "We'll go someplace else."

"This is okay for now," he called. "Only I'm not really a dancer."

"You don't have to be. Just get into the beat."

Ethan shrugged and began to move, watching her for cues. He started out hopping and bopping more than dancing, but he did have a sure sense of the beat. Stacy wasn't quite prepared for what came next. Encouraged by the in-the-cups Pedro, the professor cut loose.

He began working up a real sweat, doing odd little turns that made him look like a cross between a whirling dervish and a kung fu fighter. Any worries she'd had about Ethan Brody holding his own on the New York City club scene were being summarily swept aside. Dancers on all sides of him were cheering Ethan on and even picking up his improvised steps.

Stacy could barely keep up with him. And she couldn't stop smiling. What made it fun to dance with him, she realized, was that he was so obviously enjoying the novelty of it. His eyes never left hers, and he smiled back as he watched her move along with him within the undulating sea of dancers.

She noticed that his rough-hewn good looks were turning the heads of a number of the women in their vicinity, and that gave her a feeling of great satisfaction. *Do I know how to pick 'em, or what?* she thought. The guy had a natural charisma.

He danced closer, adjusting his rhythm to a lower-key, more intimate groove. "So this is how New Yorkers have fun," he said at her ear.

"I guess so," she told him.

He nodded happily and moved away again. Stacy realized she was still smiling. Come to think of it, when was the last time she'd had this much fun with a man?

Ethan Brody was an unending series of surprises. He'd come off as a complete space cadet when she'd met him, but he was turning out to be more...substantial. He was a little odd, yes, but he did know how to have a good time. He was a good dancer, sexy, in his way. He was probably even good in—

No sooner had she almost begun to think the thought than Stacy stopped it cold. Had she entirely lost her mind? Ethan Brody was a client, for heaven's sake, someone she was going to have to work very closely with for quite some time. And he wasn't even remotely the sort of man she could ever be romantically attracted to....

Was he?

Chapter Four

"Turn around," Stacy commanded.

Ethan frowned, then dutifully turned.

"Hole," said Russell. "Left shoulder. Well, we could cover it," he mused. "Drape a jacket over his shoulder?"

"Maybe we just go for realism," Stacy said. "After all, there's a lot of wear and tear in the jungle."

"He's not in the jungle," Russell said. "This is supposed to be how an archaeologist looks when he's back in civilization."

"I don't like the shirt, anyway," Stacy murmured. "He looks too much like a schoolteacher in that pinstripe."

Ethan cleared his throat, turning around to face the two of them with a disgruntled expression. "This *is* how he looks," he announced.

"Yes, of course," Stacy said hastily. "But this is a key photo session, Ethan. We want the image to really be ... well, perfect."

"Image," he muttered. "I happen to like this shirt. I've worn it for years."

"It shows," Russell said, and Stacy shot him a reprimanding look.

"And if it makes me look like a schoolteacher," Ethan went on, "maybe that's because I am one."

"Yes, you are," she said, placating him. "Nobody's trying to turn you into anything else." She could sense that Ethan's patience was wearing thin. They'd been having him get in and out of shirts and pants for a half hour now. She checked her watch. "And seeing as there's an hour before we're due at the studio, maybe we should just go with what he's got on, Russell. Don't you think?"

Russell shrugged. Stacy gave Ethan one of her best we're-in-this-together-please-be-understanding smiles. It worked. He relaxed visibly, the stiffness going out of his posture. "I could use some air."

"Good idea," she said. "Look, it's only a dozen blocks from here. Would you like to walk down? I'll have Russell bring the clothes over."

"Sure," said Russell, excusing himself with a little bow. "Let me just make a phone call."

Stacey nodded, glancing at the open suitcase on her desk, with the tidy little pile of shirts and pairs of pants laid across it. This was apparently half of the man's wardrobe, they'd discovered. The professor was not exactly a fashion plate. Not that she wanted him to be, Stacy reminded herself. But they did want a publicity photo that emphasized his physical appeal, and a little bit of flair in the clothing department wouldn't hurt. An idea struck her.

"There's one store I'd like us to dip into on the way," she said cautiously. "Just for a minute. In case there's something there that strikes your fancy."

"If you insist," Ethan replied. "For now, I'll change back into these," he said, picking up the pair of nondescript khakis he'd worn in to their little fashion consultation. "If that's all right with you."

"No problem," Stacy said brightly. Ethan nodded and went to the door, pants in hand. She watched him leave, headed once again to the rest room just outside. Well, he did look decent, even in his unfashionable duds. If worst came to worst, they were authentic.

She certainly didn't want to push the issue. Ethan had been cooperative over the past few days, but she was never sure exactly what was going on in his mind. She knew he was uncomfortable being the focus of this kind of attention, and an underlying tension emanated from him about such matters of appearance and behavior. On the other hand, he never objected to getting together with her and putting in the time necessary.

Stacy leaned over the desk to hit her intercom. "Charlotte, I'm going to Professor Brody's shooting," she said.

A theatrical gasp came over the little speaker. "Don't you dare shoot that man," said Charlotte.

"Cute," said Stacy. "Tell Reynolds not to wait for me on that meeting. I'll probably be late."

"Okay," Charlotte said. "Is he still here?"

"Ethan? Yes."

"I won't take my lunch break yet, then. Bye."

Stacy straightened up, shaking her head. Her secretary was mad for Ethan Brody. He was apparently oblivious to her charms, though. Come to think of it, she had no sense of the professor's taste in women. Probably went for those Bolivian amazon types, she mused, glancing at her own reflection in the mirror on her office closet door.

Stacy was looking, she had to admit, as up-to-date as Ethan was behind the times. She had on a smart black and white checked wool jacket over a white silk blouse and a high-waisted black wool skirt from Barney's. It was an outfit she especially liked for the combination of authority and femininity it suggested, casual but stylish—not too funky, not too chic. When it came to her own image, she was very much in control.

Ethan, on the other hand . . . It was possible that he had no idea what his clothes suggested about him, or even that he was particularly attractive. Well, that was refreshing in a man, in a business and a town where image counted for so much. Stacy smiled, thinking back to the other night at the Tango Club. That *had* been fun.

They'd danced for a while and had another drink—perfectly harmless, of course. In the blur of activity, the exhilaration of dancing to the din of music, a thought had strayed across her mind, true, an entirely unprofessional one. But Stacy was too smart to mistake an idle fantasy like that for anything serious. She had no romantic designs on Ethan Brody, and he didn't seem to have any of her, thank goodness. This was a tough enough job as it was.

And here he was now, looking more at ease clad in his dependable khaki pants. "Ready?" she asked, smiling. "Let's hit the street."

HE WAS DOING HIS BEST, really he was.

Considering that writing up a one-page autobiography, getting his voice recorded for a test tape and having to pose for a bunch of photographs were three things he normally wouldn't have the remotest interest in doing, Ethan was on his best behavior, indeed. For the past three days he'd been forcing himself to go along with this scheme of Stacy Morrison's, and he hadn't lost his temper yet.

How could he lose his temper when Stacy turned her thousand-watt smile on him?

It was maddening. He knew he was being an idiot, submitting himself to the indignity of "image polishing," as Russell had facetiously referred to it the day before. His motivation was hopelessly skewed, and he was setting himself up to take a fall, for sure. She wasn't interested in him. This whole thing was a waste of time and was bound to get worse before it got better.

But here he was, strolling down a sunny New York City street with a radiantly beautiful woman who was chatting on amiably about brochures, press kits and bus posters, and all he could do was smile, enjoying the warmth of her voice and the animation in her eyes, when—"Wait a second. Bus posters?"

"Yes, you know, like that," she said, gesturing at a bus that was pulling away from the curb. A heavily made up model's perfectly pearly teeth stretched practically the length of the bus. Ethan watched her frozen smile move up the street with disbelief.

"Me?" he said. "On one of those?"

"Well, maybe not that big," Stacy said. "It depends on which photo we end up using for the catalog cover. Some of the ones you gave us might be perfect, but I want to see what we get out of today's session."

Ethan felt his stomach clench. "Maybe this isn't such a good idea," he said.

"You have no idea how naturally photogenic you are," she said. "Really, there's no need to be self-conscious. You won't have to do anything silly, just be yourself."

She gave him a quick, encouraging grin, and Ethan felt his clenched stomach give way to an all too familiar, but-terfly-like feeling. Sap! Cretin! Yes, he was all of those things, but it was too late. He was hopelessly smitten. In fact, it was taking a good deal of effort to keep that little fact to himself.

The other night, when they'd been in that weirdo night-club, for example. There'd been a moment before they'd said goodbye when he'd wanted nothing more than to plant a kiss on those full red lips of hers, but he'd re-strained himself, of course. He wasn't *entirely* crazy.

And the next two days, when they'd met in the museum basement to pore over his revised notes together—that had been a challenge, all right. So near and yet so far. Every now and then he said something that made her laugh, and that wonderfully throaty music had pealed in his ears, drowning out any other thoughts in his head. Or she'd touch him, just casually putting a hand on his arm for emphasis, or nudge him with her arm when she got excited about something, and the rest of both worlds, ancient Mayan and modern American, would cease to exist for a moment.

And he had to pretend that everything was as normal as normal could be. It was a terrible situation. At the moment he was adopting a new approach, born of desperation: he focused on what she was trying to do with him, do *to* him—and did his best to resent it.

But resenting Stacy Morrison wasn't that easy. Looks aside, it was this flip, easygoing quality she had that charmed him so. Any time he started to get riled up about something, she reduced its importance with a deft sentence or two or maybe a joke, and he ended up feeling like an ogre for thinking ill of her idea.

Like this photo shoot. Why, if she had all those prints from the dig itself, did he need to dress up and pose for publicity stills? It was silly enough having to drag a suitcase over to her office and try on his own clothes as if he were some kind of fashion model, but the thought of having actually to pose—

"Here we are," she announced, and he snapped out of his mental diatribe. "Let's take a look, okay?"

He looked at the store window, confused. There was a Jeep in it, and a bunch of safari uniforms that looked as if they belonged in some old MGM desert sheik epic. He glanced up at the store's logo. "Banana Republic?"

"Yes," she said, taking him by the arm and steering him toward the door before he could protest. "Maybe we can find a little something for you here."

Ethan stifled a groan. But by that time, Stacy had her arm linked through his, and he was catching a subtle whiff of perfume that was already puttifying his brain.

He let her lead him on.

"No," ETHAN SAID, casting a dubious eye on the pith helmet in her hand. "No way. Nobody's worn one of those to a real dig since the turn of the century, Stacy."

"Oh," she said, chagrined. "Sorry."

"Some of this stuff's okay," he allowed, feeling the material on the top pile of jean shirts at his side. "But have you checked the prices? Go to any army-navy store, you'd do a lot better."

"It's on P and W," she said absently, distracted by a low hubbub over at the store's entrance. A woman in expensive clothes was attracting some attention as she walked in. She looked familiar, even in sunglasses. Heads were turning to gawk at her as she approached them.

"Whitney Houston," Stacy said, as recognition dawned.

"Who?" Ethan followed her gaze. "Friend of yours?"

Stacy shot him a look. Ethan was apparently serious. "Boy, you really have been away for a while," she said. "She's a famous pop singer."

"Oh." He gave the superstar only the most cursory of glances as she passed, intent on Stacy. "You shop here a lot?"

"Once in a while," she said, aware that while the concentration of every other man in the vicinity was riveted on Miss Houston, Ethan seemed only interested in Stacy Morrison. She couldn't help feeling flattered. "What sort of music do you listen to, Ethan?"

He shrugged. "I kind of like Willie Nelson," he said. "Ah, Ray Charles . . . and Schubert."

"Schubert?"

"Yeah, Schubert, Bach . . . you know, regular stuff."

"Regular stuff," she echoed.

"Mozart's no slouch, either," he mused, fingering a poncho from the counter. "Plenty of good tunes."

Good tunes? Even as Stacy suppressed a laugh, her inner PR Geiger counter registered: good copy. "You listen to a lot of classical music in the jungle?"

He nodded. "Down there we also listen to a lot of reggae. Buck's a big Bob Marley fan."

"Buck?"

"My bird," Ethan said. "Hey, you don't really think I need to wear any of this, do you?" he asked, a plaintive note in his voice as he surveyed the clothing emporium's plethora of "rugged" pseudo safari wear.

A few aisles over, Whitney Houston was trying on a jacket. The bevy of teenagers hanging around her in adulation were snapping photos with their Instamatics. Stacy looked them over. Half of them were clad in Banana Republic duds, looking less like teenage New Yorkers than miniature colonial explorers en route to the Congo.

She glanced around the store. Yuppie types buying army fatigues. A housewife holding up to her chest a khaki vest that probably originated in the British RAF. Stacy had a well-developed sense of how long "hip" stayed hip in this fast-paced metropolis. She turned back to Ethan.

"No," she said decisively. "You wear whatever you want to wear." Ethan was enough of his own personality without any such store-bought accessories. The more she thought about it, the more his going against the stereotypical grain appealed to her.

"As a matter of fact," she went on, "let's have you look however you want to look from here on in. Even at the press conference tomorrow. How does that sound?"

"That sounds fantastic," he said, appreciative. "Can I quote you? In case you forget you said it later?"

"Absolutely. Here, we'll shake on it." She held out her hand.

"Great," he said. Whitney Houston was heading their way, but Stacy was too distracted by the man's handshake to pay the star much attention. Her senses were occupied with the feel of his hand grasping hers as she registered warmth, strength, and a subtle caressing quality in the smoothness of his palm as it left her own.

"Let's blow this joint," he said happily, turning up the aisle.

Stacy nodded, aware that her skin was tingling and that a strange fluttery feeling had invaded her stomach.

Fluttery feeling?

Remembering Richard's sarcastic comment on the phone, she felt her cheeks redden. Honestly, how ridiculous. There was nothing wrong with her stomach that an overdue lunch wouldn't correct.

RICHARD SAT BACK behind his desk, hands linked under his chin. "Who've we got coming?" he asked.

"The three newspapers, two local stations, one major network—"

"What's with the other two?"

"They'll pick up the story if no major disaster happens. Richard, you know how that is," Stacy said, her fingers crossed. True, if tonight happened to be a no-news night, the Mayan tomb piece just might make it into the filler slot on the national networks' late-night shows.

"And?" he prompted.

"And we've got *People*, *Personality*, *Us* and *We*." She checked her notepad. "There may be other magazines and a few radio stations. In fact, I've set up an interview on WUBW for right after the conference...."

Her voice trailed off as she saw that Richard wasn't listening. He was looking at the doorway. Stacy flinched inwardly as she heard Christopher's familiar singsong greeting. "Hey, guys."

He sauntered across the carpet as Richard nodded a hello. "Richard, the Revlon people haven't got back to us yet. Should I call Carrie now or wait?"

Richard frowned, leaning forward again to drum his fingers on the desk. Neat, Stacy thought grimly. As usual, Christopher's carefully calculated timing had succeeded in drawing her boss's attentions from her current achievement to his own account.

"Oh, sorry," he was saying now. "Didn't mean to interrupt."

"That's all right," Richard said vaguely. "This all listens well, Morrison. Get back to me with a full report when it's over, all right?"

Stacy nodded. Richard's calling her by her last name was a sign of affection, she knew, and something that "listened well" meant a job well done. Somewhat mollified, she stood up and began collecting the photos from his desk.

"These the new shots?" Christopher had one of the glossies from Ethan's photo session in hand.

"Yes," she said warily.

"What's this kind of smudgy thingy on his elbow?"

Stacy held her hand out for the photo. "A grass stain," she said pleasantly. "Never seen one before?"

Christopher chuckled. "Going for the authentic look, huh? That's a good approach."

"Yes, we think so," she said, with a cheery smile at Richard, who was already on the phone. He gave her a little wave, intent on a sotto voce conversation. Stacy kept the smile on for Christopher, who was sliding into the leather chair she'd just vacated with a proprietary air.

"See you on the news," he said breezily.

"That's right," she said. Snake. She hurried out. Ethan's conference was in forty-five minutes, and she was picking him up at the hotel.

HE WASN'T WAITING outside when her cab pulled up to the curb, unfortunately, so she let the taxi go and strode into the Plaza lobby. No sign of Ethan. Stacy nervously checked her watch and headed for the main desk, about to have him paged. But there he was now, strolling past the elevator bank, an open letter in his hand.

Stacy hailed him. Ethan looked up with a preoccupied air. "Hi," he muttered as she approached.

"Something wrong?"

"No," he said, eyes still intent on the airmail stationery he was holding. "Zack's having some problems, that's all."

"Your bird."

"Bird?" He looked at her, confused. "No, that's Buck. Zack is Zachary Matthews, a colleague of mine who's at a dig down in the Imperial Valley. He's getting resistance from the Cuyapaipe."

"What's that?"

"The Indians who live there. It's the southernmost part of California," he said. "Near the Mexican border. Apparently Zack's dig is crossing the lines of some ancient Cuyapaipe burial grounds. You see, after the Mayan empire was prominent in Mexico—"

"Could we talk about this later?" she said, trying to rein in an impatience born of anxiety about this conference. "We really should get going."

Ethan put the letter away as she hustled him through the lobby. He appeared to be listening as she reviewed what they'd discussed about the conference. "They've got the slides set up over there," she told him. "We'll run through them fairly quickly, though. Most of the time is going to be spent on your prepared statement and their questions. You remember what we said about the question and answer stuff?"

Ethan nodded, squinting in the sunlight outside the hotel entrance. "That looks like fun," he said.

Stacy sighed, following his gaze across the street, where just at that moment, one of the horse carriages that catered to the tourist trade around the southern end of the park was slowly moving along the curb.

This particularly gaudy carriage was loaded down by a large family of out-of-towners, the mother and father with exquisite camera in hand, the three kids slurping at ice-cream cones. A car stuck behind it gave an angry honk. The driver atop the cab looked half asleep as he lazily tugged the aging horse's reins.

Ethan chuckled at the sight, then turned to look at her again, one eyebrow raised in an unvoiced question. Stacy bit her lip. In the first place, they were in danger of being late. In the second, such a trip was too corny to contemplate, anyway.

Ethan seemed to intuit her response. "No, huh," he murmured.

"What we need," she said gently, "is a taxi." She scanned the street for one. Oddly, there weren't any cars in the vicinity, let alone cabs. She noticed a police barricade, cutting off traffic on their side of the street. Some people were bunched up at the corner. She wondered briefly what the problem was. An accident. A parade?

Whatever it was, she wasn't going to let it sabotage their all-important press conference. "Come on," she said to Ethan. "Let's cut across the street and get onto Fifth. We can find a cab there."

ETHAN STEPPED OFF the sidewalk, Stacy at his side, still a little distracted by Zack's newsy but worrisome letter. He'd been hoping to catch up with his friend in the desert when he was done with this exhibit business, but now it seemed such a trip might be superfluous. The dig was in danger of being shut down, and that would be a disappointment to both of them. He'd wanted to get a look at the cave paintings Zack had discovered there.

Stacy was talking to him, he realized, and he tried to focus his attention on what she was saying as she hurried them across the street. Something about keeping his language simple and not getting too technical if he could help it. Ethan nodded, his attention distracted by the crowd gathered on the corner.

A man with a walkie-talkie to his face was standing in the middle of the street waved excitedly in their direction. Ethan slowed. The man was pointing to the corner. Ethan looked over, but just as he did, something quite astonishing caught his eye.

Beyond the group of people knotted behind the police barrier, a tall woman with a mane of reddish-blond hair was striding quickly up the block. No sooner had he noticed her, than Ethan realized that the lanky man in a windbreaker, jeans and running shoes at her side was— lifting her purse!

The woman let out a shriek as the man grabbed the shoulder bag and yanked. He sprinted off the sidewalk, running diagonally across the street and into Ethan's path. Ethan reacted on pure reflex. Even before he thought to, he was running as the red-haired woman yelled, "Stop! Stop him!"

Adrenaline shot through him as he put on speed. The lanky man in the windbreaker was headed for the park, but Ethan was gaining on him. He was shorter than Ethan, possibly younger, and as he threw a startled glance over his shoulder, Ethan knew with certainty that he could take him.

Voices were yelling behind Ethan, and he was vaguely conscious of someone else running toward him, perhaps another pedestrian helping his pursuit. Ethan ran harder, closing in on his prey. But just then the man abruptly changed direction, putting on speed in his turn. He was headed into the cover of the park.

Ethan cursed under his breath even as he took longer strides. A criminal like that was bound to know the ins and outs of the park better than he did. If he wasn't going to lose him, Ethan needed to gain on him immediately.

Then he saw the horse at the curb. There was a policewoman kneeling nearby it, engrossed in comforting some wailing child on the sidewalk. Ethan waved frantically at her but she merely stared at him, having looked up too late to see the darting figure of the purse snatcher, already behind her.

The whole thing happened very quickly. Before the policewoman had time to do more than yell, he was astride the horse and headed into the park. The horse snorted and shook its head in protest but nonetheless set off at a fast clip. It was obviously used to taking sudden flight, if not to its new rider.

The man in the windbreaker was running down a grassy hill, pedestrians scattering in his wake, their surprised expressions turning to shock as Ethan came cantering over the rise on horseback. The man glanced over his shoulder. He looked alarmed, and inexplicably, just when Ethan would have expected him to really make a mad dash for it, possibly zigzag out of reach, he slowed.

That was all Ethan needed. Within a few yards of a concrete pathway, he leaped forward, pulling in the horse's reins with one fist, and grabbed the flapping end of the man's windbreaker in his other outstretched hand.

"Hey!" the man yelped, panic on his face. "What the—?"

The rest of his retort was literally knocked out of him as Ethan sprang from the slowing horse. He landed on the purse snatcher in a flying tackle. Together they tumbled to the ground, the man cursing and flailing fists at him.

But Ethan kept him down on the grass, fending off the assault, concentrating on wresting the stolen bag from the man's hand before he got whopped in the face with it again.

"Easy!" Ethan barked. "I don't want to have to hurt you, but—"

Strong hands grabbed his own shoulders. He was being pulled off his captured prisoner, and even as he protested, was alarmed to find his own arms twisted behind him.

"All right, buddy." A police officer was in front of him, brandishing a nightstick and handcuffs. "Simmer down!"

It was the policewoman who had his arms pinned, he realized. Ethan stopped struggling. "I'm glad you showed up," he said, a little out of breath. "This man—"

But no one was listening to him. The man in the windbreaker was on his feet, yelling. Ethan didn't understand what the guy was talking about, or why the police were concentrating on holding him, instead. "He's a lunatic! A maniac! I could've been killed!" the man shouted.

"Take it easy," said the officer. "Hey, hey, give us some room here!"

Ethan had been conscious of a small crowd of excited people gathering around them. He was momentarily blinded by the flash of a camera and when he blinked, refocusing, he saw even more people running toward him, more cameras in hand, even a microphone waving in the air.

The man in the windbreaker was surrounded by three or four people who seemed to be attending to his injuries, including a huge man who looked like a bodyguard. Another grim-faced guy in a suit was waving a finger in Ethan's face. "We're going to see you in court!" he was shouting.

Something weird was going on here.

ONE SECOND Ethan had been standing next to her, and all had been right with the world. The next thing Stacy knew, he was gone, and even before she knew where, she'd had a sinking sensation that her best-laid plans were about to blow up in her face.

But she couldn't have imagined he'd be able to get into this much trouble this fast. She had to hand it to the man. When it came to making things go wrong, he had an instinct for the truly original approach.

At first, she too had thought that the running man was a bona fide purse snatcher. But when the red-haired woman started yelling, and Stacy recognized her as the actress Barbara Talley, and those men with the walkie-talkies had started running after Ethan, Stacy had comprehended the misguided man's grievous error.

Then she saw the camera mounted on the crane, just around the corner, and understood immediately that they'd merely wandered into one of the many movie shoots that were routinely going on around the city on any given day. But by then Ethan Brody had already commandeered the policewoman's horse and was riding into Central Park, and all she could do was look on helplessly and sigh.

If she hadn't hustled over there in record time, getting through the crowd that was already gathering within the park's entrance would've been quite a feat. As it was, she managed to push and shove her way to Ethan's side in time to hear the police officer start reading him his rights.

"Wait a second!" she interrupted. "You can't arrest this man."

"Who are you?" asked the disgruntled cop.

"I'm with the firm of P and W, and I represent Professor Brody," she began. "And he's due at a press conference even as we speak."

"Press conference?"

The policeman's skeptical tone was drowned by the two reporters who were converging on the man in the windbreaker. "Mr. DeVine! Are you hurt?"

"Hey, Bobby, over here!" The reporter's camera flashed.

The excited squeals of three teenage girls who'd spotted the actor added to the melee, so Stacy had difficulty making herself understood at first. But by the time Bobby DeVine had calmed down sufficiently to give out some autographs, Stacy had done some of the fastest talking she'd ever done in her professional life.

"I dunno, there's still the stealing of police property to consider," the officer said. He was indicating the horse, now tethered nearby.

"He didn't steal it, he borrowed it," Stacy said impatiently. "He was trying to capture a criminal, and the officer present didn't respond to his requests for assistance."

"Didn't respond?" The policewoman, indignant, turned on Stacy, her hands on her hips. "I see this lug barreling at me, waving his arms around—"

"His name is Professor Ethan Brody," Stacy said.

"Spell that, will ya?" This from a newspaperman.

"Hey, can we get Bobby with the professor?" His photographer was already snapping away.

"Back it up, back it up!" The policeman was trying to make some order out of the chaos surrounding him.

Through it all, Ethan maintained a stony silence. Stacy couldn't tell if he was angry, embarrassed or unfazed, but didn't have time to find out just then. She was too busy thinking on her feet, trying to make the best out of this potentially litigious mess. She concentrated on the man in the suit.

Fortunately Bobby DeVine's agent was amenable to reason. In fact it wasn't hard to get him to agree not to press charges, mainly because the actor himself had tuned into the absurdity of the situation. The eyes of the press were upon him, and he was savvy enough about the nature of publicity and concerned enough about his image to have shifted his stance from outrage to good-natured amusement in a matter of minutes.

Which was why, creature of the limelight that he was, Bobby didn't object to shaking hands with Ethan as the cameras flashed. By the time the photographers were asking to have shots of Ethan with the horse, even the policewoman was mollified. The magical power of celebrityhood to soothe the ruffled feathers of even the most intractable city employee was a strange and wondrous thing.

Stacy surveyed the coverage, mentally counting up the various media representatives on hand. Elation was taking the place of anxiety. Come to think of it, things had worked out even better than she could have imagined.

"Sorry," Ethan muttered, as Stacy gently but firmly started guiding him away from the crowd of rubbernecking tourists and happy press people. "We're probably way late."

"Late?" she looked up at him, shaking her head. "Don't worry about it."

"No?" His gaze was more thoroughly befuddled than the one he'd evinced while posing with Bobby DeVine.

"Honey," she informed him, "you just *had* your press conference. And it was an unqualified smash."

"I THINK my favorite is 'Mugging Mugger Mugged,'" Stacy said, surveying the newspaper clippings on her table.

At the other end of the phone, Eva laughed. "That must be the *Trib*," she said.

"Right," said Stacy. "And there's a subheading under the photo. Ready? 'Mayan Maven Mashes Macho Method Man.'"

"That's awful," Eva crowed.

"No, it's wonderful," Stacy corrected her. "They spelled 'Mayan' correctly."

"You saw the *News*, of course."

"Got it right here." Stacy patted the paper. "I wonder if the name'll stick."

"'Arizona Brody'? It does have a ring to it."

"'A real-life Indiana Jones made cinematic history today,'" Stacy read, "'by tackling Oscar-winner Bobby DeVine as the cameras rolled.' Wait," she said suddenly. "You don't suppose they...? No," she corrected herself.

"What?" Eva asked.

"I thought for a moment there might actually be footage of Ethan and DeVine," she explained. "But that's impossible. They were already out of camera range when Ethan caught up with him—" A telltale clicking on her line indicated another call was waiting to be answered. "Oh, Eva, let me get back to you, okay? That might be Channel 5."

"Sure thing," her friend said. "I'll look for you on the news."

"Eleven o'clock," Stacy told her. "Talk to you later." She pressed down the receiver. "Hello?"

"Stacy?"

"Ethan!" She gripped the phone harder, relieved and excited. "Where have you been?"

"I've been looking at flight schedules," he said dryly.

"What do you mean?" she asked.

"I mean I had to practically sneak back into my hotel room, because the lobby was full of photographers,"

Ethan said. "And my first impulse was to head for the airport instead."

"Now, Ethan," she said. "Don't be like that. What's wrong with a few photographers?"

"I'm too much of a gentleman to tell you what I think of them," he said. "The point is, didn't they get enough of me this afternoon?"

"I guess not," she said cheerfully. "You should be flattered."

"I'm not flattered," he said. "I'm...I don't know what I am."

"You've become a minor celebrity," she teased. "There's nothing wrong with that."

"There is when it's because you've made a total fool of yourself," he said darkly.

"You were not a fool," she said. "You were being very...heroic. I was proud of you."

"Sure," he muttered.

"No, really, Ethan," she said, and she wasn't entirely gilding the lily. It had given her a thrill to see Ethan jump up onto that horse, like some sort of modern-day Butch Cassidy, and take off into the park. "It was very impressive, what you did. And nobody's blaming you for doing it."

"No, they're just making fun of me," he said. "And what's with this 'Arizona Brody' bit? How'd they find out I'm from Arizona, anyway?"

Stacy bit her lip. She was the one who'd supplied the API reporter with all the salient particulars about who Ethan Brody was. But she sensed instinctively that letting Ethan know this relatively unimportant piece of information right now might set him against her, and she couldn't chance that. Not when they were on a lucky promotional roll. "Oh, you know the media," she said blithely. "Being nosy is their job."

"Yeah, well I know a few noses I wouldn't mind punching," he muttered.

"Not a good idea," she hastened to tell him. "Ethan, look on the bright side of this. What's the one thing that's in all the papers and about to be on the evening news?"

"My dim-witted visage."

"The Mayan Tomb Exhibit," she corrected him triumphantly. "Your museum show has gotten more free publicity today than money could've ever bought in a month's worth of PR. Now, isn't that great?"

"It's all right," he grudgingly allowed. "Well, at least nobody got pictures of me in action."

Which was a disappointment. Stacy had wanted Ethan to stick around, actually, so the news team could get an interview, but he'd insisted on leaving the park as quickly as possible. She'd had to settle for supplying the networks with Ethan's publicity photos. "Yes, and it's only a local story," she told him, masking her own regret over the fact.

Her phone line was clicking again. "Ethan, I have to take another call. You're back at your hotel?"

"For the moment."

"Now, come on. Don't even think about leaving town. You and I have a lot of work to do. And all that's happened today is that you've inadvertently made a lot of *my* work easier. Which I'm very grateful for. In fact . . ." She thought hurriedly. "I'm buying you breakfast in the morning. How's that?"

"Well . . ."

"Good. I'll pick you up at your hotel at nine, okay? Get a good night's sleep," she added, surmising that the one person who wouldn't be pleased by the upcoming eleven o'clock news item, ironically enough, was its subject.

"All right," he grumbled.

"Great. Take care," she said, and switched to the other call. It was Sheila Coles from MGM. She was the publicist for *City Streets*, the film Bobby DeVine was in the midst of shooting, and she'd been in contact with Stacy throughout the day. The incident with Ethan had been almost as useful to her as it had been to Stacy, and at the moment she sounded particularly excited.

"We've hit pay dirt," Sheila said. "I was just talking to Gary Becker at Channel 5—"

"I know," Stacy said. "They're definitely running the piece, about 11:22."

"It's better than that," Sheila said. "Do you know *what* they're running?"

"That clip of DeVine leaving the park, and the stills I sent over of Ethan."

"Better yet," Sheila said. "They've got your professor on the horse."

"You're kidding! How?"

"A tourist was taking home videos of DeVine on the set, and he got the whole thing, practically—at least a pretty good shot of Ethan in his cavalry charge, in focus, in color."

"Good Lord," Stacy breathed. "Do you know what this could mean—about the coverage?"

"Yup," said her MGM counterpart, and both women uttered the hallowed word simultaneously.

"National."

Chapter Five

People were staring at him.

At first Ethan thought he must be imagining it. He was walking across the Plaza lobby to meet Stacy, and two women near the front desk stopped talking to watch him go by. Ethan wondered if it was his clothes. Most other male Plaza guests tended toward suits and ties. To be safe, he nervously checked his zipper and shoelaces. All seemed to be in order, and the two women stopped watching him after Stacy greeted him, though they certainly gave her a thorough once-over.

Then, while they were looking for a cab outside, a couple with a teenage son, waiting on the steps for a valet to unload their luggage, nudged one another and fixed their gazes on Ethan. He self-consciously felt the lines of his trousers, wondering if they were ripped in the back or something. But no, that wasn't it.

He chanced giving them a tentative smile as a cab arrived. The teenage son's eyes became two large circles, even as his parents nodded and waved cheerfully. Ethan wondered if they were just particularly social out-of-towners.

He shrugged and settled into the back seat, though settling was a little difficult when only a few inches separated him from Stacy Morrison and her pair of—he couldn't help but notice—very shapely legs, encased in some black stockings that had a subtle swirly kind of pattern on them. It occurred to Ethan that he'd yet to see her twice in the same outfit.

Today she had on an orange-red double-breasted jacket with a scooped neck over a simple black blouse and a pinkish-red wool skirt. She looked...chic he supposed was the operative word, but there was something about the way she wore whatever she wore that made it seem entirely natural.

Not that these colors and that cut would've seemed natural outside of this concrete island, he reflected, sneaking a look at her shoes. Heels. Again, as he sometimes found himself doing in moments of idle fantasy, he tried to picture Stacy in another environment, say, oh, in the Central American bush country. The picture didn't materialize.

It didn't materialize because it was an impossibility. A woman like Stacy Morrison wouldn't last a minute on a genuine archaeological expedition. Transplant her somewhere that she couldn't use a charge card or get a manicure, and she'd most probably be on the next plane out at the first sign of physical hardship. It was nice to think that she was made of stronger stuff, but really he should be realistic.

She was looking at him expectantly. Had she asked him a question? "Sorry. What did you...?"

"I said, have you been to SoHo yet?" He shook his head. "I thought we'd go down there for brunch," Stacy said. "Get you out of midtown for a change."

"Fine with me," Ethan said, and then once again, he had the odd feeling that he was being observed. This was especially strange, since they were in a moving vehicle, but then he caught the cabby's eyes in the rearview mirror and realized his feeling was justified. The man squinted at Ethan, then looked away.

Ethan shifted in his seat, befuddled. Was he being paranoid? Or had someone stuck a clown nose on his face when he wasn't looking?

"Sleep well?" Stacy asked.

"More or less," he said.

"Hey, you in the movies or sumpin'?" The cabdriver's piercing baritone startled him.

"No," Ethan said.

The cabbie scratched his head. "I've seen ya before, somewhere."

Ethan shrugged, turning to Stacy. But she was staring out her side window with a preoccupied expression. "How about you?" he asked. "Sleep well?"

She nodded, then met his gaze. "You didn't happen to see the eleven o'clock news, did you?"

"No," Ethan said, frowning. He'd hoped that yesterday's embarrassment had perhaps gotten buried under items of more pressing importance. "How bad was it?"

"That's it!" The cabby slapped the back of his seat with his hand. "I seen you on TV. You're that guy, aren'tcha? Arizona Brody!"

Ethan blanched. *That* bad? He looked at Stacy, who was biting her lower lip in consternation. "I'm Ethan Brody, yes," he said.

The driver smiled broadly. "How do you like that? I knew you looked familiar. So, what's he like?"

"Who?"

"Bobby DeVine! He give you a run for your money, or what? Some of these movie guys are wimps, but I bet DeVine can really throw a punch, huh?"

Ethan sighed. "It all happened pretty fast," he said.

"I'll say! I liked the way you jumped on that horse, kaboom. It was like sumpin' out of a John Wayne picture, ya know?"

Ethan turned back to Stacy again, eyes widening. "I'll tell you all about it," she said, her voice apologetic.

"Hey, listen, while we're stuck at this light, do me a favor, willya?" The cabdriver was thrusting a pad through the open divider. "For the wife, ya know? She'd get a kick out of it." He chuckled. "Arizona's autograph!"

APPARENTLY even those who lived south of Houston watched the eleven o'clock news. Stacy had thought this part of town might be less interested in the exploits of Ethan Brody, but unfortunately, their waitress at the Cupping Room, a comfortably laid-back eatery on West Broadway, recognized him the moment they walked in.

Ethan seemed to take these attentions in stride, more or less, but Stacy was beginning to know him well enough to sense the discomfort beneath his implacable face. "Look," she said, signaling for their check, after yet another Cupping Room patron had inspected them both with the uninhibited stares New Yorkers employ for celebrities. "It's a momentary thing. By tomorrow no one will be bothering you."

"They'd better not be," he said, somewhat ominously. "This isn't my idea of a good time."

"Well, honestly, why not?" she asked. "What's wrong with people being interested in you?"

"I'm the kind of guy who likes his privacy, that's all," Ethan said. "Who wants to be stared at and photographed and followed and bugged? It's ridiculous, anyway. I didn't do anything." He stared at his plate. "All right, I did something. I acted like a horse's ass. But now that half of America knows it, anything I do is going to be material for a bad joke."

"No, it won't be that bad," she said, feeling a tug of remorse at her cavalier handling of yesterday's incident. Time for a subject change. "Then what *is* your idea of a good time?'' she asked. He shot her a look, and she realized she'd sounded flip. But it was a sincere question. ''I mean, besides going on digs in remote and foreign climates,'' she said.

''Oh, I don't know,'' he said, looking perplexed. ''In a way, my work's been my life for a while now.''

A life of rock hunting? She found it difficult to believe that there wasn't more to the man. ''No hobbies?'' she asked. ''No frivolous amusements? After all, you're a good dancer.''

''Not really,'' he said, abashed, and Stacy smiled. There was something so refreshing about a man who was genuinely modest. After all, another guy might have been perfectly happy to have his picture in the papers. His self-deprecating air made him seem all the more attractive. Idly she wondered why some woman hadn't already grabbed Ethan Brody. Maybe his profession was the problem.

''Isn't it an awfully...solitary kind of work?'' she asked.

He shrugged. ''It can be. But there's always people around, actually. Students come down to work with us. And there's Wally, of course.'' He brightened. ''He's coming in tonight, you know. You can meet him tomorrow.''

Stacy nodded. ''But I was thinking more of... I guess you're not interested in raising a family,'' she said.

''Oh.'' He looked at his plate, then at the waitress who was approaching with their check. He seemed grateful for the distraction. ''It hasn't been a main priority,'' he said, after she gave the woman her credit card. ''Hey, you don't have to keep doing that.''

''It's on P and W,'' she reminded him. ''Was it ever?''

''Hmm?''

''A priority. You know, wife and family.''

Ethan's face took on a set, you-are-approaching-the-borderline expression. "A few years back, maybe," he said guardedly. "But I've been pretty busy lately."

Aha, she thought, a woman in his past. She might've figured that. The other thing about Ethan's manner was that it brought out her inquisitiveness. She didn't mean to pry, but she couldn't help it. Sometimes he was like an open book, but at others, it was as if that open book was written in a secret language. And perversely, the less personal he wanted to be, the more she wanted to find out.

"What about you?" he asked.

"Me?" Stacy waved a hand. "I'm married to my career," she said lightly. "At least for the time being."

Ethan nodded. "Well, you know what that's like, then."

"Not that I like it, necessarily." Funny, she hadn't meant to say that, but it had slipped out. Now she was the one happy to busy herself filling out the credit card slip the waitress had handed her.

But Ethan, fortunately, wasn't being as inquisitive as she. When Stacy glanced over at him, he looked literally tongue-tied. "Ready to go?" she asked.

Some interested gazes followed them up the aisle. Stacy was glad no one had overtly pestered them. Now, if they could get back to the museum without incident, maybe she'd be able to broach her next promotional suggestion to Ethan and not get too much resistance.

"Hey, Arizona! Where's your horse?"

"Who's the hot date, Brody?"

Oh, no. It was two jackal-like members of the fourth estate, cameras in hand. They'd been waiting outside the restaurant. How had they zeroed in on this place? Ethan was already doing a slow burn as he steered her up the sidewalk.

"Hey, give us a smile, Prof!"

Stacy felt him stiffen at her side. She put a placating hand on his arm, even as she felt a sudden flush of guilt. She'd told Russell where they were going, and told him to handle any calls related to Ethan. So she was indirectly responsible, wasn't she?

"It's okay," she said. "Just keep walking and they'll leave us alone." The reporters had already gotten some photos, as soon as she and Ethan had emerged from the restaurant, so she reasoned they wouldn't be unduly persistent. Fortunately she was right. When they turned the corner heading west, the voices died out behind them.

"'Arizona Brody,'" he muttered. "It's ridiculous."

"I know," she said. "But honestly, think of all the people who'll come to see your exhibit now."

Ethan frowned, hands shoved in his pockets. "Yup," he muttered. "I guess we should wait a few minutes before going back to the main drag," he said, gesturing toward West Broadway.

"We're not in a mad rush," she assured him.

"Well, I wouldn't mind walking off those eggs Benedict, anyway." They walked together in silence for a stretch. The farther away they got from the Cupping Room, the more Ethan's mood seemed to improve. "And SoHo means what?" he queried.

"South of Houston Street," Stacy explained, pointing to the north as they strolled down Spring Street toward the river. It was a clear day with a refreshing wind.

"I'm still finding the character of this place hard to take in," Ethan said, looking up at the rooftops of the old loft buildings they passed. "Everyone's crammed on top of each other, but they seem to like it that way."

"It's not so much that we *like* it," she said. "That's just the way the city is."

"So what do you like about it the most?" he asked.

Stacy considered. "There's a lot of different cities in one, really," she explained. "Down here in this little corner it's one world, full of painters, sculptors, writers, people who stay up till dawn and rise in the afternoon. But a five-minute cab ride would take you to the heart of midtown and a whole other pace and style. If we walked farther south we'd be in Chinatown. If we crossed the street we'd find Little Italy. There's more energy on this one little island than you'd probably find in a whole state elsewhere."

"Depends the state," Ethan allowed. "But I see your point."

Stacy was gravitating toward the piers on the city's edge. You could see the Jersey shore across the Hudson there, and look back at a bit of the city's skyline. In her college days at NYU she'd lived not far from here, and she'd spent many a summer night on the piers with her school friends.

It wasn't necessarily the best area for a single woman to stroll around alone. But with Ethan at her side in broad daylight she felt absolutely safe. He exuded an air of confidence that put her totally at ease. And also, she suddenly remembered, he was armed.

They crossed the West Side Highway to the pier. "What's so funny?" Ethan asked, noticing her smile.

"I'm just remembering that doorman's face the other night," she told him. "Tell me, is that how you settle most disputes south of the border?"

"With a knife? No," Ethan said. "I tend to rely on my wits. I hope you're not getting the wrong idea about me," he said, a twinkle in his eye. "You are talking to a Ph.D."

Stacy stepped through the gate that led out to the deserted pier. "Yes, but it's hard to picture you in front of a classroom with chalk in your hand."

"I do like being in the field more than being on campus," he admitted. "Or in the newspapers," he added.

Stacy decided she'd better steer the conversation elsewhere. "But you *are* a good teacher," she said. "I'm sure that tape for the museum is something you'll enjoy doing."

"I guess."

"You know, when you were talking about the Trump Tower and the Mayan cultures and the different value systems, I could see you had very strong feelings about your work. It came across, and it was very..." She searched for the right word. "Sexy" was what came to mind as she looked at him, standing in the sunlight with lower Manhattan behind him, his hands in his pockets, the breeze ruffling his wavy hair.

"Persuasive," she said, looking away. Stacy took a seat on the wooden riser at the pier's edge, lifting the hair off the back of her neck to let the breeze cool her skin. She gazed off, self-conscious. It was getting harder to ignore the feeling that had been sneaking up on her for the past few days. Ethan was more than merely fun to be with. He was a powerfully attractive man.

"Well, maybe you're easy to talk to," he said, putting a foot up beside her. "Communicating one on one comes easier to me, anyway."

"If you'd like, I'll come to the taping with you," she said impulsively. "Then it can be as if you were talking to me."

She'd said it playfully, almost as a joke, but when she turned to look at Ethan again he seemed quite serious, nodding thoughtfully. "I'd like that," he said.

"You could probably do a tour as a speaker," she posited, trying to steer the conversation back onto a professional track. Odd, but when they had no work on a table between them or business matters to discuss, she found herself feeling a little vulnerable with him, even nervous. Maybe it was guilt over all this publicity she was willingly encouraging.

"A speaker?"

"Well, you know, if you ever decided to actually stay in civilization for more than a month," she said lightly, "you could probably hook up with a speakers' bureau and make a nice living doing the college circuit, talking about your Mayan digs."

"I'd rather do them than talk about them," Ethan said. "Although, to tell you the truth, I've been feeling like it wouldn't be the worst thing in the world to settle down in civilization for a change. You know, lead what some consider a normal life. Whatever that is."

"Right," Stacy said wryly. "You don't strike me as a nine-to-five city dweller type."

"Well, maybe it is just wishful thinking," he said. "But I do feel it's time for a change."

"Don't tell me New York City's turned your head that fast," she teased.

"No, but I think I could acquire a taste for the nightlife," he said. "Especially with a guide like you."

Stacy chanced a look at him and saw a hint of that now-familiar smile on his lips. She smiled back, tossing her hair as the breeze rose. "Yes, I bet you could," she said.

She hadn't meant to be flirtatious. Or had she? Ethan held her gaze for a long moment. She could feel nervous energy swell up inside her; he seemed to peer right into the center of her. She was conscious of her heart beating unnaturally loudly.

She would have given anything to know just what he was thinking. But Ethan abruptly straightened up, his smile fading. "I suppose we should get back to work."

"I suppose," she said. Their fleeting moment of unacknowledged intimacy had passed.

He extended his hand to help her up. Stacy took it and rose to her feet. She wasn't sure which one of them forgot to let go, but she suddenly found herself quite close to

Ethan, looking up into his sparkling eyes. There she was, gazing at him from mere inches away, her lips parted slightly as she caught her breath.

If she'd ever seen the signs of a kiss in someone's eyes, they were there in Ethan's. She could feel the subtle but unmistakable desire that radiated from his gaze, and the answering pulse of excitement that rose from inside herself. The sensation was so vivid that she imagined she could almost feel his lips already softly closing over hers.

What was so surprising was how natural the idea seemed, even though there'd been no real prelude, no self-aware flirtation. But at this moment, as the rising wind enveloped them in a small circle and the sunshine made his every feature seem aglow with a vibrant energy, having Ethan kiss her seemed the most perfectly inevitable thing in the world.

Which was why she was so shocked when it didn't happen. His hand left hers and he stepped back, looking downward with a faintly embarrassed air. "After you," he muttered, indicating the way back down the pier.

Had she imagined the whole thing? Maybe so, and if that was the case, Stacy reflected, it was just as well. Kissing Ethan Brody?

She straightened her shoulders, strolling down the pier with as casual an air as she could muster. Really, it was as if she'd lost her mind for an instant. Apples and oranges, she reminded herself. The two of them were absolute opposites, and it was silly to even conjecture where a kiss like that might have led.

Nonetheless, she couldn't help feeling sorry she'd missed it.

"WHO IS IT?" Ethan strode to the door of his hotel room. The knock had wakened him from a fitful doze in the armchair. A bleary glance at his wristwatch told him it was nearly midnight.

"Gimme a cracker!" screeched a voice from outside. "A cracker, you old coot!"

"Buck!" Ethan cried, and opened the door.

There stood Wally, duffel bag in hand and Buck perched on his shoulder. The parrot's blazing yellow and red feathers were fluffed in excitement, his little face puffed up, beak quivering as he fixed a baleful gaze on his former owner.

"Hey, Wally," Ethan said. "Hiya, Buck."

"Arp!" crowed Buck. "Blow it out your barracks bag."

Wally chuckled, shaking hands with Ethan. "Had a hell of a time getting him in here," Wally said, letting Ethan take the bag from his hand as he strode through the door. "Those guys in the suits downstairs—"

"I know," Ethan said. "They're a stuck-up bunch, aren't they?"

"Your mother!" squawked Buck.

"Not that *he* helped much." Wally chuckled. "Hey, nice room you got here. Mine's half the size."

"I did what I could at short notice," Ethan said. "We could switch, if you want. Say, what time did you finally get in? When I called the airport—"

"I know, the flight got held up in Chicago. But hey, it beats Taca, right?"

Ethan laughed. Taca was the fly-by-night airline that ran shuttles from Mexico to Belize, notorious for interminable delays and routine loss of luggage. "Then you've still got your belongings?"

"Including your precious videotape," Wally said, patting the duffel bag.

In a noisy flurry of feathers, Buck took off from Wally's shoulder and alighted on the television set. He settled on his perch, puffed out his chest, and announced in a singsong croak: "I shot the sheriff."

"Yes, Buck," Ethan said. "But? But what else?"

"'I did not shoot no deputy,'" Buck replied. This oft-quoted lyric came from the bird's favorite reggae tune.

"That's right," said Ethan.

"Bug off," said Buck.

"Well, I see being back in civilization hasn't changed him a bit," Ethan observed, chuckling. "Nor you. Ever thought of trimming that bush?"

Wally felt the bottom of his bushy salt-and-pepper beard, which came down to midchest. His eyes narrowed indignantly behind his thick bifocals. "Why should I?" he asked. "I'm not the one posing for newspaper photos."

"Oh, here we go," Ethan said. "I knew I'd never hear the end of this."

"'Arizona Brody,'" Wally said, grinning. "Boy, you've put your foot in it this time."

"Look, it wasn't my idea," Ethan said.

"No? Ah," Wally said, his thick eyebrows wiggling in Groucho Marx-like lasciviousness. "It's that woman, isn't it? The one you've been telling me about. The one on your arm in the New York *Trib*."

"You saw that?" Ethan asked, startled.

"Picked it up at the airport. She's a looker, I'll give you that."

"Stacy had nothing to do with me getting that stupid nickname," Ethan declared, instantly feeling defensive on her behalf. "She's not the one who went running after a movie actor mugger. And if anything, she respects my privacy."

"A PR person?" Skepticism wrinkled Wally's brow. "You ask me, she's making you a very public laughing-stock."

"Hey, she didn't send those newspaper guys after me. Capitalizing on what happened is part of her job. I don't blame her for that. Not that I like it."

"But you do like her," Wally said. "Come on, don't give me that look. I'm seeing all the danger signs, Brody. You're in trouble."

Ethan did his best to affect detachment. "Oh, she's all right," he said. "You'll meet her tomorrow and see for yourself. This is a purely professional relationship. Stacy Morrison just wants our exhibition to make a splash, that's all."

"Bull-dinky!" sang Buck. "Gimme a cracker."

"Hey, he said it." Wally smiled. "I didn't."

"PHOTOGRAPHERS? How many?" Stacy exchanged a worried look with Russell.

Harry Nelson consulted the memo in his hand. "There's two of them, I guess," he said.

Stacy tried to shake loose the small knot of anxiety she felt in the pit of her stomach. "Do you have a phone number for Richard?" she asked his assistant.

"No way," Harry answered. "You know how he is about his three-day hideaways. Look, what's the big deal? According to the memo, he's answering your own request."

"Well, in a way," she said, sinking into her chair. She'd complained to her boss about those *Trib* reporters hounding Ethan, asking him if he could pull some strings with his friends over there to have their photographers lighten up. And before leaving the office for one of his periodic brief sabbaticals, Richard had done as she'd asked. But unfortunately, he'd gone further than that.

Richard had hired two photographers to tail Ethan from now on. These men, on the P and W payroll, would release to the local papers only those photos that Stacy approved.

"He won't even see them, probably," Russell said hopefully.

"Right," said Harry. "Anyway, that's the word. A problem develops, you can talk to the Big P on Monday."

"Fine," Stacy muttered, as Harry left the office. "Thank you, Richard."

"Well, you *should* thank him," Russell said. "He got the *Trib* guys out of your hair."

"Yes, and now I've got two full-time snoops on my hands." Stacy sighed, the knot of anxiety now a general ache of guilt that was suffusing her innards. "If Ethan finds out about this, he'll kill me."

"I'm sure they'll be discreet," Russell said. "They'll certainly be cooler about it than those news hounds."

"They'd better be," Stacy said. "Or Mr. Arizona Brody is liable to bolt right back to Hambone."

"Hambone?" Russell said.

Stacy's phone line was blinking. "Never mind," she said, picking up. "I'll see you later."

Russell waved a goodbye. It was Eva on the phone, checking in. She'd seen the picture of Ethan and Stacy leaving the Cupping Room in yesterday's paper. "You make a cute couple."

"Very funny," Stacy said. "We are not a couple."

"Not yet."

"Eva," Stacy said, "I have no intention of getting coupled with Ethan Brody."

"Really? When you put it that way, it sounds wonderfully obscene."

Stacy paused, remembering with a little flush of embarrassment the almost-kiss with Ethan that she'd imagined yesterday on the pier. In the time since, she'd repeatedly told herself that such romantic fantasies would lead to nothing but disaster. Hadn't she only recently recovered from a relationship with a Mr. Wrong? And who could be more wrong for her than Ethan Brody?

"We're in a professional relationship," she said, with an emphasis intended for herself as much as for her friend. "There's nothing obscene about it."

"That's too bad," Eva said. "He's a hunk."

"Yes, he's a hunk," Stacy said. Rather than dwell on that fact, she forced herself to consider Ethan's downside. "But he's also an addle-brained academic with the social graces of a water buffalo. I *like* him, don't get me wrong, but getting involved with him would not only be professional suicide, it would be..." She searched for the appropriate image. "Oh, I don't know. But how can you take someone seriously whose idea of a good time is visiting the Statue of Liberty?"

Eva laughed. "But I think you doth protest too much," she said. "I know you're interested."

"Interested? Hmph," Stacy said, conscious that she'd unintentionally used Richard's sound of assent.

"Did he really visit Miss Liberty?"

"We're going this afternoon, in fact," Stacy said. "He and his partner, Wally. I'm playing tour guide, since the other professor just got to town, and he wants to see the sights. Now I'll have *two* hayseeds from Hicksville on my hands."

She glanced up. Christopher was hovering in her office doorway. How long had he been there? "Hold on a second," she said, and cupped the receiver. "Yes?"

"Your professor's in Reception," Christopher said, flashing his perfect teeth in an unsavory grin. "You might want to join him. He's got a couple of friends."

"Oh. Thank you," she said, as her intercom buzzed.

"Ethan Brody's here!" Charlotte's breathless voice called.

"Thanks," Stacy repeated. "Tell him I'll be right out."

"Get bent!" squawked the speaker.

Stacy stared at it. That hadn't sounded like Charlotte. She must have misheard it. She glanced at the doorway. Christopher had sauntered on. She wondered if he'd introduced himself to Ethan, and if so, if he'd been a slimier snob than usual. The idea irked her.

"I gotta go," she told Eva. "My tourists have arrived."

PROFESSOR Wilfred "Wally" Canfield looked like what Stacy had originally imagined Ethan Brody would. He was a hirsute man with thick horn-rim glasses, his bushy beard extending, Walt Whitman-like, over a potbelly. He wore faded corduroy pants and a cardigan sweater with patches on the elbows. The only thing that didn't completely strike a note of academia about him was the loudmouthed parrot that stayed perched on his shoulder.

Buck's language was certainly as colorful as his plumage. In addition to the standard scatological four-letter words, he was fond of more arcane and imaginative exclamations, some of which, Ethan sheepishly explained, he and Wally had taught the bird down in Belize. But since Buck wasn't mean-spirited, just conversational, the cabdriver who drove them downtown took no offense.

Neither did the various guards and officious-looking people at the World Trade Center, their first touring stop. This was fortunate, Ethan explained, because Buck tended to really dig his claws in if someone tried to remove him. Both he and Wally had some shoulder scars to prove it.

"You sure he won't fly away?" she asked, as they emerged into the winds at the Trade Towers observation floor.

"Nuts to you, bud," squawked Buck.

Stacy laughed. They'd been favored with good weather, and even she, jaded New Yorker that she was, had to admit that the view from atop the tower on a clear day like this was truly breathtaking.

"That's the Empire State Building," Ethan told Wally, pointing away with the authoritative enthusiasm that only the newly initiated Manhattanite could muster. "There's your East River, your Hudson..."

Stacy smiled, letting Ethan take charge, since he was obviously enjoying himself. She liked seeing him with Wally. He seemed more relaxed, less self-conscious and jittery around his old friend. Wally himself was a likable, unpretentious guy. This outing, which she'd thought would be a horrible bore, was actually starting out as a nice mini-vacation from their drudge work in the museum.

She glanced at her watch, making a mental note to steer the two anthropologists uptown before midafternoon. There were some things she had to attend to back at the office. But while she was out here, she might as well enjoy the sunshine. Stacy turned back to rejoin Ethan. That was when she noticed them.

To the unpracticed eye they were just a couple of men, lounging about near the door to the deck. But she immediately intuited—and it was a guess confirmed by the bulky camera cases slung around their shoulders—that these were the two photographers Richard had hired.

Even as she stared, dismayed, one of them was taking out a camera. Stacy looked over to Ethan, still animatedly pointing out sights. What if he saw them?

Her momentary panic abated as she realized that most of the other people up there had cameras to their eyes. In this environment, at least, the men wouldn't excite Ethan's suspicions. Nonetheless, she rejoined her charges and hustled them back to the elevators as soon as she reasonably could, pointedly ignoring the photographers. Maybe if they kept moving, she could eventually shake them off.

Their next stop, after a prolonged debate about choosing between the Staten Island ferry and the one to Liberty Island, was a hot dog stand. "Give him one with everything," Ethan instructed the vendor. "Stacy?"

"Just mustard, thanks," she said, peering over Ethan's shoulder. There they were again, camera cases and all. Stacy stifled a groan. There really was nothing to be done. They were clearly determined to dog "Arizona Brody" every step of the way.

Frankfurters in hand, tourists, bird and slightly distracted tour guide strolled to the dock where people were lining up for the next Liberty ferry. En route, a fourth person tried to join them—a man in a ragged and filthy clothes whose shoes were held together with masking tape.

He wanted money, of course. Ethan gave him the once-over. "Money for what?" he asked.

"Food," said the man.

Ethan was now apparently an old hand at dealing with New York's beggar patrol. "Here," he said. "Take this, then." He handed the man his hot dog.

Stacy heard the telltale click and whir behind them and stiffened, forcing herself not to turn around. "Wow, man, thanks," the beggar was saying, moving away. Ethan peered over Stacy's shoulder, frowning.

"Look at that," he said.

Stacy took a cursory look behind her. "What?" she asked, all innocence.

"Some guys with cameras," he said. "You don't suppose...?"

"Probably tourists," she said. "Come on, we've got to get tickets or we'll miss this boat."

Once they boarded, she lost sight of the men and even briefly imagined that they'd stayed on the mainland. But no, as they approached the statue, Ethan lining Wally, Buck and Stacy up against the guardrail to get a photo of his own, Miss Liberty hovering in the background, there they were again, cameras in hand.

This time the noise of the wind and the crowd drowned any telltale clicks. Stacy put on her best smile, which soon gave way to a genuine full-fledged giggle as Buck began singing at her ear. The bird apparently knew only one song—a reggae number by the Wailers—and only a few lines of it. But the expressions on the faces of their fellow travelers as Buck crowed, "I Shot the Sheriff," were priceless.

Ignore them, she kept telling herself as they landed on Liberty Island. Ethan and Wally were having a good time, and if it hadn't been for the photographers casting shadows on their sunny day, she would have been enjoying herself thoroughly. She hadn't been to see Miss Liberty since she was a teenager, and the newly refurbished torch glinting in the sun was a sight well worth seeing from close up.

She didn't even mind the long interior climb, since Ethan's boyish enthusiasm buoyed her own spirits. She joined in the teasing of Wally as he huffed and puffed his way to the top. The delighted laughs of the schoolchildren that accompanied them as they heard Buck talking away inside Miss Liberty's crown added to the lighthearted mood of the gorgeous spring day.

Strange to contemplate, but Stacy Morrison, the chic cosmopolitan sophisticate, was actually enjoying being a surrogate tourist. For a while she could put aside her work and the tensions it generated. Ethan was more talkative than usual, regaling her with anecdotes about Wally among the mestizos. At one point the two men got her laughing so hard that she had to stop on a landing and let other people pass.

Emerging into the bright sunlight at the statue's base, Stacy felt a pure exhilaration that was overpowering for an instant—until it evaporated.

"Hey," Ethan said, scowling, as one of the two photographers snapped another picture. "It's those guys again. I knew it! They're not tourists, they're—"

"Don't worry about it," she said, pulling Ethan back. "Look, going over there and giving them a hard time is no way to handle this. That's just what they want, don't you see?"

Ethan glowered at the men, then looked at her, still unconvinced. "Maybe a good dunking in the river would take care of it." Wally nodded, apparently ready to help.

"Bug off," said Buck pleasantly. "Cracker?"

"Ethan, please," she said nervously, having learned by now that such an activity would be entirely natural to Ethan Brody. "If you ignore them, they'll go away, eventually. You're not doing anything newsworthy. They'll get bored."

Ethan reined in his irritation. She could see it took some effort for him not to say a word as they continued to the ferry, passing the photographers. Her own stomach was tied up in knots. Paranoid, she slunk past, positive that they'd sing out, "Hi, Miss Morrison" or "How are we doing?"

But no, they barely gave her a glance, and mercifully once they were on board again, faded into the background. But Ethan's mood had shifted, and with it, the weather. On their return the skies were as gray as they'd been blue going over. Stacy did her best to keep Wally amused, and Buck continued to attract the admiration of the schoolchildren, but Ethan was preoccupied, now looking at anyone who had even an Instamatic in hand with evident mistrust.

Once ashore, they hurried toward a cab. The plan was to walk through Rockefeller Center before ending up at the museum. But just before she was about to climb into the taxi's back seat, Ethan suddenly grabbed her arm. "Over here!" he whispered. "Come on, Wally!"

Bewildered, she stumbled after Ethan. He was waving at a bus that hovered nearby, discharging passengers. It wasn't until he'd hustled them aboard and was chuckling happily, slapping hands with Wally and waving past the impassive bus driver at someone in the street that she realized what he'd done.

"Lost 'em," Ethan announced, immensely pleased. Stacy peered out the window in time to catch a glimpse of the two photographers standing by the open doors of another taxi, at a loss what to do.

There was room for all of them in the back of the bus. Crammed in together, with Buck taking a few experimental pecks at her hair, Stacy shared Ethan's relief. He was happy again and so was she, for the moment freed of guilt.

Unfortunately the patter of drizzling rain on the bus's roof forestalled their plans. "We'll save Rockefeller Center," Ethan said. "We can walk there from the hotel tomorrow, anyway."

"Are we near the hotel?" Wally stared myopically out the window. "If we are, I think I'll get off," he said, stifling a yawn. "Jet lag's catching up with me."

"No, it was that climb in the statue, you old blowhard," Ethan said.

"Blow it out your barracks bag!" squawked Buck.

"Army expression," Ethan explained. "Here, just press that thingamajig. They'll let you off on the corner."

Wally bade them a hurried goodbye and trundled up the aisle with Buck. Ethan settled back into his seat with a satisfied smile. "This has been great," he said.

"I'm glad you had a good time."

"Wally doesn't get out nearly enough," Ethan said. "And he wasn't too whipped up about coming here. So this was just what he needed. You know, to feel welcome."

There it was, that infectious smile of his. She smiled back, pleased. "And me, too," he went on. "If it wasn't for those photographers..." He shook his head. "Ah, it doesn't matter. Anyway, you've been a great tour guide. I owe you one, Stacy."

"Don't be silly," she said, embarrassed.

"Boy, it's really coming down now," he said, moving to the window. "We're gonna get soaked."

Stacy nodded. "Well, they'll let us off right in front of the museum," she said.

"Damn," he muttered.

"It won't be so bad."

"No, it's those guys."

"What?" She slid down the seat, following his gaze. There was a taxicab driving alongside them, and sure enough, even in the rain, the side window was rolled down enough to allow a camera's telephoto lens through. "Oh, no," she said.

"Oh, yes." Ethan looked to the front. "Where are we now? Seventy-something?"

Stacy nodded. "Look, once we're in the museum they're bound to go home for the day—"

"Maybe," he said. "But even so..." He got up, taking her hand. "Come on. If we get out at this corner we can lose 'em again. They'll probably tail the bus without us on it."

"Ethan, what difference—?"

But he was a determined man. Stacy stifled a sigh and followed him down the aisle. The bus slowed. Ethan was poised in readiness at the back door. "Okay," he said. "Let's scoot!"

Stacy scooted. Together they dashed into the down-pour. As they rounded the back of the bus, Stacy could see that Ethan had been right. The taxicab was still with the bus, already headed up the block.

"Come on!" Ethan yelled. "We're free at last!"

Chapter Six

They were running for the museum side entrance on Seventy-seventh Street. The rain beat down even harder, as if some perversely playful rain god had decided that Ethan and Stacy's exit from the bus should occasion the first real full-fledged downpour of the afternoon.

"Last one in is a drowned water rat," Ethan called, laughing as he raced around the corner with her.

"No kidding," Stacy yelped, dashing past him down the sidewalk.

"Here, take this!" He was waving a newspaper at her, holding it up as an impromptu umbrella.

"No, thanks." Stacy shook her head as they trotted past the southeast corner towers of the rambling building. Her hair could stand a little frizzing, and she didn't want to chance having it festooned with soggy newspaper bits.

A flash of distant lightning was followed by a bellow of thunder that sounded scarily close. Startled, she increased her speed, then stumbled as her heel caught on an uneven block of pavement. She gave a little cry, only barely managing to regain her balance.

Ethan was instantly at her side. "You all right?"

Stacy knelt down to inspect her shoe. The heel had come loose. "Great," she muttered, as another peal of thunder sounded and the rising wind blew rain and hair into her eyes. "I can't run with this, only limp."

"Take them off?" he suggested, holding the opened newspaper above her like a tiny tent.

Stacy frowned, surveying the sidewalk. It was a surefire way to ruin a pair of stockings. She straightened up, momentarily stymied. "I don't know—" she began.

"All right, come on," Ethan said, sliding his arm around her.

"What? Wait!" But her protest turned into a gasp as she was lifted into the air.

"Hold on," he said, already moving down the sidewalk. Ethan had a firm grip on her, one arm under her legs and the other around her back. Stacy instinctively clung to his neck, her other hand still gripping the damaged shoe.

"You didn't have to do this!"

"It's good exercise," he said with a chuckle.

She could *feel* that chuckle, she realized. It was vibrating from his chest to hers. But then all of her senses were being bombarded at once with all kinds of sensations that were totally disorienting.

There was the feel of his strong arms encircling her body in sudden intimacy, the heat of him as he held her close, the feel of his wet hair beneath her fingers as she tightened her grip around the back of his neck. There was the chill of the wind and the warmth of his skin against hers. And a dizziness that came not only from being carried at a fast clip down the curving slope of driveway that led to the side entrance, but from the realization that she was entirely his captive.

Which wasn't such a bad thing.

It seemed only natural to rest her head in the crook of his shoulder, though when she was aware that she'd done it, she instantly lifted her head. She could feel her own heart beating a mile a minute, and the rapid beat of his heart against her breast.

"We're almost there," he assured her, his voice a husky rasp at her ear. Stacy was sure she was blushing an indigo red. Blood was pounding through her tingling body, making the points of her breasts taut against the thin material that seemed to barely separate skin from skin. The clean but musky scent in her nostrils that she recognized as his, mingling with her own, was a heady combination.

The rain was blurring her vision as she tried to catch her breath, but she could see, as they hurried toward the doors, a group of school kids in raincoats gathered in the foyer. They were staring up at Ethan and her like a colony of awestruck munchkins, and the teachers shepherding them looked even more aghast.

"You can put me down now," she gasped, as they cleared the steps to the entrance.

"Soon enough," he said mildly, apparently not at all discomfited. "Get that, will you?"

He was indicating the door. Stacy reached out to pull it open for them and he eased them inside. "It's probably a good idea," she murmured, as the schoolchildren parted, a Red Sea of yellow, red and blue slickers around them.

"Are you sure you can walk?"

Am I sure I can think? she wondered, slightly dazed. Much as she was embarrassed to be seen like this, a part of her was finding the experience . . . well, it was downright arousing. She struggled to maintain composure as a museum guard smiled in evident complicity with Ethan's show of macho gentlemanliness. "I'll limp," she said weakly.

"You sure?"

He was already whisking her past the gigantic replica of a seagoing canoe full of Indians that graced the south lobby. The brave at the prow seemed to watch her go by with interest, but fortunately this part of the museum wasn't particularly crowded.

"Yes, I'm sure," she said. "Really, you can put me down now."

"Where are we?" he said, still carrying her onward.

"The North American Forests," she said, reading the sign on an approaching wall. They were entering a winding corridor full of glass-encased dioramas.

"Well, it can't be too far to the main lobby," he mused. "Okay."

As they came around a bend in the exhibit, he slowed, then stopped and gently lowered her to the floor. "Thank you," Stacy said, noticing that her voice was coming out oddly high and tremulous. Her heart was still pounding away at a record speed. Ethan was looking at her with a peculiar expression. Self-conscious, she put a hand to her wet hair. "I must look like...I don't know what," she said.

"We'll find you some paper towels or something," he said.

Stacy wasn't able to suppress a giggle. Ethan himself was looking rather comically bedraggled, his hair plastered over his forehead and his wire-rimmed glasses partially fogged. "I'm sure we make a very attractive pair," she said.

"Oh." He sheepishly drew a hand through his hair. "Well, we're certainly unphotogenic," he noted.

"And certainly safe," she said, her feelings of guilt somewhat assuaged. "They won't follow us inside here."

"Good," he said. "Come on. You know your way around here?"

"No," she admitted. "To tell you the truth, I haven't been through this wing since I was a kid."

"I think it's fantastic," he said, glancing around with a look of great interest. They were parked in a quiet corner where various panoramic views of forestry and nature gleamed from behind panes of glass. "I wouldn't mind taking a thorough, leisurely tour. But right now we should get ourselves . . . Wait a second," he said, and dug into his shoulder bag. She stepped out of her other shoe as he produced a denim shirt. "Here," he said, holding it out. "For your hair."

"Oh, no, I couldn't. It's a clean shirt."

"Come on," he said. "You'll catch a cold."

"No, really," she began. But in the next moment her face was suddenly engulfed in denim. Ethan was toweling her hair with his shirt. Yet another protest died on her lips as his strong but gentle hands moved rapidly over her head. But after a minute of watching the blue material dance in front of her eyes and enjoying the somehow illicit pleasure of his fingers lightly kneading her scalp, she took over, stepping back and whisking the shirt from his grasp.

After a few more practiced rubs with it over the back of her head, she removed the towel-shirt altogether and handed it back. "Thank you, sir," she said, smiling as he looked her over with evident amusement. "How do I look now?"

THE THING WAS, she looked so damned beautiful that it was almost criminal. Her long blond hair was tousled and free, cascading over her shoulders and puffed about her head in a kind of a gossamer halo. Her eyes were sparkling and her skin had a lovely sheen. Ethan had to bite his tongue and silently command his feet to stay right where they were. Otherwise he'd be within an inch of sweeping her into his arms again, and not because her shoe had a broken heel.

"Fine," was the one-syllable answer he was able to come up with. Stacy smiled, self-conscious, smoothing back her damp hair. Ethan decided that rather than just stand there and stare at her, he was better off drying his own hair, so he did that.

When he emerged from under the shirt, she fixed a critical gaze on the top of his head. "Hold still," she commanded. Stacy reached up and pushed down the rumpled hair above his forehead. He felt an involuntary shiver at the casual but intimate touch of her hand. Stacy stepped back, nodding.

"Better," she said.

It occurred to him that one reason she looked like some kind of gauzy soft-focus vision was that his glasses were fogged. So he took them off, and wiped them on the shirtsleeve. When he replaced them she still looked good, gazing around her with a preoccupied air. "I think we go this way," she said, pointing.

Ethan nodded and fell into step beside her. Think about your work, he reminded himself. "I'm supposed to hook up with Dr. Carver today," he told her. Carver was the anthropology curator, in charge of the permanent wing of Middle and South American Culture that their exhibit was a small, temporary adjunct to.

Stacy nodded. "He should be in his office," she said. "Tell me something."

"Anything," he said, and then realized that might have sounded funny. But thankfully she didn't notice.

"Don't you ever get stir-crazy and lonesome down in the jungle? I mean, don't you ever feel like you're missing something, being away from the rest of the world for so long?"

Ethan shrugged. "Yes, there's some lonely stretches," he admitted. "But what would I be missing, specifically?"

Stacy shook her head. "Oh, I don't know." She seemed about to ask him something, then thought better of it.

"Are you having a decent time here? I mean, besides that publicity stuff?"

Long as I'm hanging out with you, he thought, and said, "Sure." Again he had the distinct impression that wasn't the question she'd wanted to ask, but she was silent, and he followed suit. Stacy limped her way through the rest of the North American Forests, but as they entered the hall of the Invertebrates, she paused to take her shoes off altogether.

"No one'll notice, I don't think," she said.

Normally he would've liked to have checked out the exhibit more thoroughly. But the presence of Stacy was too distracting. He'd gotten an immense charge out of carrying her around. It was something he hadn't minded doing and would've easily done again, if asked. She wasn't too heavy, and she smelled better than any woman who wore a suit had any right to.

Ethan tried to remember if he'd ever been attracted to a woman who wore suits. None came to mind. This particular one she had on, a double-breasted deep purple thing over a short matching skirt, shouldn't really have struck him as sexy but it did, regardless. He didn't even mind the shoulder pads. He was trying to reason out for himself what it was that most New York City women saw in shoulder pads, when he caught a glimpse of the biggest whale he'd ever seen in his life, and stopped short.

"Oh, it's the famous whale!" Stacy said, turning to follow his gaze. With a childlike absorption, she half ran, half skipped in her stocking feet to the entrance of the darkened hall where the giant blue whale, nearly a hundred feet long, hung suspended from the ceiling. "Isn't it amazing!"

"Yes," he agreed. On all sides of the whale were dioramas of underwater scenes featuring a variety of marine life, with larger ones on the floor below. The whole vast chamber was dimly lit in a deep blue color, so that it felt like a subterranean environment.

Stacy was poised at the railing, staring at the whale. "I remember this from when I was a kid," she whispered. The few other people looking at the exhibits were also speaking in hushed tones, he noticed. The atmosphere in this Ocean Life room made a normal speaking voice seem too abrasive.

"My dad took me here once," she went on. "My little brother got scared of the whale, so my dad had to take him into the other room. And I got to walk around here by myself. It was kind of spooky," she said, smiling. "But I remember I was so proud of myself for not being scared like David, my brother, and being on my own...." Her voice trailed off as she gazed down into the lower level. "And there was this polar bear I fell in love with, and the cutest baby seal. I wonder... There!" She pointed.

"Let's take a look," he said.

"You want to? I know we should be getting back to the basement, but—"

"Dr. Carver can wait," Ethan said. He'd never seen Stacy in this particular mood before. She suddenly didn't seem at all like the sophisticated city woman she normally was, more like the girlish version of herself she'd been describing. She even *looked* smaller. Because she wasn't wearing shoes, he realized, as she smiled and started down the stairs beneath the whale.

Ethan followed. Stacy made a beeline for the diorama, which did indeed contain a huge white polar bear, amazingly lifelike against its painted Arctic backdrop. She stopped in front of it, then turned with an embarrassed grin as he joined her. "Silly, huh?"

"No, it's actually an amazingly lifelike job."

Stacy laughed. "I meant..." She shook her head and turned back to gaze at the bear, arms folded across her chest. "Not exactly your habitat, is it?"

"No," he agreed, looking at the ice.

"But you'd go if you had to. If they suddenly discovered a frozen Mayan mummy up there."

Ethan chuckled. "Not highly likely. In fact, it would be impossible. Mayan 'mummies' don't keep. And anyway, the very first people who settled in North America crossed a land bridge from Siberia to Alaska about, maybe twenty thousand years ago, but their Mongoloid culture isn't really within my area of expertise."

Stacy sighed. "You certainly know a lot about, um, what there is to know about."

Was she making fun of him? "In a very limited way, yes," he said.

"When it comes to the larger things," she said. "The historical perspective and all. I envy you that."

"Oh, come on," he said. "It's a lot of useless information, really."

"No," she said, still staring at the polar bear. "It's very admirable. I admire you for it."

"That's funny," he said. "I've been feeling like I don't know much at all." She met his gaze as he stood beside her, her face a soft pale blue in the diorama's glow. "You're the one with all the inside dope on life in the real world."

Stacy smiled. "The real world," she murmured. "Is that what we're in?"

At that moment he couldn't tell. It seemed to him that any world besides this dreamlike deep marine one didn't exist. When they were so close that he could smell the rain on her still-damp hair, and her eyes were gazing up into his, her lips half parted in an odd little smile, the world appeared to consist of the two of them alone.

"I hardly know which world I'm in, these days," he said, and it was the honest truth.

She nodded, the smile disappearing, and she considered him in silence with a look that was almost grave. "Do you miss it? Belize and all that?"

He shook his head. "Not at the moment."

Stacy looked back at the bear. Then she turned away, beginning to walk on to the next diorama. "It must be frustrating for you," she said, as he followed her along the wall. "Having to work on this exhibit with a total novice like me."

"Not at all," he protested. "Look, I get my quota of academic discussions filled with Dr. Carver and Hugh Russell upstairs. My work isn't what I like to think about twenty-four hours a day, you know."

"No? But you'd probably prefer a woman—that is, a person to work with who knew more about what you did."

He couldn't imagine whom he could possibly prefer more. But he wasn't about to say that. "I like the way you think, though," he said. "I mean, you bring a fresh slant to things."

"Honestly?"

"Yes, you're . . . you're bright, and sharp . . ."

"And totally exploitative," she muttered. "You hate the way this exhibit's being handled, I can tell."

He was surprised to hear a note of insecurity coming from her. "I wouldn't say that," he protested. "Look, I told you I didn't blame you for trying to make this show a success. That's your job."

"My job," she echoed, nodding.

"And you're doing a good job, so far. Even Wally's impressed."

"Really?" She turned to look at him.

It suddenly occurred to him that this most tough-skinned of New York career women had an endearing vulnerability hidden beneath the surface. He nodded encouragingly, secretly flattered that his opinion should mean something to her. "I think we make a good team," he ventured.

She cocked her head slightly, a surprised smile on her lips. "We do?"

Ethan nodded. "Sure."

Her smile deepened. Then her eyes widened, caught by something behind him. "Oh, look!" she cried. "There he is!"

He turned as she whisked past him in the semidarkness, headed for another diorama. This was a smaller one, he saw, featuring only a lone baby seal, who was taking a little bath in a hole cut in an ice floe. The sleek, almost puppylike mammal was lying on its back, flipperish feet sticking up from the water, an expression of pure contentment on his wet face.

"Oh, look at him," Stacy breathed with a delighted laugh. She put a hand on his arm, squeezing it in enthusiasm. "Isn't he the most adorable creature you've ever—!"

Ethan felt a rush of warmth surge up through him in a wave. His hand was at her waist, instinctively resting there in a caress almost too casual to be called that. But her hand on his arm, her smiling face so close to his, the damp halo of her hair, the fresh rain and perfume of her—it was all too much for him.

"No," he said, before he could think to stop himself. *You* are, were the words poised on his tongue.

Her face tilted to see his, eyes startled. In that instant, which suddenly seemed an elongated eternity, he knew that he absolutely had to kiss Stacy Morrison. He no longer cared what consequences he might suffer, including an incredulous rejection. There was only so much a man could stand.

His other hand stole out to gently cup her chin. Amazingly, she was staring into his eyes, lips parted breathlessly, almost as if she, too...

"Look! Lookit!"

The piercing squeal of a little boy's voice from behind her was like a dash of cold water on Stacy's upturned face. One second she'd been poised on the brink of surrender to what had promised to be a kiss—it could only be that, she hadn't been imagining it this time—and in the next instant she was taking a step back, startled and embarrassed.

There were actually three or four of them, a gaggle of school kids scampering right at them, intent on the baby seal—although one of the children, a little girl who had large braided pigtails, was staring at Stacy and Ethan in blatant, wide-eyed fascination.

A teacher was bringing up the rear, shushing the kids with an apologetic smile. Ethan, too, had taken a step back. She looked at him and saw her own embarrassment mirrored in his expression.

"We should probably be moving along," he said.

"Yes, we should," she quickly agreed.

They exchanged a glance that Stacy intuitively understood. It was as if they'd made a tacit agreement: that—whatever "that" was, really—hadn't happened. He hadn't been about to kiss her. They hadn't been about to fall into a passionate embrace underneath the giant blue whale.

Still, as she fell into step with Ethan's swifter, more resolute stride out of the Ocean Life room, now echoing with the giggles and cries of myriad schoolchildren, she couldn't help trying to reconstruct the moment in her mind. She'd said something about the seal, about it being cute, or, no, adorable, she'd said, and then he'd said—

No? It wasn't? That was the odd thing. She might have been imagining it or projecting her own fantastical, vain thoughts onto him, but she could have sworn that what he'd meant, what he'd been about to say, was . . .

Stacy shook her head, rushing to catch up with him. Ethan was certainly a man in a hurry, all of a sudden. They were almost out of the Biology of Invertebrates hall, headed toward what was undoubtedly the main entrance. She stole a glance at him. He was frowning, looking around to get his bearings.

Could she be totally off base? Had she entirely misinterpreted what had—hadn't—happened? Honestly, over the past few days the man had hardly been acting as though he was smitten with her. Clearly her imagination was merely inventing romantic fancies.

Just then Stacy caught a glimpse of what looked like an elevator around the corner, and reached out to tap Ethan's shoulder. He jumped at her touch, as if she'd given him an electric shock.

"The elevator," she said as she met his nervous gaze. And in that instant, suddenly her instincts were absolutely confirmed. Ethan Brody *was* attracted to her. It was as clear as the flush on his face.

What an interesting development! But Stacy was even more surprised by her own automatic response. She suddenly felt happier than she'd been in years.

"SUCKER!"

"Shut up, Buck," Ethan said tersely. He was trying to wrestle into submission a black bow tie, and so far the bow tie was winning. The last thing he needed was peanut-gallery ragging from a parrot.

"Hey, lighten up," Wally said mildly, puffing on the pipe clamped between his lips as he settled back into the hotel room's overstuffed armchair. "You've been a real pain all day, you know that?"

"If you had to get into a monkey suit and go smile at a bunch of rich socialites for God knows how many hours, you wouldn't be kicking your heels up either," Ethan said, with a morose stare at his reflection in the closet door's mirror. He simply wasn't built for a getup like this.

"You look fine," Wally said, puffing away. "Besides, you've been a major grouch for two days now. It's not this fund-raiser that's really put a bug in your ear."

"Bug off!" squawked Buck.

"No?" Ethan said, tugging the recalcitrant tie into place. It still looked lopsided, and he could barely breathe with the collar so tight.

"Nah, it's that Morrison woman."

"Says who?" Ethan grunted.

"Oh, come on," said Wally. "She's gotten under your skin, that's easy enough to see. Why don't you just own up to it and go after her, if you want her?"

"I don't want her." Ethan frowned again at his reflection. He could see Wally shaking his head in the mirror. "Well, I don't," he persisted. "It would just be Lucille all over again. Another woman who's about as right for me as . . . I don't know what."

"Uh-huh."

Wally kept a tactful silence after that. He knew about Lucille Bender. He knew how Ethan had fallen for her, a young anthropology student whose first love was photography. And how he'd taken her with him on that trip to Peru. And then how she'd used Ethan's connections to wrangle an exclusive deal with a friendly rival of his in the field, Harry Golwin, to do a coffee-table photo book on the Peruvian ruins . . . and had abandoned Ethan shortly thereafter.

It had seemed so clear-cut to a woman like Lucille. Use what you need to use to get what you want, and then move on. That he'd totally trusted her and been completely in love—that had seemed irrelevant. She had her $25,000 advance and a career in exotic travel photography launched. And he'd been left with a broken heart. . . .

Ethan snapped back to the present. "The only reason I'm, ah, infatuated with Stacy," he informed Wally, "and that's all it is, an infatuation," he declared, "is that I spent one year too many in the Belizean bush."

"Right."

"She's a good-looking woman, that's all, and I'm a red-blooded American male, you know? But nothing's going to come of it," he said. "Not if I can help it. My life's turning into a farce as it is, with every other thing I do showing up in the damned newspapers."

"Oh, I don't know," Wally said mildly, indicating the *Trib* that had been unceremoniously dumped into the wastebasket. "I thought we looked pretty good on page six, you and me and Miss Liberty."

"Right," Ethan said, grimacing. "What time is it?"

"Time for you to go pick up your hot date and meet the Rockefellers."

"It's not the Rockefellers," Ethan said. "I don't even know their names. And she's not a hot date, she's a professional colleague."

"Gimme a cracker," said Buck.

THE FUND-RAISER wasn't being held in the museum proper, but in the town house of Dr. Carver, a few blocks down on Central Park West. Considering that she didn't usually hobnob with this level of New York's social elite, that she was bound to be surrounded by women in dresses that were worth more than one month of her salary and men whose names appeared in the nation's newspapers every day, Stacy should have been nervous.

Oddly enough, she wasn't. And taking into account all the things that should have been on her mind, such as how to "work the room," once they got inside, whom to pitch what to, and whether the press coverage would be adequate, et cetera, Stacy should have been distracted and preoccupied.

Strangely, that wasn't the case, either. No, the only thing that seemed to be on her mind was the singularly fascinating fact that Ethan Brody looked tremendously handsome in black tie.

It was funny how these things went, she mused as she climbed out of the cab that Ethan had picked her up in, and nodded a thanks to the uniformed man who opened the door for her. Barely a few days ago, the only notice she'd taken of Ethan's clothes was whether or not they'd look good in a black and white newspaper photo. But now whatever he wore was of a different kind of interest to her.

She looked him over with a proprietary air as he joined her at the foot of the steps. The conclusion she reached was that Ethan Brody could probably look sexy in a clown suit or scuba gear. His frame and face were fashion-proof.

"You ready for this?" he asked, pulling at his bow tie.

"Yes," she said, leaning over to realign it for him. "Are you?"

"Absolutely not," he said with a tight little smile. "What am I supposed to do here, again?"

"You just smile—maybe a bit more convincingly," she added. "And pretend to be interested in what these fuddy-duds say to you, no matter how bored you get. That may be hard, but it'll all be over in a matter of hours."

Ethan sighed. Stacy slid her arm through his, and was rewarded with a telltale stiffening in his posture. It wasn't fair, really, almost cruel in a way, but ever since that moment in the museum she'd been unable to keep herself from subtly testing Ethan's responses.

Like someone who'd received a large and mysterious gift that promised to be fulfilling beyond his or her fantasies, Stacy was unwilling, as it were, to rip off the wrapping paper. The idea that Ethan Brody was attracted to her filled her with an illicit excitement, but she wasn't going to *do* anything about it, not yet. The situation was too complicated.

To begin with, her own emotions were complex enough. For the past two days she'd been trying to figure out why, beyond mere vanity, she was so pleased by his interest, and had come to an inescapable conclusion: she was just as interested in him. But that disturbed her for a number of other reasons.

First and foremost there was their professional relationship, and jeopardizing it would be madness. Especially because now, even as these thoughts whizzed through her recently recoiffed head on the way into Dr. Carver's town house, she and Ethan were right in the middle of selling the Mayan tomb to Manhattan. And there was nothing like a volatile affair to sabotage a carefully orchestrated PR campaign.

Or to sabotage her own still-precarious and hard-won sense of well-being. She'd sworn since the breakup with Stanford that she wasn't going to allow emotional upheavals to wreak havoc with her life. At least, she fantasized, until she was a vice president at P and W and living in her nice new co-op apartment. At the moment her life was directed, clear, uncomplicated, and she wanted to keep it that way.

Why not just sleep with Ethan? was another oft-thought, annoying question. After all, once he left town, he'd be gone for good, and any attendant romantic complications would be gone with him. Well, the answer, simply enough, was that she liked him too much. Besides the fact that she was by nature monogamous and never prone to one-night stands, she already had a feeling that Ethan wasn't the kind of man you trifled with like that.

And she wasn't that kind of woman. Something told her that once she and Ethan started something, as strange as the idea might have first appeared . . .

So in lieu of opening up the whole tantalizing gift package that might be a wonderful fling with a very appealing anthropologist, Stacy was for the moment content to savor the time spent with Ethan—time charged with a subtly erotic undertone, now that she'd let herself tune into the chemical reaction already crackling away between them.

She found, for instance, that the simplest things, like touching Ethan's shoulder while they were in the midst of talking to Carver at the museum, or holding his gaze in a moment of quiet, gave her a little thrill of pleasure. It almost always rendered Ethan speechless, the poor fellow. Now, for example, the simple act of walking arm in arm with him was clearly making him break into a sweat.

"Relax," she murmured into Ethan's ear.

"Right," he said. He was still bearing himself with a stiffness that suggested any sudden movement might cause his suit to fall off, so she figured she'd better help him out. Stacy gracefully removed her arm, putting him more at ease. But she couldn't resist reaching up to smooth back a lock of hair from his forehead. She'd been wanting to do that for twenty minutes.

She was rewarded by an embarrassed smile that was nonetheless more genuine than the grimace he'd been wearing. "You look fine," she assured him.

"You look great," he said, his eyes evidently arrested by the dress she'd worn. It was your basic black party dress, strapless, clingy, its simplicity augmented by some long silver hoop earrings and silver bracelets on her arm. One never went wrong with the basic black dress, especially when one couldn't hope to compete with the bejeweled Ralph Laurens and Armanis that were floating around this joint.

"Thanks," she said. "Let's mingle, okay?"

THEY WERE always pushing cocktails at you, along with good-looking hors d'oeuvres that tasted okay but left you wondering what they were. Ethan decided, beginning his second glass of champagne, that the people were pretty much the same. They looked good, but you wondered who they really were.

He'd been introduced to so many that there was no use in trying to remember names. It was a buffet dinner kind of thing, and he didn't have an official seat anywhere. That was just as well, because he was feeling out of his element, to say the least. These guys mostly looked as if they *lived* in black ties and suits, and the women... Well, there were some knockouts among them, but they all looked as though they'd spent the day getting put together for this.

Stacy, on the other hand, looked like Stacy to him, even though she'd done something to her hair. Whatever it was was okay by him, and he tended to follow her lead as the evening progressed. He found it hard to orient himself at first, because she kept guiding him from one group of people to another, but after a while he was on his own.

This wasn't his idea of fun. The main thing that kept bothering him was the way people stared. He felt he couldn't do a thing without finding some other person watching him. He had a sense, not entirely paranoid, that he was being talked about when he left a given clique. It was unnerving.

Worse, the people he did talk to seemed to know too much about him. Did everybody in New York read the *Trib*, even these high-class socialites? He would've thought they'd ignore that rag, but no, he was always being asked about Bobby DeVine and the Statue of Liberty, nonsense like that. Whenever he tried to turn the conversation back to his work, they tended to listen politely for a second and then ask him where he'd gotten the nickname "Arizona" or something.

Ethan didn't like being patronized. After a while his blood was set on low simmer. At the few other functions like this he'd ever attended in his life, he'd been able to hang out with a couple of academic cronies and fade into the background. But tonight he felt as though there was a spotlight trained on him all the time. And it wasn't a warm light.

Ethan settled down at one of the tables with Dr. Bruford, the other curator he was acquainted with at the museum, a couple of guys in monkey suits who were with the mayor's office—or the governor's, he hadn't been able to get that straight—an elderly woman swathed in pearls named Beatrice, who'd apparently been a close personal friend of Margaret Mead's and was completely deaf, and some other total strangers.

Here at least, people weren't watching him like a hawk, and he was able to talk quietly with Dr. Bruford. But not for long. One of the strangers, a man named Daryl with a deep tan and wearing a white suit, was a famous writer, and his friend Rob, who sported a walrus mustache and was also nattily attired, owned some magazine or other. He'd found it hard to pay attention to the details, because they tended to talk at the same time and laugh a lot at each other's jokes. But suddenly he found himself the center of their conversation.

"Belize used to be British," Daryl was saying.

"Plimpton was down there last summer, in the Cays," Rob said, fixing Ethan with an expectant gaze. "Did you see him?" He'd been drinking a bit, Ethan could tell, both from the slight slur in his voice and the redness of his bulbous nose. Ethan assumed they meant the writer Plimpton, who traveled in vastly different circles than he did. And the Cays was the part of Belize that catered to the moneyed tourist trade. "No," he said. "I didn't really get up to that part of the coast much."

"Great fishing there, apparently," Rob told Daryl.

"Of course, you were much too busy," said Daryl to Ethan. "Digging."

He pronounced the word with a strange combination of relish and distaste, as if "digging" was an activity that was extremely bizarre. Ethan felt his hackles rising.

"Guess you've got to keep in shape for that kind of work," Rob said.

"Yes, that's how he was able to make mincemeat out of Bobby DeVine," Daryl interjected. "We were all very impressed, following your exploits in the papers."

Both men were smiling, but Ethan didn't like the tone of this conversation. He was aware of Stacy hovering nearby, and reminded himself to just relax and smile back, but that didn't come easily. Especially since there was a photographer looking their way; Ethan had already had enough of the man's flashbulbs going off in his face this evening.

"We understand you've been seeing quite a lot of the sights of our fair city," said Rob.

"Yes, do tell us—which did you find the more impressive, the Empire State Building or the Twin Towers?"

Ethan looked at Daryl, who seemed to be asking the question with genuine interest. "Well, I don't know," he said warily. "One's taller. But the other has more class, I'd say."

"Well put!" crowed Rob. The guy wasn't British, but he had that strange snooty accent Ethan had encountered now and then from upper-class New Englanders. It set his teeth on edge.

"Mr. Brody is a writer," Daryl told Rob.

"Really?" Rob raised an eyebrow. "Maybe he'd like to do a piece for us about his experiences here."

"I don't really write," Ethan said hurriedly. "I mean, I've published some pieces in the anthropology journals, but—"

"He's published?" Daryl said. "Well, then he's more of a writer than some of *my* best friends."

This witty remark occasioned gales of laughter from his companions. Ethan glanced up at Stacy. She had her eye on Daryl and her own smile seemed pretty perfunctory.

"What are some of your titles?" Rob was asking.

"Titles?"

"What was the last piece you wrote?" Rob said. "Something on the Mayans, no doubt."

"I don't think you'd be interested," Ethan said shortly. "It's pretty dry stuff."

"Well, the folks back in Baconville—I'm sorry, what is that town, the one where you grew up?"

"Hambone," Daryl interjected. "The professor hails from Hambone."

"Hambone, of course," Rob said. "They must be pretty proud of you, for all your various achievements."

Ethan looked at Rob. He looked at Daryl. He looked at all the guests at the little table, dressed to the nines as they were, and was filled with an overwhelming urge to get out of their sight as fast as possible. "I wouldn't know," he said. "But I'd appreciate it if you'd stop making my hometown the butt of your jokes."

"Really, Professor Brody," Rob said, looking at him askance. "There's no need for you to take—"

"There's no need for the likes of you to be talking to the likes of me," Ethan said. "You've made that much clear. So if you don't mind, I think I'll move along." He rose from his chair.

"Come on, Brody," Rob huffed. "No one meant for you to take any offense."

"No, you were just having some laughs at my expense," Ethan said. "And if you were more of a man and not two-thirds booze at the moment, I'd ask you to step outside."

"I am outraged," Rob announced matter-of-factly, and pulled his chair away from the table. "And I am perfectly capable and willing to defend myself."

The guy could barely get to his feet. Ethan clamped a hand on his shoulder. "Sit down," he told Rob. "You're in no condition to—"

But the blustering magazine magnate had already lost his balance. Though Ethan made a grab for him, Rob went flailing backward into Beatrice's lap. She shrieked. A flashbulb went off. And Rob hit the floor, looking more like a beached walrus than ever.

People were getting up, waiters hurrying over, and more flashbulbs were popping, but Ethan wasn't wasting any time. Stacy had been standing behind Beatrice the whole time. He grabbed her hand and propelled her out of the developing melee. "Let's blow," he said.

Stacy was looking over her shoulder. "Oh, Ethan . . ."

"I'm sorry," he said. "I know that's exactly what I wasn't supposed to do, but—"

She let out a helpless giggle. "Sorry? That was wonderful."

Surprised, Ethan paused in his stride to stare at her. They were nearly at the door, where an imperturbable waiter at a small table full of glasses looked up at them, a freshly opened champagne bottle in his hand. "Champagne?" he asked.

"Thanks," Ethan said, and took the bottle from his gloved hand. And with Stacy's renewed laughter ringing in his ears, they headed out into the night.

Chapter Seven

"So you're not upset?"

"Are you kidding? Ethan, if anybody in that room deserved to end up on their butt, it was Rob Koppleman." Stacy giggled as they crossed the street. "He's one of the most pompous people in the business, and the expression on his face was priceless."

She smiled at Ethan, but he looked worried. "I don't want you to get the wrong idea about me," he said. "I mean, I don't get into fights, usually."

"It's really okay," she assured him. "As far as the rest of the evening went, it was very much a success. Money was raised and people got to meet you, and that's all to the good." She paused, uncomfortable. "Of course, there's bound to be another picture in the paper," she said. "That's the only downside."

"Why do they let those guys in, anyway?" Ethan said. "Don't people like being able to eat in peace, without someone shoving a lens in their face?"

"It goes with the territory," she said, knowing full well that Richard had pulled some strings to get his own photographers access to the dinner.

"I'll probably get sued or something," Ethan said ruefully.

"You didn't hurt him, really," Stacy said.

"Yeah, but you know what it'll look like in the *Trib*," he said. "'Arizona Brody Attacks Author,' or some nonsense like that."

He was probably right, but she didn't want to dwell on it. "Anyway, I'm glad you stood up to him," she said. "I couldn't stand the way he or that windbag crony of his were talking to you."

Ethan shrugged, but she could tell he was pleased. "Didn't mean to cut the evening short. And most places must be closed by now," he said, looking up the Avenue. "Here we are, all dressed up . . ."

"Ethan, this is New York," she said. "We could do pretty much anything we want to do until all hours of the morning. What are you in the mood for?"

"Well, what goes best with this?" he asked, holding up the champagne bottle. "I realize I snatched you out of there before dessert was served."

"We can't really bring that into a restaurant," she mused.

"Why not have a little park bench picnic?" he said. "The park's only a block away."

"That's a great idea! Come on, we'll take a look over here," she suggested, indicating one of the many Korean greengrocers that had sprung up on corners all over the city.

They browsed through the brightly lighted aisles of the store. "Splurge," Ethan instructed. "This particular meal's on me." Stacy picked out some fresh strawberries, vanilla ice cream and some Pepperidge Farm cookies, which was certainly a splurge, considering the diet she was supposed to be on.

Illicit dessert delights in hand they headed back toward the park. "This is much better than having to hang out at Dr. Carver's," she said.

"Think so?" he asked.

"Absolutely," she assured him. "Look, I don't enjoy hobnobbing with those stuffed shirts any more than you do. It's true," she added, as he shot her a surprised look. "When you work for a firm like P and W, you're always having to be on good behavior, going out and meeting people you don't necessarily care anything about. It gets wearisome. I much prefer..."

Her voice trailed off. *Spending time with a person I really do care about, like you,* was what she was thinking. "...being with friends," she finished uncertainly. Strange, but her earlier resolves about keeping a good professional distance from Ethan were seeming harder to keep by the minute.

The problem was, he kept doing things that made him all the more attractive. What other man in New York would've stood up to Koppleman like that? All the ones she knew would've been too concerned about their careers and reputations to say "boo" to him.

"I'm flattered," Ethan was saying. Stacy looked at him, startled. Had he been reading her mind? "I mean, to be considered a friend," he said.

"Oh. Well, we are, aren't we?" she said lightly. "Friends."

Ethan held her gaze a moment. She couldn't tell what *he* was thinking, though she had some suspicions. Then he nodded and looked away. "Light's changing," he noted.

Stacy smiled to herself as she crossed the street with him. He was really such a shy man. Yet another lovable—no, likable—thing about him. She regarded him in his suit as he looked up and down the sidewalk bordering the park. In a way it was too bad that they were getting along so well. It suddenly occurred to her that when Ethan did leave town she was liable to miss him.

"Not too many available benches," he observed. Stacy followed his gaze. The bench in front of them was occu-

pied by a sleeping bum. The next one down had been
claimed by two teenagers with a radio playing soft salsa
music. On the other side sat a couple involved in a conversation.

"We could walk uptown a ways."

"Your ice cream'll melt," he said. "Come on, we'll go
into the park. Not far, just to where we can have a little
peace and quiet."

Stacy nodded. Normally she wouldn't have ventured
into Central Park at night if she'd been paid good money.
But with Ethan at her side she felt protected. They strolled
up the path that led in. The night was clear and the distant streetlights cast a nice glow around the treetops. An
old woman in a jogging sweat suit came trotting by with a
dachshund on a leash, giving them a friendly wave. Stacy
waved back, instantly glad they'd decided to do this.

"There's a nice spot," Ethan said, pointing to a hill a bit
farther on. "Can you handle it in those heels?"

"No problem," she said. Otherwise he might try to
carry her over there. Though that wouldn't be the worst
thing in the world.

They settled in under the lone tree atop the hill, so they
could look down on the surrounding greenery and the
winding path below, with its single dim street lamp. Ethan
broke out the ice cream, strawberries, cookies and champagne, pouring the latter into the two plastic cups they'd
picked up at the grocery store. He raised his in a toast.

"Here's to having our own party," he said.

"I'll drink to that," she said, and took a sip. "Um. I
think it tastes better in these cups."

"Definitely." Ethan grinned, then put his cup down as
a warm breeze rose. Stacy felt her carefully combed hair
swept into instant disarray. But it didn't really matter, and
she gave up trying to fix it. As she smoothed her bangs

back out of her eyes, she saw Ethan looking at her in silence.

"I'm a mess, right?"

"Wrong," he said, his eyes still intent on her. She felt her heartbeat quicken as he reached forward to brush a leaf from the edge of her dress, and when he didn't move away again, she felt a tingle of anticipation.

"Now I want to do something I've been wanting to do all night," he said quietly.

She looked at him, her throat tightening. "Yes?"

His eyes glimmered in the soft light. "This," he said— and yanked loose his bow tie before sitting back against the tree with a satisfied sigh. "That's better," he said, unbuttoning his collar. "You don't mind, do you?"

"Of course not." She took another sip of champagne, feeling more than a little foolish. Maybe she'd been wrong about Ethan, and he wasn't that attracted to her, after all. Maybe she was only playing a silly game with her own imagination. After all, Ethan hadn't made a single move in her direction since that moment in the museum. He probably had the same reasons as she did for avoiding any more intimacy.

Ethan cleared his throat. "Tell me something."

She selected a strawberry. "Hmm?"

"Am I getting to be a nuisance?"

She tried not to choke on the berry. "What?"

"Well, I mean, it seems like you end up having to spend a lot of time carting me around places, outside of office hours," he said, inspecting a cookie with great intensity. "I'm probably interfering with your social life."

Stacy smiled. "I'm not exactly living in a social whirl these days," she said dryly. "So, no, you don't have to worry about that, really."

Ethan nodded, still intent on examining the cookie in his hand. "And your friend doesn't mind?"

"My friend?" She looked at him blankly.

"That guy Phil you introduced me to, at the Tango Club."

"Oh!" So maybe that was what was holding him back. "Phil's just a guy I go out with, now and then. It's nothing, you know, serious."

"Oh." Ethan nodded, then put the cookie down without eating it.

"I'm not involved with anyone, remember?" she said. "I'm married to my work."

"Right," he said. "Like me. We're just a couple of confirmed bachelors." Stacy laughed. Ethan smiled, then picked up the cookie again. "But you weren't always like this," he ventured.

"If you mean, did I get serious once and did I get burned? Then, yes," she said. "How about you?"

"Ditto," he said. "You still licking your wounds? Or was it a while ago?"

"It's been long enough," she said, aware of the ambivalence implicit in that phrase.

"Long enough for what?" he asked, picking up on it.

"Long enough to be over it...and immune to romance," she said, though she knew she didn't really mean that. She looked at Ethan's profile in the moonlight as he bit into the much-examined cookie at last, then glanced up at the moon, just breaking through a bank of fleecy clouds in the dark sky.

She'd never be entirely immune, that was the problem, she mused. She'd seen too many romantic comedies on late-night television, studied too many of them in her film school days. She couldn't help thinking that a night like this was made for the whispering of sweet nothings, and that Ethan, minus bow tie but still looking smashing in his formal suit, was made for sweeping a woman off her feet.

But she'd been swept up once, swept away and then dis-carded. . . .

"Who was the guy?" Ethan asked softly.

"His name was Stanford," Stacy said.

"Want to give it to me in twenty-five words or less?"

"Sure. He came from money and he wanted to make more. I think we were both a bit too career-obsessed to be able to make a real commitment. God, that sounds like something out of a magazine," she said wryly.

"Does it have to be mutually exclusive?" he asked. "Career and commitment, I mean."

"Well, look at you," she said, defensive. "Isn't that the choice you've made?"

Ethan shrugged. "Doesn't mean I've made my peace with it," he said.

"I see." He'd turned his attention to spooning out some ice cream now. She still couldn't figure out what his boundaries were, Stacy realized. It was hard to tell how personal you could be with a man like Ethan. "And what was *she* like?" Stacy asked. "The woman you were with?"

"Lucille," Ethan said.

"Twenty-five words?"

"Smart, sophisticated, successful," he said, looking at her directly for the first time in a while. The inference didn't escape her, and she was all the more intrigued. She'd assumed that Ethan's former "significant other" would be some academic with matching wire-rims and a pith hel-met.

"And?" she prodded him.

"And our paths diverged," he said. "I wanted to go into the Third World, and she wanted to go into what she called the real world."

"Which was?"

"Commercial photography," he said. "She puts books out. And when push came to shove . . ."

"Careers came first," she said. "Sounds oddly familiar. Wounds healed?" she asked.

"Sure," he said, with a little smile. "Oh, it was all for the best, I suppose."

She had a feeling there was more to that story. "Well, we really are a pair, then," she said, surprised and pleased to think of them as having such a similar history in affairs of the heart. "We're peas in a noncommittal pod."

Ethan chuckled. "Well, as one pea to another," he said, lifting the champagne bottle. "What do you say we have another round?"

"I say put that bottle down and shut your mouth, man!"

The voice hissed out in the darkness behind them. Stacy froze. Ethan paused in midpour. Only when he turned to look did she allow herself a frightened glance over her shoulder.

There were two men standing beside the tree, and one of them had something in his hand. A knife! It was glinting in the moonlight as he stepped forward.

"I just want the wallets," he said. "You hand yours over and the lady's bag, and we won't have any problems, okay?"

Ethan sighed. He put down the bottle and slowly got to his feet. "Look," he began. "I'm not in the mood for—"

"I'm not in the mood for nothing!!" the man with the knife said hoarsely. She couldn't see his face well in the darkness, but what she could see didn't look at all intimidated. "So don't mess around, just do it!"

Ethan, hands on hips, wasn't doing anything. "Ethan," she whispered nervously. "It isn't a movie this time."

"I don't wanna hafta use this thing," the man with the knife said. His companion was edging cautiously forward, his gaze fixed on Stacy's handbag. Stacy's eyes darted nervously to the footpath below, but there wasn't a soul in sight.

"And I don't want to have to use these," Ethan said quietly, his hands clenching into fists. Stacy felt her heart give a lurch. She could see the headline: "Would-be V.P. Dies in Central Park Mugging Massacre." She wanted to say something to stop them, but her mouth couldn't move.

Their assailant had also stopped in his tracks, eyes widening in incredulity. "Man," he said. "What the—? Don't be a fool."

"Hey!" his companion exclaimed. "It's him!"

"Huh?"

"It's that guy, from the news! Arizona Brady!"

The man with the knife took a step back, staring at Ethan. "Nah, it can't... Wait a second. Your name Brady?"

"Brody," Ethan said.

"It's him!" the other repeated. "What'd I tell you?"

The man with the knife suddenly broke into a grin. "Too much!" he said. "What are you doing in a monkey suit, man?"

Ethan sighed. "Put that thing away," he said evenly.

"Sure, no problem," the man said with a casual wave of the knife.

"Let's get outta here!" his companion implored.

"You shouldn't be hanging around the park this time of night," their would-be attacker said. "You could get into trouble."

"He doesn't know anything, he's from Arizona!" said the other. "Come on, let's split!"

"All right, all right," the man said. "Sorry to bother you, Brady. But really, you gotta watch yourself. There's some dangerous dudes around here after dark."

"Come on!" His friend was growing frantic. "This guy's crazy, man!"

"So listen, no hard feelings, right? We gotta go." The man waved his knife again in a friendly salute, then turned around at last as his companion hurried down the hill. Stacy stared after them, her heart still racing. Their voices floated out of the darkness as they retreated.

"Go back, whaddya mean, go back?"

"Hell, we shoulda gotten his autograph!"

"Come on!"

Once they were out of sight, Stacy looked at Ethan. He was still holding his ground, fists clenched. He turned to look at her. "Are you okay?"

"I'm fine," she said, her voice tremulous. They stared at each other in silence. "Ethan," she began, "did that really just happen?"

Ethan's face finally relaxed into a smile. "Hard to believe," he said, chuckling.

Stacy laughed, giddy with relief. Ethan joined in, sitting down again in the soft grass next to her, his deep laugh booming out through the darkness. He was leaning close to her, his shoulder against hers. It seemed only natural to clutch at his arm as she tried to catch her breath. She realized that even though she'd been scared, she'd somehow trusted that Ethan would take care of her, and a warm feeling of gratitude surged up through her.

That was why she gave him a little hug, of course. It was only natural. But somehow, no sooner had she done that then her breath was quickening again, and she had to move away from the nearness of him to get her bearings.

Not that it mattered, she thought as she looked up into his smiling eyes. Something seemed to have given way inside her; some last barrier had dissolved. She was feeling a closeness with Ethan she didn't even want to define, but knew instinctively that their night together was far from over.

"The ice cream's melting," he noted.

"Yes, but I have my handbag and we're both alive and healthy," she reminded him. "Ethan, I should have said something. You just don't go wandering into the park at night, usually."

"Hey, you're with Arizona Brady," he said.

"Right," she said. "Maybe we could return to the brightly lit pavement now. What do you say?"

Ethan frowned. "We don't seem to be able to stay put anyplace tonight," he said. "What's next?"

Stacy got to her feet, Ethan putting a hand out to steady her. The champagne and the excitement had definitely gone to her head. Otherwise the next words she uttered would never have come out of her mouth so easily, so spontaneously, as if it were the most logical thing in the world. "Why don't we go back to my place?" she suggested. "It's not far from here."

ETHAN WAS DOING HIS BEST not to jump to conclusions.

He hadn't really thought about this evening out with Stacy as a date. He'd accompanied her to the fund-raiser—or vice versa, to be more accurate—for professional reasons. When they'd left early, it had only seemed natural to finish off that champagne together. And after going through what they'd gone through in the park, it would've seemed unnatural to say good-night and leave it at that.

And they were having a good time together. The way friends did, he reminded himself, as the cab wended its way uptown. Hadn't they established that they were friends? So there was really no reason to get anxious about taking Stacy home or to have any expectations. He'd go up and have a last glass of champagne with her and then leave. It was really quite simple.

That was what he kept telling himself as they arrived at her apartment building, paid the cabdriver, bade a cheery hello to the doorman and then took the elevator up four floors. Stacy seemed perfectly at ease, even a little giddy, for which he couldn't blame her. She'd probably been frightened out of her wits in the park.

She certainly wasn't being provocative. Just friendly. He tried to keep this thought firmly implanted in his own relatively sober brain as they entered her apartment, even as Stacy kicked off her shoes, headed straight for her stereo system to put on some soft, bluesy jazz music and only bothered to turn on a solitary lamp.

"Welcome to your first bona fide New York apartment," she said. "This is how we live."

Ethan looked around. Everything looked tasteful and well put together, like something out of one of those glossy home magazines he never bothered to read on airplanes. It made his own barely furnished, thrown-together digs in California seem absolutely hovel-like. "Nice," he said.

"Boring," she said. "Here," she added, handing him a champagne glass. "Don't search for compliments. I'm moving anyway."

"Oh?" He was still clutching the half-empty bottle inside his jacket. Ethan removed it now and poured them both another glassful. "Where to?"

"Across the street," Stacy said. "Isn't that silly? Here." She raised her glass. "To terrorizing the dangerous dudes of Central Park." She clinked her glass against his.

Ethan nodded and sipped. "Still bubbly," he noted.

"Yes, me, too," said Stacy.

He peered at her in the dim light. How much *had* she been drinking? "Are you really moving across the street?"

Stacy sighed. "Maybe," she said. "It seemed very important up until recently. But let's not talk about me." She drank the rest of her champagne and put down her glass. "Let's talk about what you think about me. Just kidding," she added quickly, since his face betrayed his confusion.

"I think you've had a good amount of champagne," he ventured.

"I'm not drunk, if that's what you think," Stacy said, with an indignant look. "No, I'm just happy that everything turned out okay tonight. Come to think of it, it's been a perfect evening."

"Oh." He still couldn't get used to the idea that she really didn't mind the kinds of crazy things he always seemed to get them into the middle of. "You mean, even with that Koppleman character taking a fall and us nearly being mugged? That's your idea of a perfect evening?"

"Uh-huh." Stacy nodded, then suddenly turned toward the music, her face brightening, eyes aglow. "Oh, I love this song," she said. "Gershwin." Then she moved away, swaying to the music as she walked across the carpeting toward the window.

Seeing her lithe figure silhouetted in the moonlight, Ethan couldn't help but follow, drawn as if bewitched. He was almost at her side when he forced himself to pause. This was not at all what was supposed to be happening, right? Wasn't this a good time for him to maybe talk about heading out?

But she was still swaying to the music, humming along, slightly off-key, and as if he'd been hypnotized, Ethan found himself walking right up to her. The next thing he knew, she was sliding a hand around his shoulder and lightly fitting her body to his with a little smile on her upturned face. "Yes, thanks, I would like to dance," she said.

Ethan cleared his throat, slipping an arm around her waist. "So would I, I guess."

"So you are," she said. "And you move pretty well for an anthropologist."

"Thanks," he muttered. The music was all muted horns and tinkling piano. He could glimpse the lights of the city sparkling behind her as he placed his other hand on her shoulder, pressing his body gently against hers. "But you know..."

"What?" she murmured, intertwining the fingers of her right hand with his left.

"I really should be going," he said.

STACY BLINKED, wondering if she'd heard him right. Going? Now? Was the man crazy? Didn't he know what she knew by now? Wasn't it obvious that no matter what kinds of rational obstacles either of them had put up between them in the past few weeks, an irresistible, wonderfully irrational force was propelling them together? Somewhere inside, she'd already surrendered to it.

"Go where?" she asked. "Have you got a hot date with a hunk of postclassic limestone or something?" She could feel Ethan's heart beating, feel the subtle shift of her own heartbeat as it joined his.

"No," he said. "But..."

She looked up at the handsome face only inches from her own. His eyes gazed steadily into hers as they swayed slowly together, but his expression seemed thoughtful and wary. What was wrong with the man? She couldn't help but be aware of her breasts pressing against the firmness of his chest, couldn't shut off the lightly insinuating movement of his firm thighs against her own, and didn't want to.

"But what?" she asked.

He frowned, and when he spoke it seemed as though the words were being pulled out of him. "A guy could get the wrong idea," he said. "I mean, here we are..."

"Yes?" She leaned back slightly in his embrace.

"Alone in your apartment after midnight, dancing like this...."

"Mmm-hmm." She could feel her body relaxing under the subtle pressure of Ethan's warm hands on her back. Relaxing? That wasn't the proper word. Her body was melding to his, and she was anything but relaxed.

"And if I didn't know better, I mean, if we hadn't already made it pretty clear that neither one of us is interested in anything other than being..."

"Friends?" she supplied.

"Right, friends," Ethan said nervously. "But here we are, you know, and if I stick around any longer..."

"Something might happen?" Lazily she moved her hand on the back of his neck, gliding her fingers through his soft, thick hair. Ethan nodded.

"Exactly," he muttered.

"Ethan Brody, you big dope," she said. "It's already happened."

His eyes widened slightly. "I don't..."

"I'm not saying I planned this or anything," she went on, unable to stop her hands from straying over the strong, smooth contours of his neck and shoulders. "But something's been happening between you and me for a while now. Hasn't it? Or am I crazy?"

"Something," he murmured. "Well, yeah, I suppose something has."

"Something good," she said. "Only it's seemed like it might be bad. To let it be good, I mean."

"I'm not sure I follow you," Ethan said, his voice sounding huskier as he held her tighter.

"I think you do," she said softly.

"Are you saying," he said, his hand sliding more possessively to the small of her back, "that if I let myself do what I've been wanting to do...?"

"It might turn out to be what I've been wanting you to do. Yes," she said.

She could see her own excitement and anticipation mirrored in the glimmering depths of Ethan's dark eyes. "Then let's stop talking about it," he murmured, and his lips closed over hers.

Fireworks? Not exactly. It was more like a slow-burning fuse that had been sparked. At the first touch of his soft lips she was surprised at how perfectly natural it seemed to be doing this. As the kiss deepened, and the fuse that seemed coiled at the center of her began pulsing with a steadily rising heat, it seemed strange that she'd held off so long.

In another moment she was fitting her body even more tightly to his, and again the fit seemed perfect, inevitable somehow. They were still on their first kiss, but it might have been a dozen of them, for all she knew. His warm wet tongue was gliding between her lips, sliding deep within to find her tongue, and Stacy felt herself give way, felt a renewed exhilaration blossom within her.

She arched her back, her palms tightening on his shoulders, her tongue seeking his now. Savoring the salty sweetness, she pressed herself to him, eyes shut tight, senses reeling. There was a great relief in no longer pretending. This was the feeling she'd been secretly aching to feel for days, and she could sense his excitement matching her own.

A soft moan escaped her lips as his mouth left hers at last. "Stacy?" he inquired.

She opened her eyes again. He looked concerned. "Ethan?"

"Are you okay?"

Okay? Her whole body seemed to be shivering and pulsating in his embrace. Her mind had floated out into the moonlight and had settled back into place again only because for some reason he was back to talking instead of kissing. "I think I'm more than okay," she told him.

"I mean, you're not...? This isn't because of all that champagne?"

"Ethan, if I'm drunk on anything, it's the way you just kissed me," she confessed, and leaned forward to settle her face in the crook of his neck. He smelled wonderful right there, and his skin was surprisingly soft below the subtly ticklish scratchiness of his shaved whiskers.

"I know what you mean," he said, his lips brushing her forehead as his hand slid through the silken curls of her hair in a gentle caress. "I just wanted to be sure."

"Ethan," she said, smiling into his neck. "Stop being such a gentleman. I mean, it's very appealing, but..."

"I should shut up and kiss you again?"

"Mmm," she murmured, and thankfully, he did.

It was even better the second time.

THAT PERFUME was one thing. But she *tasted* good. Her lips really did have a sweetness to them. Once he was kissing her, it was hard to stop. And there was so much else to take in, there were so many other sensations—the softness of her skin, the suppleness of her body molding with surprising ease to his—that his senses were starting to reel.

And the look of her when he managed to come up for air—the way the moonlight made the paleness of her naked shoulders glow like living marble above the line of her black dress—it was all a bit like a dream. He didn't want it to end, but at the same time could feel himself fighting the pull, the passionate feeling that was like an undertow.

The last time he'd felt anything like this... Well, he'd never felt anything quite like this. Kissing Lucille had been heady stuff, true, but he felt he'd entered another realm here. Maybe it was the years in the jungle, deprived of any feminine affection, that were making this seem so especially overpowering. But no, it was how he felt about Stacy.

And if he felt that strongly about her, considering the circumstances they were in, wasn't he setting himself up to take another fall? He wasn't the kind of guy who slept around for the hell of it. He had to genuinely like a woman to want to be intimate with her, and he more than liked Stacy. And if that was the case, wasn't he going to want to stick around and be with her?

Wasn't that a preposterous concept? For that matter, wasn't it going to make working with her a risky proposition?

Anyway you looked at it, making love to Stacy Morrison was bound to create some real problems. "Stacy," he said, as she settled herself around him with feline grace. "You know, this may get us into trouble."

"I know," she murmured, her hand working a bewitching magic on the back of his neck, every hair standing up at full attention as her fingers caressed the sensitive skin there. "Maybe you ought to talk us out of it."

Ethan took a breath. Her hand was still making shivers go down his spine. His left hand, as if on automatic pilot, was sneaking across her back to lightly stroke the soft skin above the line of her dress. It was as if their two bodies were tuned to some magnetic frequency, and any caress she made had to be answered by one of his.

"Aren't we, ah, in danger of jeopardizing our professional relationship?" he asked.

"Definitely," she said, her lips bestowing a feather-light series of tiny kisses on the nape of his neck. "I'd say this is entirely unprofessional."

"We'd really be better off maintaining some distance," he said thickly, his hand exploring the soft contours of her shoulders.

"I couldn't agree more." Her other hand was playing with the top button of his shirt, undoing it, and then sliding down to undo the second one. He made an inarticulate noise of surprised pleasure as her warm hand slipped inside his shirt to play with the curls of hair on his chest. Those nails! He suddenly understood their attraction.

"It's not that I'm not enjoying this," he said weakly.

"Of course," she murmured, and bent her head to follow with her lips the course of those lightly raking nails.

"But I've really been enjoying our working together," he persisted, one hand tangled in the exquisite softness of her hair and the other sliding, as if impelled, past her shoulder to the silken-smooth swell of her breast.

"Me, too," she breathed. "It's been an…intellectually stimulating experience."

"So changing the nature of our relationship," he continued, though he was finding it more and more difficult to talk as more buttons came undone beneath her fingers' deft manipulations. "It's not the best idea."

"No," she said, lifting her face to kiss his chin.

"So since we agree," he said, "don't you think that we ought to…" Her lips brushed his and she exhaled softly as his hand closed over her breast. He could feel the taut stiffness of its tip beneath the thin material. "…that we ought to…" Her lips nuzzled his earlobe. "…lie down?"

He hadn't meant to say that. Stacy pulled back to look at him, her hooded eyes exuding a smoky, sensual radiance. "Professor Brody," she whispered. "I thought you'd never ask."

Chapter Eight

He was right, of course. This was the wrong thing to do. And she appreciated his bringing it up. But now he was carrying her in his arms, headed toward her bedroom. And that was something so right, so much righter than anything else she could think of, that the best course of action was to enjoy it. Which was easy.

"I think I could get used to this kind of transportation," Stacy murmured, nestling her face into the hollow of his shoulder. "You do it so well."

"Thanks," Ethan replied. "Watch your feet."

She tucked them in as they cleared the doorway. Her bedroom was in shadow, but a rectangle of moonlight fell across the end of the bed. "The place is a little messy," she said.

"Not by my standards." He slowly lowered her onto the moonlit quilt, but she didn't relinquish her grip on his shoulders. That was a nice idea, it turned out, because he slid right onto the bed alongside her.

"And what are your standards?" she asked dreamily, as he kissed the rounded softness of her shoulder.

"I'm used to a dirt floor and a hammock," he said.

"Oh." The problem was, she wanted to kiss him everywhere at once. And there was all this clothing they had on. But as problems went, it wasn't a bad one.

"This is quite a dress," he said, his hands moving over the sheer material, raising goose bumps on the skin below.

"Glad you like it."

"But I've been wondering all night," he said, his lips moving from one shoulder to the hollow of her cleavage. "What have you got on underneath it?"

"Not much," she told him and smiled, her eyes half closed in pleasure. "Isn't that nice?"

"Uh-huh," he murmured, his hands sliding around her back to find the zipper. She moved with him, rolling forward until he was beneath her and the zipper undone. His hands traced the line of her bare back. More goose bumps, and a sudden wave of impatience.

"You look good in that suit, too," she said. "But it's a little formal for this occasion."

He lifted his head to look at her. "I hear you," he responded.

It was interesting how quickly two people could get undressed when they put their minds to it. Of course, the process kept getting slowed down considerably, because they kept helping each other along with a lingering kiss or a caress. But Stacy wouldn't have been surprised if the material had just melted away from their bodies. Such was the heated intensity she felt when they were finally skin to skin.

It was then, when she slipped beneath the covers with him and felt his nakedness enveloping hers, that any last vestiges of pretense evaporated. She was suddenly overwhelmed by wanting him, and trying to be casual or coy about it was simply out of the question.

She felt desperate for the taste of him, for the exquisite pleasure she felt when their tongues touched and as the soft curves of her body molded to his. No longer concerned with phantom do's or don'ts, she gave herself over to this spiraling, reckless feeling of abandon.

She returned each of his kisses with a breathless fervor, her arms gliding up to encircle his back, hands restlessly feeling the hard lines of his shoulders. Beneath the quilt, Ethan fitted her to himself, a gruff moan of arousal escaping his mouth as their thighs and hips aligned.

Then he slipped away and she opened her eyes in dismay. "What's wrong?" she whispered.

"Wrong?" His chuckle was a husky rumble in the darkness. "Not a thing. But I have to see you, Stacy. It's not enough just feeling you."

She understood, and offered no resistance as he slid down the sheet past the splash of moonlight on her legs. His hand returned to glide over the tingling nakedness of her taut belly, caressing her hip, stealing over the soft skin of her inner thighs.

"That feels like heaven," she murmured.

"I think I'm *in* heaven," he said. "Damn!"

"What?" She saw that his brow was furrowed as he looked down at her, his hand's gentle caresses making her shift restlessly beneath him all the while.

"Are you allowed to look this beautiful? It seems almost criminal."

Stacy smiled. "You've already gotten this far without flattery," she teased. "But do go on."

"Oh, I'll go on," he said, the words ending in a little growl as he bent to kiss the taut peak of her breast. Stacy heard her breath catch as his hand glided upward to cup the soft mound. The combination of lips and fingers was almost too arousing.

She pulled him down to herself again, her mouth hungry for his. Desire overtook her and she went with it, drinking in the taste and feel of him. When he lifted his lips from hers at last, having savored and seduced every pore of her mouth into vibrant, tingling awareness, his fingers lingered over her hair, brushing back a stray lock from her cheek as he gazed at her.

Time seemed suspended, her pounding heartbeat the only constant. "You don't know what a job it's been, not kissing you," he murmured. "Keeping my mind on our work has been more work than the work."

"I know the feeling," she replied.

He looked surprised. "I didn't think you would."

"Neither did I," she told him. "Until recently."

"We do make an unlikely couple," he said.

"Not at the moment," she answered, stretching against him, pleased by the way he stiffened with pleasure as she fitted her soft contours to his.

"True," he murmured. "And as long as we stay *in* the moment..."

"...we're liable to make each other very happy," she whispered. Her lips longed for his kiss, already impatient to taste him again. Her blood seemed to hum in her veins beneath the gentle exploration of his fingertips. As his luminous gaze held hers, she knew his impatience matched her own.

"You know, I think I've been wanting to be with you like this for so long that it was starting to become physically painful," he murmured.

She smiled at the earnest look on his face and nodded. "Let's ease that pain," she suggested.

Ethan's lips found hers once more. Moonbeams seemed to dance on her half-closed eyelids. Exquisite pleasure billowed up from deep inside her, spiraling still higher as his lips descended to the cleft between her breasts, then sought and claimed their rounded fullness, explored each trembling tip with a velvet tongue.

Next he kissed a glistening, shiver-provoking path between them and over the curve of her belly, tracing a warm wet path in deliciously erotic slow motion down her trembling thighs. Stacy shook with an arousal that seemed to inflame every nerve ending. The feel of his lips gliding over each newly kissed inch of her was almost too much to bear.

Then it was she who covered his chest with a fiery trail of kisses, her fingers playing with the curly thatch of hair, then finding places to tickle and tease him into groans of arousal. Gaze locked in his, she stroked his taut belly, enjoying his shaky intake of breath as she explored each beautifully shaped plane and contour.

Each kiss gave way to another. It was as if they wanted to devour each other. His dark eyes glittered with passion as he slid his supple hands over her body in a ceaseless, eager exploration, and she tried to cover his every inch with her hungry lips.

And when she heard his voice again, it was almost like hearing her own, the words the same, the feeling identical. "I want you," he was whispering. "So much. . . ."

"Yes," she whispered back, and it was all she could say, since his fingers were working an erotic magic at the core of her that made her body convulse, liquid fire coursing through her every limb. "Yes," she repeated. "Yes. . . ."

Ethan gathered her tighter to him. Lost in sheer ecstatic sensation, she clung to him, breasts crushed against the soft curls on his chest, her hands moving eagerly over the smooth muscles of his back. His body slid over hers, poised in arched arousal. And then as their eyes locked gazes once more, their bodies merged at last.

Joined, united in a passion that knew no bounds or limits, they seemed to leave the world behind. They were alone in the darkness, rapt in ecstatic discovery, this melding of body and soul all that existed. And as they loved each other, forming one entity that seemed to blaze like a shining star, she wondered dimly how she had ever lived without this feeling.

Now that she had felt it, would she be able to live without it again?

A WARM BREEZE wafted through the open window of her bedroom, and outside the sky had turned a pale blue gray. The city was stirring. The two bodies in the thoroughly disarrayed bed, in contrast, were finally still beneath the tangle of sheets. They had drifted into a brief slumber after hours and hours when sleep had been inconceivable.

Stacy stretched her wonderfully exhausted limbs, enjoying the lingering glow of contentment she still felt. With a little sigh she rose to one elbow, brushing the tangled bangs from her eyes, so that she could better study the chiseled features of the man who was now snoring softly beside her.

She examined the soft but masculine line of his lips, the rugged cheekbones, the unkempt shock of hair over his high forehead. She decided that without glasses, he could definitely give Gary Cooper a run for the money.

Stacy tugged the edge of the sheet past his hip, her gaze reveling in the sculpted planes of his broad back and shoulders. For a moment she marveled at this specimen of sheer masculinity. He was almost perfectly proportioned, a strong man, but capable of such tenderness.

She couldn't stop herself from caressing him again, kissing him lightly on the shoulder, even though he was asleep. The desire he'd awakened in her was still just as strong, as were the softer, warmer feelings that went with it. Even watching him sleep gave her a rosy glow inside, though it was very tempting to wake him, so that they could...

Stacy sat up slowly, frowning. How far gone *was* she, exactly? When all of this had begun last night—and that fund-raising dinner already seemed weeks, ages ago—she hadn't given much thought to the morning after. But here it was. Now she couldn't imagine things being any different than they were. She couldn't imagine not waking up without this man beside her.

Had she lost her mind?

If only there was something horribly wrong with Ethan Brody. If only he hadn't made her feel more fantastically fulfilled than any man ever had before. If only she wasn't . . . in love with him.

She wasn't! Stacy drew her knees up to her chest, swallowing a lump in her suddenly tightened throat. What a ridiculous idea. Lust, maybe. That was it. She was feeling lust for the man, and who could blame her, when he was such a good lover?

But even as she thought it, she knew there was more. Lust couldn't really account for the intensity of feelings she'd felt, in between their passionate bouts of lovemaking, in the pauses between whispered conversations in the darkness. And in a way she'd known the moment she'd awoken, know it even sooner, when he'd first merged his body with hers. It *was* love. And it was that very intensity she immediately wanted to flee from, as soon as she dared acknowledge that dread, oh-so-problematic word.

Stacy pulled up her portion of sheet, imagining an early-morning chill that wasn't really there. Well, there was clearly only one solution: she had to get away from this gorgeous hunk of manhood before things got any more complicated than they already were.

Watching the curls of soft dark hair on his chest slowly rise and fall, she tried to recall her earlier convictions. What was it she'd been telling herself since the breakup with Stanford? That she needed to stay single for her own well-being, had to live her own life, make her career flourish before even considering losing herself again in the treacherous waters of an emotional commitment.

And all she could think about now was being with Ethan.

And being with Ethan was an improbable, nay, impossible proposition, wasn't it?

Life was unfair, Stacy mused ruefully. Just when you thought you were free and clear, independent and happy to be that way, love came whizzing down around you like a golden net, and you were caught. Suddenly feeling a panic of imagined claustrophobia, Stacy contemplated escape.

Let Russell take over the museum account, now that things were well underway? That was risky, but it was conceivable to finesse a less intimate involvement in the exhibit. The rational, calculating part of her mind that was used to contemplating the politics of business had to be nudged woozily into gear.

But her inner computer refused to boot up, as it were. How could it, when she was contemplating Ethan's peaceful repose? She tore her eyes away, staring out the window at the brightening skyline. Separation from a daily work relationship, that would be imperative. If she escaped now she'd get out with a minimum of damage....

"Hey." The one sleepy syllable from Ethan's lips startled her. She turned guiltily to find him looking up at her with a lazy smile. "Was I asleep?"

"Uh-huh," she said, thinking, *if I'm going to even attempt to put some distance between us, I'd better leap out of this bed immediately.*

Ethan reached out to grasp her knee. "Sorry," he said. "What'd I miss?"

There was a wonderfully husky rasp to his sleepy mumble that made it harder to move from his gentle grip. But she'd lost her chance, anyway. Stacy knew that as soon as she gazed into the long-lashed dusky eyes peering up at her under his tousled hair.

"Not a thing," she told him.

"Seems a shame to waste any of this time sleeping," he said, his soft palm caressing her knee and then moving higher. Stacy felt a warm flush of pleasure crest like a wave at the touch of his fingertips. "You seem awfully far away," he noted.

"I was..."

"Going somewhere? You look a little cold."

Stacy glanced down at her nudity with a self-conscious smile. "Well, I figured I'd put some clothes on."

"Terrible idea," he said, gently pulling her leg closer.

"It's morning," she began, but there was no power in her protest.

"Barely," he murmured. Ethan captured her waist and, with a gentle tug, brought her sprawling on top of him.

Laughing, Stacy fought off his tickling caresses as they rolled about in the sheets. Her blood was already simmering with arousal, skin tingling as he rained quick kisses over her nakedness. "Stop," she protested breathlessly. "We'll never get out of here."

"I like the sound of that." Ethan's eyes gleamed with amusement and desire. Albeit pleased, she was a little taken aback. After endless hours of passion, Ethan was showing no signs of exhaustion, but in fact, evidence of a healthy arousal himself. "Why go anywhere else?"

The prospect filled her with both excitement and trepidation. "Wait," she protested weakly. "Aren't you hungry?"

Ethan grinned. "I'll avoid the obvious clichés," he said, his hands cupping her breasts, his fingers' caress eliciting a soft moan from deep in her throat. "Let's just say there's more than one appetite to take care of at the moment."

Stacy glimpsed her clock at the bedside table. "Some of us do have work to do, Professor," she said, squirming to get free of his embrace.

"Work," he sighed. "Can't it wait?"

Richard. The office. Christopher. The film festival. She invoked every one of these usually all-important words in her dazed mind, trying to force herself out of this bed through sheer willpower. It was tough going. The feel of Ethan's arms around her was overpowering.

But just then he relaxed his grip. "Okay," he said. "I don't mean to be greedy." Ethan lay back, crossing his arms behind his head. "Go," he said.

Stacy stared at him. Of course now she had no intention of leaving. "It's fine with you?" she inquired, in a tone of reproach that was only half facetious.

Ethan grinned. "Suit yourself."

"You're mean," she sighed, and then snuggled up to him under the sheets with a little sigh. "All right," she said, as he hugged her to him, his hands playing with her hair. "Just for a few minutes. We won't do anything."

"Nothing?" he teased, his other hand roving over the curve of her hip.

"Just talk," she suggested.

"Ah," Ethan said. "Yes. Let's talk about us."

Us. The word suddenly had a meaning to it and a resonance that was a bit overwhelming. "You and me," she said cautiously.

"I don't think there's anyone else here." He lifted her chin with his thumb and forefinger, looking into her eyes. "What's wrong?"

"Nothing, yet," she said, wondering how he'd so swiftly become adept at reading her inner thoughts.

"You're worried," he said.

"A little," she admitted.

"I want you to know something," he said. "Much as I hate to admit it, I've been stuck on you for quite some time. I didn't plan on being able to be with you like this," he continued, his hand gently stroking her shoulder beneath the sheet. "Though I'll admit it's something I dreamed about."

Stacy's throat was tight again. Even his light caress was sending little tremors of sensation through her body. But what did he mean, exactly? Was it only a physical experience he'd wanted, only her body that he'd dreamed of "being with"? She wanted to believe it was love she saw glowing in the dark velvet depths of his eyes—but no, she'd rather it wasn't! She didn't want to get pulled into the whole maelstrom of loving and being loved, the giving with the taking, all the sacrifices such a commitment implied.

"Well, I didn't plan on any of this, either," she said, trying to adapt a detached, unemotional tone.

"No, wait, listen to me," he said, and the urgency she heard in his voice was arresting. "The point is, now that I have, I don't see why I have to pretend anymore." He took a breath, and his brow was furrowed as he spoke again, as if the words were hard to say. "You're the kind of woman any guy in his right mind wouldn't want to let go of," he said. "So I want you to know that's not what I have in mind."

"What do you mean?"

"I mean, this is all kind of scary, if you want to know the truth, but Stacy—" his hand tightened on her shoulder "—I don't know how things are going to go for us from here on out. I know neither of us planned this or expected it or even know what to make of it, but—oh, hell!"

He was shaking his head. "What? What is it?" Stacy demanded.

"I'm in love with you, damn it." He said this with a scowl. "You can make fun of me all you want, but that's the truth." He closed his eyes, looking like a man who expected a blow to fall on his head.

Looking at him, she was filled with a surge of feeling that was—oh, hell! as he had said—unmistakable in its intensity. She wanted nothing more than to kiss his worries away and have him do the same for her. She wanted to sink right into his very skin and feel that love and lose herself inside of it and—

Scary, he'd said. Terrifying was more like it.

Stacy suddenly realized that she'd been repressing her deeper emotions so routinely, for so long, that until last night she'd almost forgotten she had them. And now that being with him had put her in touch with those feelings, she was frightened that they might be hard to control.

Right now, the only way to keep that fear at bay was to cling to him. "I wouldn't dream of making fun of you," she whispered, sliding her arm around his neck, pulling him closer to her. "Oh, Ethan..."

"What?" he whispered.

"I don't know what's going to happen, either. But for now—just kiss me again, okay?"

"That's all I want to do," he said. And did.

FOR EVERYONE ELSE at the office building on Madison Avenue it was probably just another day. For Stacy it felt like a day that existed outside any calendar.

As she walked up the street toward work, the sun seemed to sparkle on the pavement. Anyone she looked at, from a tousled-haired teenager handing out flyers on the corner, to the balding executive occupant of a sleek limousine parked by the curb, appeared to be lit in an ethereal glow.

That the sky was blue and absolutely cloudless was a marvel to her. What a deep blue! Stacy couldn't remember the last time she'd looked up at the tops of the skyscrapers around her workplace, but today they shone with a radiance that astounded her. It was hard to believe everyone didn't stop what they were doing to gaze up at that amazing blue sky pierced by the towering spires. For all their nonchalance, you'd think it was there every day.

People were smiling at her when she walked into the building. Maybe that was because she was smiling at them. She couldn't help it. She had to resist an impulse to tell the man behind the newsstand in the lobby that whatever was on the front pages was entirely irrelevant. She, Stacy Morrison, was in love. What could possibly be more earthshaking news than that?

She was late for work. Let 'em sue her. The extra hour she'd stolen in Ethan Brody's arms was worth it. She'd finally tumbled out of bed into a shower and then into her clothes in one mad scramble. The thing that had propelled her forward was the promise that she and Ethan would be meeting after work. With that exquisite and erotic carrot dangling at the end of the day, she'd been able to tear herself away and face the office.

They'd walked out together, she more floating than walking. Ethan had hailed her a cab and then kissed her goodbye. On her way across town, Stacy had tried to remember the things they'd said. She wanted to get it straight in her mind. They'd made no promises, no rash declarations of undying love, but she knew that what was happening between them was capital *S* Serious.

The only plan, such as it was, was to take each day as it came and see what happened next. As long as what happened next was that she'd spend another night with Ethan, that was fine with her.

Stacy was almost at the elevator when she remembered that there actually would be something in the papers that concerned her. She dashed to the newsstand for the morning *Trib*. Back in the elevator she found what she was looking for within the first few pages, and had to laugh aloud.

The picture of Rob Koppleman, looking bug-eyed and apoplectic as he stared up from the floor, was truly priceless. And although the caption was typically hyperbolic and inaccurate—"Koppleman K.O.'d by Bridling Brody"—she didn't think there could ultimately be any harm in it.

The little article represented more free publicity for the Mayan tomb exhibit, and nothing but amused respect for Ethan. The *Trib* was having a grand old time with Arizona Brody, but to this paper's purple prosers he now seemed less a figure of fun than a genuine folk hero. She doubted that even Ethan would be upset this time.

It was odd to read about him in print like this, when the touch of his gentle fingertips still seemed magically imprinted on her skin. Delicious memories only hours old stirred in her mind, so she was still smiling when she strode into the P and W office. She gave a cheery hello to the front desk receptionist and was humming to herself as she approached her own outer office.

Charlotte's pale and frowning visage was the unexpected thing that stopped her in mid-hum. Her secretary rose from her desk as soon as she caught sight of Stacy. "The phone's been ringing nonstop," she said grimly. "I've been stonewalling everybody, but I'm sure glad you're here."

"Sorry I'm late," Stacy said uncertainly. "But what's going on?"

"Haven't you seen it?"

"Seen it? Oh," Stacy said, remembering the *Trib*. "Sure. But why so many calls?"

"Well, it's the museum people, mainly, along with some of the other magazines. I can see why they're upset," Charlotte said, still looking uncharacteristically glum. "Richard's okay about it, though. I think he's even pleased. But he does want to see you."

"All of this over another silly photo?" Stacy said. "I don't get it. Is Koppleman suing? He couldn't be that stupid."

"Koppleman?" Charlotte stared at her. "What are you talking about?"

"What are *you* talking about?" Stacy countered, bewildered.

"This!" Charlotte was holding up a copy of *We* magazine. Stacy looked uncomprehendingly at the cover, which featured Princess Di. Then she remembered.

"Oh! The piece on Ethan—it's in this issue?"

"Then you haven't seen it." Charlotte shook her head, looking all the more pained. "It hit the stands this morning. Here. Page 68."

"What's wrong with it?" Stacy asked, alarmed, taking the glossy magazine from her outstretched hand.

"Oh, the main article is fine," Charlotte said. "But you'd better take a look at that insert on page 70. The one that talks about us."

"Us?" She nervously flipped pages. "What do you mean?" The whole of page 68 was taken up with one of Ethan's expedition stills, him looking oddly dapper in his trademark khakis, Buck on his shoulder, shovel in his hand. The article was headlined "Arizona Brody and the Mayan Tomb," with the words mocked up to look like a movie title. She skimmed the opening paragraph. So far, so good.

"It's in a box at the end of the article," Charlotte said. "'How Mad Ave Makes a Myth.'"

"Oh," Stacy said, finding the page in question. Half of the page was set off in another style of print beneath that title. Filled with foreboding she began to read.

"You'd better sit down," Charlotte said, then left her side to answer the ringing telephone.

Stacy read, feeling for the arm of the chair and sliding into it as her eyes zipped across the two columns of print. The first two paragraphs talked about the art of creating and promoting instant celebrities, and cited P and W among other "hot" agencies who did this with panache. No wonder Richard was pleased. But then why—?
Her heart gave a sudden lurch as she read on.

The people at P and W lost no time in capitalizing on their professor's unwitting penchant for colorful publicity. Within hours of the Bobby DeVine incident, Powell hired two photographers to tail Brody around the clock.

Stacy winced, her fingers tightening on the page. She hadn't had a chance to tell Ethan about that yet, hadn't even really thought to. And now he was going to find out in the worst way possible—through the very media he'd been so annoyed by. How would she explain?
She bit her lip, heart pounding. Of course that had all been before last night. And the idea had been Richard's. She could say she hadn't—no, she wasn't going to lie about it. She'd just have to tell him the truth, as difficult as that would undoubtedly be. She'd have to own up to having lied to him, and hope that the feelings they felt for each other now would somehow be strong enough to make everything all right.
Would they be? Would he understand and forgive? She thought of the look in Ethan's eyes when he'd kissed her goodbye, so tender and so trusting. Oh, he'd have to! She'd make him believe, make him know how much she cared. Buoyed by her own optimism, she read on. If that was the only hurdle they had to face—
Stacy froze as she continued skimming and caught a phrase in passing. Uh-oh. The "junior executive" at P and

W—that could only be her. What was she doing there on the page? She'd only spoken briefly to that reporter from *We*, and hadn't said anything that was remotely quotable, had she?

No. Oh, Lord, no—

That the denizens of such celeb factories as P and W are ruthlessly cynical about their work should come as no surprise. "Ethan Brody is an addle-brained academic with the social graces of a water buffalo," the junior executive who has been handling the anthropologist at P and W was quoted as saying. "How can you take someone seriously whose idea of a good time is visiting the Statue of Liberty?" But such personal opinions haven't kept the P and W people from seeing to it that Brody's public shenanigans receive maximum media exploitation.

The magazine slipped from Stacy's white-knuckled fingers. She rose abruptly from the chair, her stomach turning. This was a nightmare, right? Any second now she'd wake up and find herself in that warm and wonderful bed with...

Ethan. She had to speak to Ethan! She had to tell him immediately, before he read this horrible thing, that she'd never made a statement like that, never would or could've said those things. But even as she turned toward her office, a horrible thought occurred to her.

She *had* said them. She'd known those were her own words as soon as she'd seen them. But when? To whom? And how had they ended up in print, on the glossy pages of a national magazine?

Charlotte was fielding yet another phone call as Stacy rushed past her into the safety of her office, her mind whirling. By the time she was seated behind her desk with the door closed, she had it. Eva. She'd been talking on the phone with Eva, two, maybe three weeks ago, and she'd said those things.

But Eva wouldn't repeat them. No, especially because she knew as well as Stacy did that she hadn't really meant them. She'd been putting Ethan down in the context of not wanting to be involved with him. She'd been—what was that Shakespearean phrase—protesting too much. Because even then she'd sensed how attracted to him she was, and she'd been trying to resist that attraction.

But if Eva hadn't repeated her words, then who?

Stacy's fist came down on the pane of glass atop her desk with such force that she nearly cracked it, but she barely noticed. "That snake," she muttered, grabbing the phone. "That slimy, eavesdropping, Machiavellian— Hello? Christopher, please. This is Stacy."

"I'm sorry, Ms. Morrison, but he's away from his desk just now. Can I take a message?"

"Tell him," she said between clenched teeth, "that I want to see him." Dead, she nearly added, before slamming down the phone again.

With the detachment that only comes in the eye of a storm, she had to give Christopher his due. This little piece of mischief-making really was a thing of beauty. He'd been jealous of her success with the Mayan account and of Richard's tacit approval. In seeking a way to muck things up, he'd found a handy means of both souring her relationship with her client and making her look bad to her employer. Nice work.

Someone was knocking on her door. "Not now, Charlotte," she called, but the door opened and there was Richard himself. "Oh, hi," she said, automatically getting up, feeling the blood rise in her face.

Richard waved her down, shut the door behind him and sauntered over, hands in the pockets of his cardigan.

"How's tricks?" he inquired blithely, and sat on the edge of her desk.

Stacy cleared her throat. "All right," she said. "First I want to get some facts straight. I did *not*, I repeat, not, talk to that reporter from *We* about Ethan Brody. Anything I said was said in absolute—"

"Hey, take it easy," Richard said. "Your name isn't in the article. *Our* name is, though, many times. And that's fine with me."

"But I-I-" Stacy stuttered.

"Admittedly, if prospective clients were to get the impression that we routinely talk about them to the press in a derogatory fashion, it would be bad for business," he went on mildly. "But I think it'll be understood that this is a special case. And the important thing is, the writer points out that regardless of private feelings, P and W gets the job done."

She stared at him. "Then you're not—I mean, it's okay?"

"Hon, I must say you've stumbled upon a gold mine with this Brody character. Our business has just gotten a major profile boost. 'Ruthlessly cynical,'" he said, and smiled. "Stacy, in our profession, that's a sort of high praise."

Great. Stacy couldn't even manage a smile in return. The phrase he was so pleased with might well be a kind of professional accolade. But in her personal life it could only sound a toll of doom.

Chapter Nine

Ethan felt not unlike a kid playing hooky from school. He'd decided to take a leisurely walk from Stacy's block to the hotel, and it had turned into a wonderfully aimless stroll through Central Park. There was no one with a knife in residence on this sunny spring day, just a lot of mothers with babies in strollers lining the benches, and old men and women who favored him with wrinkled grins when he nodded a hello in passing.

If he had been a better than average whistler, he would've been whistling his favorite melody from Schubert's *Trout* Quintet. That was what came to mind as he surveyed the shiny waters of the pond beside the park's winding path. But as it was, he chose one of Buck's favorite reggae tunes. Taking responsibility for having shot that mythical sheriff seemed a perfectly jolly thing to do today.

With this jaunty melody issuing from his pursed lips, Ethan strolled around the pond, realizing only when he smiled at the same nanny sitting by a pair of twins in matching Apricas that he'd gone in a complete circle and was no closer to his destination than before.

Not that it mattered. He knew he should get back to Wally, who was helping him prepare the necessary speech for the opening ceremonies at the exhibit tomorrow night.

He had many phone calls to make, including an attempt to reach Zachary Matthews. But he wasn't in a rush to do anything that smacked of work just now. He wanted to savor the moment.

As moments went, this was fairly peak, Ethan reflected. He'd stopped whistling long enough to purchase a big soft salty pretzel from a vendor, and was enjoying the first tasty chew as he stood on a little bridge overlooking the water. The luxury hotels that ringed the southeast corner of the park were visible above the treetops, and the perfectly blue sky above made it all look like a picture in a magazine. He was filled with a sudden affection for this city. It was an okay place after all, really—because hadn't it produced Stacy Morrison?

One could even contemplate... No. The thought buzzed through his brain and out again. He couldn't really take it seriously. Yes, John Dumont at Columbia had talked seriously about a teaching fellowship for him, but Ethan had privately dismissed it out of hand. How could he possibly make New York City his home, even for a year? It just wasn't his kind of place. But then again, if he and Stacy...

A memory of Stacy smiling up at him from her rumpled pillow as she slid into his arms once more filled his vision and heart. Ethan fixed the image in his mind, filing it for later contemplation. His smile grew wider as he realized that later he could contemplate the real thing. Life was good.

A phantom vision of her face seemed to linger over the water for a moment. What a face. But it wasn't Stacy's physical beauty that was running circles around his heart, Ethan mused. No, he'd seen quite a lot of gorgeous women in New York, arguably prettier in a plastic, model sort of way. The thing was, Stacy's beauty seemed to come from who she was, and when he thought about it, it was her inner qualities he really prized.

Who else had stood beside him during this whole misbegotten trip? Sure, it had been great to have Wally around again this past week. But Stacy had been practically the only person he'd met in New York who really seemed to care about his feelings. That had been the thing that had first attracted him to her in earnest, this sensitivity he knew she possessed, this feeling he got from her that she could see past surfaces to understand a little of what made him tick.

And to think he'd been so wary of her, comparing her to Lucille. Ethan shook his head as he wandered down the path. Lucille had been an opportunist, a woman whose calculations had ultimately overtaken her emotions. She'd used him to meet the people she wanted to meet in academic circles, and then as soon as she'd turned her attention to another sphere of business, she'd pulled up her stakes and moved on.

Only not soon enough, he remembered grimly. The fact that she'd been so duplicitous as to have gotten involved with Golwin and not let on until months later—that basic lack of trustworthiness was what he'd held against her most. Well, it was partially his fault, he reminded himself. He'd been so lost inside his work, he hadn't paid her enough attention.

And the whole thing was water under the bridge, anyway. Why was he dredging up thoughts about Lucille on a beautiful new morning like this? Such comparisons were odious. At a fork, Ethan chose the path that led out of the park. He'd dawdled half the day away. Ethan started to whistle again, amused at the thought of Wally's face when he strolled into his hotel room. His friend would give him a teasing hard time, no doubt. But he could take it. On a day like this, Ethan felt nothing short of invincible.

ODDLY ENOUGH, Wally didn't say a thing when Ethan knocked on his door. Buck gave him the customarily noisy greeting, but Wally seemed preoccupied.

"Sorry I'm late," Ethan said, plopping himself into the armchair.

Wally tamped down his pipe tobacco and lighted a match. "I'm afraid to ask you where you've been," he said.

"I'll give you a hint," Ethan said expansively, stretching out in the chair. "I did not sleep alone."

Wally merely blinked behind his glasses, puffing away in silence. "Oh," he said finally.

Ethan looked at his friend's frowning visage, perplexed. "Well, don't call out the brass band or anything," he said. "I mean, it's only the first time I've been this happy in a decade or so."

Wally's frown deepened. "You were with that Morrison woman, is that it?"

Ethan sat up. "Stacy," he said. "Last I remember, the three of us were on a first-name basis."

"You spent the night with her?"

Ethan peered at Wally. He was acting like the belligerent father of a wayward teenage girl coming home late from prom night. "You get out on the wrong side of your own bachelor bed this morning?" he asked.

"Yeah, I did. Something wrong with that?"

"Hey, pinhead," squawked Buck. "Buck wants a cracker."

"Been to a newsstand this morning?" Wally asked.

"No, thanks," Ethan said. "I've given up on reading the local tabloids. But let me guess. Rob Koppleman's on the front page with an imaginary broken jaw, is that it?"

"Who's he? Oh, him," Wally said. "No, he didn't sustain any major injuries. You're the one I'm worried about."

"Me?" Ethan chuckled. "That fop never laid a glove on me, Wally. What are you talking about?"

Wally trundled over to the desk in the corner. When he came back, he was holding out a copy of *We* magazine. "I guess I should be the one to break it to you," he said darkly.

"What, that Princess Di's on a diet?" Ethan took the magazine from him. "She looks good, I'll say that."

"Page 68," Wally said.

Ethan looked up. "Uh-oh. It's me? In here?"

Wally nodded gravely. "It's no worse than any of the other slop they've been printing," he said. "But you're not going to like what's on page 70."

"Today I can handle anything," Ethan told him, opening the magazine.

"Blow it out your barracks bag," said Buck.

"Thank you, Buck," Ethan said, turning to page 68. "Well, there we are. I'm kind of getting used to this, you know. But I wish they'd dig up a different picture. You look like Bigfoot's kid brother in this shot, you know that?"

"Keep reading," said Wally.

"All right, all right," said Ethan. He read.

A few minutes later he put the magazine down. Getting up from the chair was a difficult thing to do when he felt as though he'd just gotten the wind knocked out of him. Wally was holding out the little silver flask he'd always carried in Belize. Ethan took it from him without a word and downed a stiff, stinging shot of something that didn't do a thing for his state of mind.

"She wouldn't say that. It can't have been her," he said, but he could hear the lack of conviction in his own voice.

"You know it is," Wally said quietly.

Ethan was at the window, looking out on a sunny morning that suddenly might as well have been as gray as a gravestone. He felt as if someone had put an ice pack around his chest. "Their own photographers," he muttered. "But maybe she didn't . . ."

"She knew," said Wally. "How could she not?"

Ethan turned back to survey the hotel room. He looked at the phone on the table by the bed. A part of him was already dialing it and talking to her, and listening to her explain it all away, so things could magically be back to the way they'd been only hours, no, minutes before.

But another part of him had already gone. "This joint has been getting on my nerves, you know?" he said. "What do you say we get the hell out of here?"

"HE WON'T BE THERE," Stacy said tearfully.

"Nonsense," said Eva. "Hold still."

"Not that I blame him," Stacy went on, as Eva worked the fasteners at the back of her friend's dress. "But I wish he'd given me a chance to explain!"

"I know," Eva muttered. "So you keep saying." She stepped back. "There, you're all together now."

"I'm not together," Stacy said, blinking back a tear as she looked at her reflection in the mirror. "I'm a wreck." She'd bought a new outfit for this occasion, a Donna Karan black wool crepe body dress with white silk crepe collar and cuffs, which had cost an arm and a leg. At the moment she'd just as soon have been wearing a plastic bag with hair-shirt trim.

"You look very good for a wreck," her friend noted. "Except for the red-rimmed eyes."

"There's nothing I can do about that." Stacy sniffed, getting yet another Kleenex from the already depleted new box.

"Yes. You can stop feeling sorry for yourself and look on the bright side," Eva said.

"There is no bright side."

"A vice presidency practically plopped in your lap? That sounds pretty bright to me," Eva said.

"He didn't say anything definite," Stacy murmured, and blew her nose.

"But you know he will," Eva said.

Stacy sighed, examining her makeup. They were due at the museum within the hour. Richard would be there. The press would be there. The mayor would be there. Even Wally, if she could believe the terse phone message she'd received that morning at the office, would be there. But the evening's featured attraction?

She had been trying to get to Ethan Brody since yesterday afternoon. At first she thought he'd merely been avoiding her. And then she'd thought there'd been some mistake over at the hotel, when they said the Brody party had checked out. When they insisted on it, she panicked and cabbed over there in person.

It had been an entirely useless trip. Ethan had indeed checked out only an hour or so earlier, and hadn't left any forwarding address or number. Stacy had known he'd be upset, but had counted on at least being able to talk to him. The idea that he wouldn't even want to see her was devastating.

She'd returned to the office and had a few words with the smarmy Christopher, who actually denied having leaked her words to the press. "I might've said *something*," he mused, feigning great confusion. "I mean, I did talk to the guy. But I honestly don't remember. Why, is there a problem?"

The immediate problem for Stacy had been how to keep herself from strangling the man on the grounds of justifiable homicide. But she'd managed it somehow, and she'd managed to get through that awful afternoon, taking care of the myriad phone calls and the mountain of preparation she had to do to be ready for tonight's opening.

She'd rushed home as soon as she could get free, after having beeped into her answering machine every hour, hoping for some word from him. She'd fantasized that he might call her there, had even had Chinese food delivered in and kept her line free, still hoping against hope that he'd phone or show up. But no, it was just herself and her conscience in the apartment, and a night of what seemed like only minutes of fitful sleep.

She alternated between bouts of fury at herself, at the unjust media and at him. Why didn't the thickheaded lug at least give her a chance? What was with this disappearing act, and at a time like this? Was he deliberately trying to make her sweat?

"If he waltzes in there tonight as if nothing's happened, I'll break a champagne bottle over his head," she told Eva.

"No, you won't," Eva said wryly. "You'll collapse into his arms, begging forgiveness."

"*After* I break the bottle over his head," Stacy said. "Well, come on, we might as well get into gear."

"Got an extra handkerchief?" Eva asked. "If he doesn't know, you'll probably need it."

IT WAS A GOOD CROWD at the museum. As Stacy surveyed the reception area, she couldn't help but feel a bolstering thrill of pride. At least she'd done her job well. Her personal life might have been completely ruined, but judging by the attendance alone, the Mayan Tomb Exhibit was off to a smashing start.

She made her way through the crowd in a kind of haze, as if she was watching the whole spectacle from somewhere else. She smiled the right smiles, traded witty banter with the right people and said the right things to the nervous museum officials. Many wanted to know where Professor Brody was. At Eva's suggestion, Stacy had manufactured a plausible excuse for the occasion. The overworked professor had come down with a cold, and might very well not be able to make it tonight.

Meanwhile, she kept anxiously scanning the entrance-way. If not Ethan, then Wally should certainly be here by now. She checked her watch again. So far the exhibit had been officially open for thirty-nine minutes. There was still hope that Ethan might show.

Stacy sighed in exasperation at the workings of her own mind. Someone was at her side with a glass of something. His face was familiar. Eva was at his side. It was Andrew, that screenwriter she was going out with.

"We thought you might need this," he was saying with a friendly smile, holding out the glass.

"Thanks," Stacy said, taking it from him.

"Champagne," Eva said.

"Champagne?" Stacy echoed, looking down at the glass in her hand. Her throat constricted. Her eyes grew blurry. The last time she'd had champagne, she'd been so incredibly happy. And now...

"Oh, no. What's the *matter*?" Eva peered at Stacy.

"I don't want it," Stacy said, swallowing and blinking back her tears. She handed back the glass to a perplexed Andrew.

"Good grief," Eva murmured. "You really are far gone, aren't you? It's all your fault," she added, turning to her boyfriend.

"Me?"

"Men," Eva said. "I don't know why we have anything to do with you at all."

"She's only teasing," Stacy said, seeing the alarmed look on Andrew's face. "Here, have you seen the exhibit yet? I'll take you on a little tour."

"Just got here," Andrew said warily, as Stacy took his arm. "You don't have to—I mean, aren't you busy?"

"She's not busy enough," Eva said. "Come on, let's see the ancient artifacts."

Stacy steered her friends through the first room. Here were the larger stone pieces, with photo blowups of the dig in progress adorning the walls. A glass case in the center of the room had attracted the most attention, as it featured some of the intact Mayan weaponry.

Andrew and Eva made the proper noises of interest as they continued. Stacy was glad of the distraction. She did her best to avoid lingering over the photos of Ethan and Wally that popped up in the next room, and concentrated instead on showing off the cases that held some gold pieces and Mayan decorative jewelry.

In the connecting hall that followed was the actual skeleton of the Mayan warrior prince, and farther on, his death mask. This room was bottlenecked just now with genuinely fascinated spectators. Stacy was pleased to hear comments that praised the display as she guided her friends onward. Things were definitely going well. She tried to bear that uppermost in her mind as they moved into the final room.

Here was the ongoing slide show and the small black-curtained area where the anthropologists' on-site videotape was running. "Maybe you'd like to hang out here for a bit," she suggested to Eva. She didn't want to spend more than another minute in there. It seemed as though Ethan was everywhere she looked.

"Fine," Eva said, picking up on Stacy's discomfort. "We'll hook up with you out there."

Stacy nodded and made her exit. This evening was taking on a nightmarish quality. Everybody was smiling at her, and she had to keep smiling, while ghostlike images of Ethan Brody hovered on the periphery of her vision. She wondered how much of this she'd be able to endure. She especially wondered what had happened to her, so quickly and so intensely, that she should feel this badly. Hadn't she only been toying with a casual flirtation?

Oh, sure.

Richard was waving at her from a small knot of dressed-up people. She waved back and started to move in their direction, then caught sight of a familiar beard in the main reception area. Stacy immediately swerved and changed course, making a beeline for Wally.

It occurred to her that Richard might very well be affronted, but at the moment she couldn't care less. "Wally," she said, her hand on his arm.

The professor turned from his chitchat with one of the museum people, and Stacy received the dubious reward of seeing his smile disappear in record time. "Ms. Morrison," he said, with a little nod. He immediately turned back toward the goateed museum man, ready to resume their conversation, but Stacy was too determined and too quick.

"Excuse me," she said, giving her most charming party-host smile to the man. "I need to kidnap the professor."

"Of course." He smiled back.

"Ms. Morrison—" Wally was protesting.

"I'll bring him back as soon as I'm done with him, no worse for wear," Stacy said, still all dazzling charm, and steered Wally away from the man's side with an iron grip on his arm. There was a small area beyond the velvet-roped entrance where only a tuxedoed attendant was in evidence. "Wally, where's Ethan?" she asked, as soon as they were beyond the rope and out of earshot.

Wally looked around him with an air of earnest distress that was so obviously feigned she might have laughed, if she'd been in a laughing mood. "He's not here?"

"You *know* he's not here," she said tersely. "Come on, Wally. What's going on?"

"Well, Ms. Morrison—"

"And since when did you forget my first name?"

Wally looked abashed. "Listen, Stacy, I really don't want to, ah, get in the middle of this."

"Well, then you should have pulled a disappearing act like your partner did," she said grimly. "But since you at least had the professional courtesy to honor a commitment, I'm afraid in the middle of it is where you are already."

Wally frowned. "I wouldn't start talking about things like professional courtesy, if I were you," he said. "If you ask me, your professionalism is what's messed things up around here."

That stopped her. Stacy felt her righteous indignation fade as a blush rose in her cheeks. "Wally..."

"And just for the record," he went on. "I think my partner's done more than his share in making this exhibit happen. There wasn't any contract that said he had to show up here to be gawked at tonight. It's been enough of a circus as it is, don't you think?"

Stacy stared at him, chagrined to feel tears welling up again in her eyes. Damn! What had she turned into, a walking faucet? Well, he was right, of course, but that only made her feel even worse. "I'm sorry," she blurted. "I didn't mean... I only hoped he'd be here," she said miserably.

Wally looked at her, concerned. "Oh, no, look," he said, with that frightened look she'd sometimes seen on the faces of men who couldn't deal with a woman on the verge of weeping. "Don't get all..." He was nervously digging into his pocket for a handkerchief.

"I can't help it." She sniffed, coming up with her own handkerchief and quickly dabbing it at her right eye, which for some reason always seemed to be the one that spilled first. "Wally, where is he? I've been calling half the hotels in New York, I've been sitting by my own phone, I've been going half out of my—'' She bit her lip, dabbing furiously at her eyes again, the left one having joined in now.

Wally was looking around him with a trapped expression. Clearly he was far less accustomed to dealing with the opposite sex than his partner. ''I didn't mean to upset you,'' he said, looking even more hangdoggedly contrite by the second. ''But you know we're talking about my best buddy here, and after that stuff in the magazine . . .''

''I know!'' she wailed, then quieted as a few heads in their vicinity turned briefly in her direction. Stacy swung Wally around, so that he stood between her and the reception area, a stocky human shield. ''Wally, those things, those quotes they attributed to me—I never said that to any reporter. Those were some things I said in a private conversation to *my* best friend, and I didn't even mean them then!''

Wally fixed her with a dubious gaze. ''No?''

''No! That was before I hardly knew Ethan, and the whole point was, I was only trying to convince her and myself that I wasn't attracted to him, even though I already knew I really was—only I didn't want to admit it.''

Wally's eyes blinked furiously behind his thick glasses. ''I'm not sure I follow.''

She was alarmed that he sounded so mistrustful. If Wally didn't believe her, how was Ethan likely to react? ''The point is, I never meant any of those things I said.''

''Uh-huh,'' Wally said. ''And you didn't know that the photographers who were giving Ethan such a hard time, feeding all those pictures to the *Trib*, were hired by your firm?''

Stacy swallowed. ''No, I did know that,'' she said quietly, finding it hard to meet his eyes. ''It wasn't my idea, and I even tried to stop my boss from doing it, but it wasn't in my power to call them off,'' she said. ''I was just as embarrassed by the whole thing as Ethan was.''

Wally shrugged. "Didn't seem to hurt, though, did it?" he said, gesturing at the people who were still streaming past them into the exhibit area.

"Well, it hurt Ethan's feelings," Stacy said. "And believe me, that's the last thing I wanted to see happen. Really, Wally."

He looked at her in silence, stroking his beard. "He's pretty unhappy," he said at length.

"Oh, Wally, why won't he just let me...why can't I talk to him?" she said. "I'm dying to talk to him in person. Where is he staying?"

Now it was Wally's turn to look embarrassed. "Well, I can't really say," he muttered, stroking his beard almost manically now.

"Oh, come on," she said. "This is silly. I want to apologize. I want to..." She stopped, feeling that seemingly endless inner reservoir of tears threatening to brim over yet again. "I want to see him," she said softly.

"Well, it's just not possible," Wally said.

"You guys and your stupid pride," Stacy muttered. "Why not?"

"Because he's not going to be here."

"Then I'll talk to him tomorrow."

Wally shook his head. "I mean, he's not in New York," he said uneasily.

"What? He left? Already? Without—?"

Wally nodded vigorously. "Yesterday," he said.

"But..." She stared at him, crushed. She realized she'd been suspecting as much, but had been afraid to really think about it. "He's gone," she asked, knowing how silly she must sound. "Where?"

"That's what I can't really say," Wally said.

"Wally," Stacy said. "Tell me."

"That's just the thing." He shifted his nervous fingers from beard to mustache. "Ethan was real specific on that.

He made me swear up and down that I absolutely wouldn't tell a single soul where he'd gone off to.''

"If he's worried about the press, he's being paranoid," Stacy said. "There's no reason why—"

"That's not it," Wally interrupted. "He knows that your media buzzards have already had their bellyful of this little human interest story." He paused with a pained expression. "It's you. You're the one he doesn't want trying to find him."

Stacy had thought her spirits had already sunk as low as they could go, but now she felt them sag right through the floor. "No," she murmured. "It's not fair."

Wally sighed. "Oh, hell, I don't know about fair or unfair or any of this nonsense," he said. "The guy got his feelings hurt. So he took off. Maybe it's all for the best, you know?"

"No, it isn't," she said dully, staring at the floor.

"Look, the show's a success. You got half of New York here to look at our stuff. Personal feelings aside, I think you did a fine job." Wally managed a somewhat crooked smile. "So at least one of us rock hounds is happy. And you should be, too."

"Why?" she said, still listlessly examining her feet.

"Well, it all worked out. Mission accomplished, right?"

Stacy finally looked up at Wally. He seemed perfectly sincere. "You don't understand," she said, trying to keep the tremulousness out of her voice. "I don't care about all this anymore!"

"No?"

"I love him!" she blurted out. "And now that he doesn't want to have anything to do with me, I—" She shook her head. Here came those insufferable tears again. Stacy rushed past Wally, headed for the sanctuary of the nearby ladies' room.

After a few minutes in there, putting her makeup back together, Stacy decided she'd better make the most of the rest of the evening. She'd do it on automatic pilot. This was an executive skill she'd perfected over the years, an almost Zenlike exercise in blanking out huge portions of one's mind and heart. You just kind of shifted into neutral and floated through. It worked with crowds like these.

Ten minutes later, anyone greeting or meeting Stacy Morrison would've met a perfectly composed and gracious PR woman. Only Eva perceived what was going on, and shadowed her friend around the room with an air of thinly disguised concern.

"I'm fine," Stacy insisted, after Eva once again asked her if she wanted to go home. Eva was tugging at her sleeve, though. Stacy followed her friend's eyes. Wally was approaching her. Stacy steeled herself, smile in place. "Professor Canfield."

"I don't know how much longer I'll be staying," he said, extending his hand. "So I wanted to say good-night."

"Thank you," Stacy said, shaking his hand. Wally nodded, but stayed right where he was.

"It's too bad Professor Matthews couldn't be here to see this," he said. "One of our colleagues. A close friend of Professor Brody's."

"Oh," she said, wondering why on earth Wally was lingering to chitchat.

"Yes, he's on a dig of his own," Wally went on. "An interesting one."

"I see," Stacy said.

"That's Zachary Matthews," Wally said.

She nodded, perplexed by the rather intent look on his face. "Well, I hope I didn't make your stay too uncomfortable," she said.

"You did fine."

"If you ever pass this way again, please give a call," she said. "And if you do speak to your partner...please let him know...I asked for him," she finished, afraid her voice might falter if she let her guard down any further.

"All right," Wally murmured.

Richard was approaching with Russell and one of the museum curators. Stacy smiled at Wally. "Well, I'm glad you were able to make an appearance. I really appreciated it."

Wally nodded, muttered a goodbye, and stepped back as the other guests moved in. It was only when she glanced over again at his retreating back that a glimmer of understanding shone in her troubled mind.

He'd been trying to tell her something, that was it. That talk about a fellow colleague...Professor Matthews. Zachary Matthews. Why did the name sound vaguely familiar? The automatic-pilot-driven part of her continued smiling and nodding as Richard and the curator traded anecdotes, but in Morrison brain computer central that name was being processed and examined at a rapid clip.

Where had she heard it? Who had mentioned it and why? And why was Wally...?

"Got it," she said suddenly. Her companions looked at her, startled, Richard pausing in mid-witty repartee. Stacy gave them a wider smile, which was absolutely genuine for the first time that evening. "Sorry," she said. "Excuse me," she added, looking wildly around for Wally as she grabbed Eva's arm. But of course the professor had already gone.

"What is going on with you?" Eva gave her a worried look as Stacy pulled her aside.

"I know where Ethan Brody is," she whispered excitedly. "Wally told me! At least, he gave me a hint, that lovable old weirdo. He's on a dig with this Zachary Matthews! I remember Ethan saying he wanted to visit his friend's site.''

"I don't know what you're talking about," Eva said. "But whatever is it, it's finally making you look less like a *Night of the Living Dead* zombie."

"Don't you see? I can get in touch with him now—I think," Stacy went on, realizing at the same time that she hadn't the slightest idea where Matthews was. "No, I will," she said, clenching a fist in determination. "I'm going to track that man down in record time, you watch," she announced.

"And then?" Eva asked.

"And then," Stacy echoed. "I don't know. All I know is I'm not letting this thing end like this!"

"I'M NOT SURE EXACTLY," said the dry-as-sandpaper voice under the crackle of long-distance static. "I believe they were in the Imperial Valley."

"Were?" Stacy cradled the phone between shoulder and ear, the pen scanning the page full of notes she'd amassed thus far. "You don't know if they're there now?"

"Well, you're really in the wrong department," the man at the other end told her. "Have you tried the Indian Studies people? Let me see if I have that extension...."

"Thank you," Stacy said, suppressing a sigh. This was perhaps the fifteenth phone call she'd made. It was after sundown in New York City, but there was still one working hour left in California. She'd been chasing Zachary Matthews all day long, and would be crushed if she didn't get a concrete lead at last.

So far she'd been running through a long-distance academic labyrinth. Matthews taught at UCLA, but he hadn't been on campus since early last year. Red tape alone had flummoxed her for hours, but now she was homing in. The administrative secretary of the chairman of Anthropology was back on the line.

"Try Simone Valary," he told her now, giving the extension number.

Stacy thanked him profusely and dialed again, well aware that she'd already doubled her phone bill in one afternoon. Scrupulously ethical, she'd even charged the myriad phone calls she'd made from P and W to this number.

It wasn't just ethics, though, but guilt. Today should have been a day of triumph at P and W. Richard had invited her into his office for morning coffee, taking a leisurely half hour to debrief her after last night's opening. He'd been visibly pleased with their success. So pleased that he'd asked Stacy to attend a lunch that Friday with Carl Bennett.

Carl Bennett! The British film scholar who was one of the high-muck-a-mucks on the film festival advisory board. And that could only mean one thing. Richard was tacitly letting her in on the festival account. He hadn't made any mention of anything specific, that would've been un-Richardlike, but the dangling carrot was clearly now in position, right over her very own plate.

Stacy should have been thrilled. But oddly enough, she'd felt only a minor tremor of excitement. She was too distracted. In fact, during the entire meeting in Richard's inner sanctum, when she should have been glowing over the good report card she was getting, she was wondering when a certain underassistant administrative secretary from a satellite branch of the University of California would be returning her call.

She was obsessed. Until she was able to talk to Ethan, she wouldn't be able to rest on any laurels or get excited about winning new ones. It was as simple as that. She'd never felt someone's absence so keenly before. There was no logic, nothing remotely rational about it, but there it was.

"Yes, this is Simone Valary. Can I help you?" This woman was French, friendly, and at last, knowledgeable. She'd spoken to Matthews only a week earlier. "They've been staying in Jacumba. It's a small town near the Mexican border," she said, adding pointedly, "He and Mrs. Matthews. His wife. You did know he is married?"

"No," Stacy said. "Why?"

Simone laughed. "You sound so intent on finding him. And he is such an attractive man."

Stacy assured Simone that she had no designs on Professor Matthews. She hurriedly jotted down what was sheer pay dirt—the location of the archaeological site and, most importantly, the phone number for the hotel where members of the Matthews party were staying. Simone had heard rumors that Ethan Brody was expected there.

"Are you sure?" Stacy's heart was racing.

"Well, if he was coming, he would be there now," Simone told her. "They are planning to head north after the weekend."

"This weekend?"

"Yes, I know that they are finishing up with their work. The Kuneyaay caves. You are interested in stone painting?"

Stacy's line was beeping, the signal for another incoming call. "Simone, you've been a great help," she said. "Is it all right if I call you again?"

"If you need more information, I will be happy to help you. Good luck!"

Stacy picked up her other call, noting that her hands were shaking and that she'd practically chewed the end off her pen in her excitement. "Hello?"

"Stace? It's Ceil!"

Cousin Ceil the realtor. Stacy's mind suddenly switched gears. Ceil had overseen her application to the co-op people. Stacy had completely forgotten to return her call from earlier. "Hi, Ceil. I'm sorry I didn't—"

"Great news, sweetie. The board will see you! They're very interested, and I think it's in the bag. They just need to meet with you, you know, for an informal interview."

"That's great," Stacy said, wondering if she should use her real name when she called the hotel in Jacumba. What if Ethan wouldn't accept a call from Stacy Morrison?

"Friday afternoon, three o'clock sharp, dear. Be sure you're prompt, because they can be very fussy about these things. And dress nicely, will you? Nothing too fancy, but something that's, well, tastefully expensive...."

Ceil rattled on, but Stacy wasn't paying much attention. What time would it be now in Jacumba? She hurried off the phone with Ceil and immediately made what she hoped would be her last long-distance call.

There was indeed an Ethan Brody registered at the Las Palmas Hotel. He wasn't in. Stacy deliberated, then left her name and number. Before hanging up, she got one other vital piece of information out of the laconic desk person. Brody, Matthews and the whole contingent were scheduled to depart at twelve noon on Sunday.

This was Wednesday night.

TWENTY-FOUR HOURS and two more messages later, Ethan Brody had not returned her call.

Stacy paced her apartment, head whirling and stomach upset. What now? Telegram? What would that do? And what would it say? "Ethan I didn't mean it stop I love you stop?" She actually considered sending such a missive, then decided it just wouldn't do. But what would?

An hour later she was on the phone with Eva. "I'm about to do something that's entirely insane," she told her.

"So as my best friend, it's your duty to calmly and rationally talk me out of it. Okay?"

"Okay," said Eva. "Shoot."

"I've just booked myself a flight to San Diego. The only one I was able to get leaves tomorrow at two in the afternoon. That gives me something like forty-eight hours to drive out to the middle of a desert, find Ethan Brody and apologize."

"Uh-huh."

"And he hasn't returned any of my phone calls and isn't expecting me to show up there and probably won't want to see me even if I do."

"Check."

"And Friday happens to be one of the more important business days of my life, but I wouldn't be here for it. Which means I may be blowing my entrée into that co-op building and jeopardizing my next gig at P and W," Stacy went on. "For a wild-goose chase that could be absolutely disastrous."

"I see."

"So this is clearly the wrong thing for me to do, right? All I need for you to do is to tell me I'm crazy, and I'll listen to you, stay here, and everything will work out for the best. Okay?"

"You're in love with this guy," Eva said. "Like truly, madly. For real."

"Well, yeah," Stacy replied without hesitation. "But—"

"Stacy," said Eva. "Go."

Chapter Ten

Stacy looked at the key in her hand. She looked at the steering wheel of the car. She looked through the rolled-down window at her side to the dusty shack of a building with the neon Rent-a-Heap sign on the roof. The taciturn dark-skinned man in the cowboy shirt behind the desk was pointedly ignoring her, feet up on the counter as he watched his color TV.

Surely she could start this car. She was an account executive at one of the sharpest agencies on Madison Avenue, possessor of more than one collegiate degree, a smart, sophisticated and self-sufficient woman, was she not? There was no way she was going to get out of this car again and ask that guy what she was doing wrong.

Stacy wiped the sweat from her brow with the back of her hand, peering through the windshield at cracked asphalt that appeared to shimmer like a mirage. It was not only one of the hottest Fridays San Diego had seen this spring, but one of the busiest. And fate had conspired to make it, for Stacy Morrison, one of the most difficult.

How was she supposed to know that the friendly computer she'd made her reservation with would've magically lost it, so that no car awaited her when she arrived? Or that a coincidental convergence of business conventions would've booked almost every other automobile in existence?

Or that the remaining rent-a-car agencies she went to didn't accept the one major credit card she had, since the other one had expired this month and in her haste to leave she'd forgotten to put the new replacement card in her wallet? Fortunately, Rent-a-Heap, though not at the airport proper, had been accessible by courtesy bus. They took her card and they'd had this car.

All of these mishaps wreaked havoc with her already precarious emotional state, but now the real challenge was in front of her. To be precise, she was in it: a 1973 Volvo that truly lived up to its current owner's name. The heap was all in one piece, true, and though it didn't have a radio or back windows that rolled down, she'd been assured it was perfectly capable of making the two-hours-plus trip out to Zachary Matthews's desert location.

It had air-conditioning. So what if the side view mirror seemed affixed to the car with gaffer's tape? Or that the interior smelled faintly of cigars and that the upholstery in the back was almost *all* gaffer's tape? The main problem was that she hadn't driven a stick shift in about ten years.

"It's like riding a bicycle," Stacy assured herself aloud, and once more attempted to start the car. This time she got the motor revved properly and was rewarded with an ear-splitting scream of improperly shifted gears as she attempted to get out of neutral.

What she'd thought was first turned out to be reverse. The car bolted backward, she braked and the engine stalled. "Piece of cake," she announced to her imaginary audience as she broke into a fresh sweat. Fortunately no other heap had been parked behind her. All right, she'd get the hang of it, given a few minutes of practice.

Come to think of it, when was the last time she'd driven a car? New Yorkers didn't drive, unless they were astronomically wealthy—to afford the parking—or terminally masochistic—to bear the *search* for parking, the traffic, the broken windows, stolen radios, etc. The thought of actually taking this vehicle out onto a highway filled her with vague dread. But once you got into fourth gear, you could stay there, right? No problem.

Ten minutes later she really was on the road, and she'd only stalled at one stoplight on her way to Route 8. From the little she'd glimpsed of it, San Diego seemed a nice enough city, small and much lower to the ground than Manhattan, of course, but cheery-looking. It was hilly, and there were distant mountains, and the air itself seemed different somehow, the quality of light brighter. But civilization was almost behind her already as she drove east.

She had a map spread out on the seat beside her, sunglasses perched on her nose, a bottle of Evian spring water in her bag and a feeling of grand optimism inside as she settled into high gear, following signs to El Cajon. Driving wasn't all that hard, especially now that she'd taken her shoes off. She'd eaten a creditable lunch on the plane and she was more or less on schedule.

In a sense getting there wasn't the hardest part. No, it would be that moment when she came face-to-face with Ethan Brody again. Compared to that, mere logistics of travel were a snap.

AN HOUR AND FORTY-FIVE MINUTES later she wasn't so sure.

Stacy peered nervously through her dust-laden windshield at the alien landscape surrounding her on all sides. Outside of telephone poles and the occasional road sign, there was no indication that she was even in America, as she knew it. She was in a country of sand, dirt, cacti and tumbleweed.

Heading down Route 8 toward the Mexican border she'd passed through a disorienting contrast of environments. There'd be nothing but desert flatland for miles, and then a sudden plethora of rolling greenery, neatly landscaped, which would go on for a mile or two and then abruptly stop again. She understood that the land down here had been irrigated, and what she'd passed were crops, probably grapes and apricots.

But now, snaking up past Ocotillo toward Plaster City— where did they get these names?—the sight of a lone green bush or two was nothing short of extraordinary. This was, after all, the desert, according to her map, a part of the Sonoran desert. It was one thing to think of it abstractly. It was another thing entirely to find oneself *in* it.

Because there was nothing there.

Only hours ago she'd been in a city where there were more people and traffic in one square block than there appeared to be in this entire county. The raw emptiness of it all was a little daunting. This was the kind of country you drove *through*, she mused. But she was going to actually park, get out of her automotive sanctuary, and walk right out into it.

Exactly how crazy an idea had this been?

Stacy glanced nervously at her new map, hand-drawn on the back of a place mat by a friendly waitress in the small diner she'd stopped at briefly outside Jacumba. She'd made the turn off 98 now and this road was smaller, even more desolate. According to Maria the waitress, who knew of the Matthews expedition, she just had to follow this squiggly penciled line another few miles south, then slow down and look for a Land Rover, trailer, truck and Jeep parked together.

Simple. Stacy shifted down as she hit a few potholes in the weathered road. Her sturdy Volvo wasn't doing any complaining, thank goodness, but she didn't want to take chances. She gazed at the straggly, bramblish things that were the one kind of vegetation, if you could call it that, along the way and wondered who on earth would want to come out here for fun and entertainment?

It's his job, she reminded herself. He was visiting a friend and colleague—who was hunting around in caves, apparently, also an odd idea of having a good time. "Oh, stop it," she muttered aloud. Being judgmental at this point was a waste of time. She'd made her proverbial bed and was about to lie in it.

That particular old metaphor gave her a little shiver of anticipation. It was bizarre, really. She'd gone so long without much sensual pleasure in her life that she'd almost thought it wasn't that important to her. Then one night and morning with Ethan Brody, and suddenly she was craving that pleasure with an intensity that took her aback.

She'd given up analyzing the logic of her heart. Her heart was in control now, having wrested her abruptly from the familiar comforts of her cosmopolitan existence to deposit her here on the edge of a mammoth sandy wasteland. She wasn't about to question that decision now.

Some distant rock formations were breaking up the sandy landscape now, and, incongruously, railroad tracks. She crossed them, driving even slower as the hills rose up to her left, craggy stone ledges visible above the low sandy peaks. A bunch of black dots off the roadside ahead suddenly took shape, and she put on her brakes.

Yes, there they were—a trailer, a Jeep or two, a dust-covered truck! Stacy steered cautiously to the side of the road and then off it altogether, following tire treads to what looked like an impromptu parking lot some hundred yards from the road.

She pulled up behind the trailer, eagerly scanning the vehicles for signs of life. There were none. But they couldn't be far, could they? Heart pounding with excitement, Stacy turned off the motor, opened her door, and stepped out.

Heat hit her in a palpable wave. Even with her sunglasses on she had to blink as she gazed out at the shimmering dunes. Without even thinking twice, she got back into the car and shut the door.

The lingering air-conditioned air was some relief. Suddenly she was aware of the absolute silence that was surrounding her. With the motor off, there was only the wind in the mesquite bushes to make a sound. Stacy took another sip of water from her dwindling supply and considered her next move. Wait here?

But for how long? It was four in the afternoon. Did that mean they'd be almost done with the day's work and due back momentarily? Who even knew what a day's work entailed and when it had actually started?

Some ten minutes later, she braved the great outdoors again, after having changed into a pair of khaki shorts and the Adidas sneakers she'd wisely packed as ostensible hiking shoes. She kept on her blue button-down shirt, sleeves rolled, and added a little tennis visor she'd brought along, anticipating this kind of sun. Slinging over her shoulder her bag containing the bottled water, she took a deep breath and locked up the car.

Why was she locking the car? Stacy shrugged, noting that citified habits died hard. Then she turned to face the desert.

Which way? She contemplated giving a good loud yell to see who might answer, but decided that was a bit silly. And she was still determined, for whatever perverse sense of drama, to come upon Ethan Brody unawares. It seemed to her that surprise was an important element here. Before he even had time to get all huffy and defensive, she'd be there, right in front of him, living proof that to her he was the most important thing in the world.

Clearly he'd have to take her into his wonderfully muscular arms right then and there, murmuring that all was forgiven, and this trek would have been completely worthwhile.

These were the thoughts that cheered her as she began trudging into the desert. Fortunately there was evidence, at least at the beginning, of some kind of trail. Things had been dragged over this area. Footprints were visible in the gritty sand. The general direction was toward those rock formations she'd noted earlier.

Caves? Well, that was where they had to be, surely. Stacy walked onward, feeling the sun beat down on her shoulders even through the cotton material. At least where there were stone outcroppings, there was bound to be shade. That was some consolation.

She'd been walking for a while when she thought to look back. Her car and the others had virtually disappeared from the horizon, just a little black cluster. She turned round again. Those rock formations didn't seem that much closer.

She fended off encroaching panic by humming a bit of Gershwin. Then she realized that the tune she'd picked was "Summertime," and decided to choose something less heated in tone. "A Fine Romance" came to mind.

Humming along, and not unaware of the possible absurdity of her appearance, she kept her eyes on the stone hills ahead, since there were no longer any footprints or tracks to guide her. What had looked like low stone hills were looming larger now, in reality a series of sloping sandstone cliffs glinting bronze in the late-afternoon sun. But there were still no signs of any people around them.

She paused for another drink of water and looked behind her once more. Now she hadn't the slightest idea where the car might be. She'd lost all sense of direction. What if these weren't the cliffs where the caves were? The movement of a lone bird in the cloudless sky above caught her eye. What was that? A *vulture*?

Now she could see it all. The *Trib* would have a rhyming headline:

Would-be V.P. Dies of Heatstroke
   Only the skeletal remains and Bloomingdale clothing labels identified the long-missing account executive. Why she had chosen a remote stretch of desert to wander into is still baffling police. A suicide attempt? Or something more—?

Stacy stopped in midfantasy. She'd heard something. She peered at the looming stone cliffs, straining her ears to catch that phantom noise again. There it was. A clink—the kind of sound a metal instrument made hitting metal.

Excited, she renewed her stride at a faster pace. Clearly there was somebody doing something somewhere close by. And even if she couldn't see them, she could hear...

It had stopped. Stacy slowed, frowning. She listened, and heard only wind. Had she imagined it? Was she already hallucinating, a victim of aural desert mirages? No. They'd left cars and trucks back there, hadn't they? She was in the right place, wasn't she?

As if in answer, she heard the unmistakable sound of human laughter. It was distant, barely audible, but it was a laugh, all right.

Relieved, she trudged on, aiming now for the edge of the rock formation. Her guess was that Matthews and company were on the other side of it. That was the most reasonable explanation. Excitement kept her pace up, even though her ankles were already starting to hurt. Maybe sneakers hadn't been the smartest choice for hiking across sand dunes.

Now she was almost at the cliffs, their stone bases ringed with prickly green cacti and sagebrush. That metallic tapping sound continued, and other voices came to her on the wind. A trick of hearing made it seem as though the noise was coming from directly in front of her, but there was only the striated sandstone rock face there. She marched resolutely around the mesalike stone cliffs.

There was a man in T-shirt and jeans with a camera up to his face. Stacy had to hold back from yelling a hello as she came around the bend. He hadn't seen her yet, intent on photographing the rock face. Stacy headed right toward him. There was another man nearby, holding some sort of metal tool in his hand. Their attention was trained on the sandstone cliffs. Stacy paused and followed their gaze.

Now that she was on this side, she was surprised to see that a large scaffolding had been erected alongside the sheer face of the rock. The network of metal pipes ascended some twenty feet up, stopping just below the protruding lip of a dark hollow in the rock. On a wooden platform atop the scaffolding were two more men.

Stacy's heartbeat accelerated as one turned back from surveying the cave. For a moment she thought it was Ethan up there, but then she realized it wasn't. This man had similar dark hair and skin, and was dressed in the kind of khaki pants Ethan favored, but it was probably Zachary Matthews. As she craned her neck, looking up, he caught sight of her.

"Excuse me." The voice at her side made Stacy jump. She turned to see a bearded young man in T-shirt, shorts and hiking boots staring at her in some perplexity. "Can I help you?" he inquired.

Now she was aware of many eyes upon her. Activity that had been in progress around the base of the scaffolding had ceased. Without much comprehension she registered a few men standing with shovels in hand around a roped-off rectangle dug in the ground nearby, and a pair of pup tents some yards beyond, with the charred remains of a camp fire in front of them.

"Well, yes, I guess," she said uncertainly. "I'm looking for Ethan Brody."

"Brody?" The guy was looking at her as if she'd just landed from a spacecraft. For a moment she had a terrible feeling she'd come here too late. But then he nodded, still staring. "He's up there with Matthews in Aida."

"Aida?"

"The cave," the young man said, and turned abruptly, a hand at his mouth. "Hey, Zack!"

"Who's that?" Zachary Matthews's voice boomed down from above them.

"Someone here to see Brody."

The dark-haired archaeologist peered down at her with an amused grin. "Looks like she's here to play tennis," he noted, then called over his shoulder. "Brody, c'mere."

The chuckles from the other men brought a quick blush to Stacy's face. She immediately regretted the sun visor and sneakers, but couldn't help feeling a flare of indignation. Men! They all looked like a bunch of unkempt desert rats.

Stacy turned back to gaze up at the cave's entrance. This time the figure who emerged was instantly recognizable. He leaned forward over the platform's edge, not seeing her at first, but then their eyes met. Even from this distance she registered the look of absolute shock on his face.

Now, of course, that handsome visage would relax into a welcome smile. He'd climb down that scaffold and be at her side in an instant, and—

He was frowning, his lips set tight, then disappearing from view altogether. Where had he gone? Back into the cave? Now Zachary Matthews appeared again. "He'll be down in a minute," he called. "Hey, why don't one of you good-for-nothing goof-offs get the lady a soda? She looks a little parched."

Gratitude for the man's hospitality took a bit of the sting out of Ethan's reaction. But the blush hadn't faded from her face. She gazed down at her feet, wondering if she'd made a horrible mistake.

The young man who'd first greeted her had scurried off toward the others, one of whom was opening a plastic cooler. She heard the swish and rustle of ice and was suddenly aware of just how thirsty she really was. "Thank you," she said, as the man appeared again, a Coke in his outstretched hand. She usually drank Diet, but now was no time for being choosy.

"My name's Pierce," he said.

"Stacy," she said, after taking a gulp of delicious cold soda. "I didn't mean to...um, interrupt anything—"

"No, no, we were just finishing up for the day," Pierce said, glancing over her shoulder. "Where's Nadine?"

"Nadine?"

"You didn't come with her?" Pierce asked. "Then how'd you find us?"

"I...got directions," Stacy said uneasily, as a new nightmare scenario suddenly occurred to her. Nadine? Was it possible that Ethan had already taken up with another woman? Why else would Pierce have assumed Stacy had come with her? The thought was chilling.

"Well, here he is," Pierce said, nodding toward the scaffolding. "'Scuse me." He hurried off to join another man who was packing up a tripod a few yards away. Stacy braved a look behind her.

There was Ethan, climbing down the last few rungs of metal pipe. She steeled herself as his feet touched ground. His face betrayed no emotion. Maybe that was worse than anger, she wasn't sure. But wasn't he even the least bit happy to see her?

She turned to face him as he approached, hands on his hips. She was trying to think of a suitable greeting, but he beat her to it. "What are you doing here?" he asked brusquely, his voice low and hard-edged.

Stacy swallowed. "What do you think?" she said. "I came to see you."

The furrows in his brow deepened. "And what in God's name gave you the idea that I'd...?" He paused, and evidently self-conscious, started walking away from the site proper, indicating she should follow.

Stacy trudged after him, her heart sinking. So much for her fantasized reunion. He seemed about as happy to see her as he would've been to see a desert sandstorm, apparently. When they were nearly at the edge of the sloping rock formation, well out of earshot of the rest of the party, he turned to face her again, jaw still set tight.

"Who told you I'd be here? Did Wally?"

"No," she said quickly, since it was almost the truth, and she certainly didn't want Wally to receive Ethan's wrath. "He refused to tell me where you were. But I pieced it together out of some things he'd said. And *you* said," she added quickly as his scowl deepened.

"Well, you're wasting your time," he said, avoiding her eyes.

She tried to ignore the sting of those words, but a knot was tightening in her throat. "You're not giving me much of a chance," she said.

"No, because I'm not about to let you talk me into anything," he said curtly, still staring at his boots. They had metal tips on them, she noticed. No wonder they were all scoffing at her sneakers.

She did her best to rein in her emotions. "I didn't come here to talk you into something," she said, as evenly as she was able.

"Good. Because I don't have any intention of going back to New York City for another round of Celebrity Circus," he said.

That hurt. She bit her lip. "Look," she began, "I know how you must feel—"

"Don't tell me you came all alone," he interrupted, looking past her now, still avoiding her eyes.

"Alone?" she repeated, puzzled.

"Where have your two friends gone? Found another photogenic sitting duck?"

Stacy winced. So that was it. But did he honestly think she'd have the nerve to be after him now for professional motives? Good Lord, how bad a person did he think she was? "Ethan, I only came here to apologize!"

His eyes flickered briefly toward hers, then darted away again. But in that briefest of instants she had a glimpse of the pain hidden in their dark depths. And that, more than anything, made her feel still worse.

"Oh?" he said, not giving way an inch. "I thought maybe you were interested in furnishing the papers with some material for a follow-up story. Is the attendance at the exhibit dropping?"

"No," she said. "The exhibit is a smash, and nobody has asked me to do this, Ethan."

He met her gaze again, but this time his face was such a mask of disinterest that she wondered if she'd only imagined the vulnerable look she'd seen moments ago. "Then what are you doing here?" he said.

"I told you," she said. "I wanted to apologize."

"For what? You were only doing your job, obviously."

Boy, this wasn't going to be easy. He was seeing to that. In spite of herself, Stacy could feel her anger starting to surface. "You don't seem to have any problems in thinking the worst of me," she said.

Ethan shrugged. "I've gotten used to it, I guess."

It was like taking a clean left to the jaw. "Have you ever heard of the concept, 'innocent until proven guilty'?" she asked, bridling. "You know, you might have had the decency to hear my side of the story before you just disappeared on me like that."

"I thought I had heard your side of the story," he said evenly.

"Well, maybe you shouldn't believe everything you read!" she said hotly.

There. A chink in the armor. For a moment he looked confused, and he held her gaze long enough for her to recognize a little of the Ethan she knew and loved in his expression. "Are you telling me you never said those things?" he asked warily.

Stacy sighed. "Well, no, not exactly," she told him. "But I was quoted very much out of context. A very important context," she said pleadingly, as she saw the imaginary stone visor descend over his face once more.

"And you didn't know about the photographers," he said, but it was less a question than a disbelieving statement.

"Well, no," she said, miserable. "I mean, I did find out about them, after the fact—"

He was already turning away. "But it wasn't me, Ethan. I never hired them and I never wanted..."

"Save it," he said. "Maybe instead you ought to be upfront about your real reasons for being here. What is it this time? The continuing adventures of Arizona Brody? The Mayan Tomb Coloring Book?"

"I'm not here to exploit you," she said, exasperated.

"Then why?" he challenged her.

Because I'm in love with you, you idiot, was the thought uppermost in her mind. He *was* acting like an idiot, and he wasn't giving her a chance to be honest with him. "I told you," she said, trying to keep her rising anger in check. "I wanted to tell you I was sorry."

"And now that you have, does that make it all okay?" he challenged her again.

"If you'd give me a break," she snapped.

"You think it should be that easy?"

"Oh, think what you want," she said, fed up. She gazed blindly around her, trying to remember which way she'd approached the rocks. The best idea was a hasty exit. The sooner she put this whole mess behind her—

"Where are you going?" Ethan's hand was on her arm as she started to walk away.

Stacy turned around, shaking off his hand with a vehemence that surprised her. Now she was the one avoiding his eyes. "Back to where I came from, I guess," she said. "After all, there doesn't seem to be any sense in trying to talk to you."

Ethan cleared his throat. "Look, Stacy..." He paused, seemingly at a loss.

"What? You don't want to hear what I have to say, Ethan, so what's the use?"

"Well, you're here now," he said. "I'm sorry if I sound angry, but damn it, I *am* angry."

"I'm well aware of that," she said stiffly.

"Nonetheless, you're right," Ethan admitted. "If you've come out all this way to talk to me, I shouldn't be jumping down your throat."

"Well, gee, thanks," she said. "That's a considerate thought.'

Ethan shook his head. "We're off to a fine start," he muttered. "Come on. I've got to help clean up camp here."

"I don't want to be an inconvenience, to you or your colleagues," she said, still struggling with her feelings as they began to walk back toward the site. "I'm perfectly willing to leave you alone. If you just point me in the right direction—"

"How *did* you get here?" he asked as she looked around again, trying to get her bearings.

"I flew and I drove," she said shortly. "My car's where yours are. Which is . . . ?"

Ethan was shading his eyes as he gazed past her. Stacy was suddenly aware that she'd been hearing a distant motor. Now as she looked, she saw a silver and black Land Rover lurching over the sand toward them. It hadn't occurred to her that she might drive right out to the site. But then, her old Volvo didn't have four-wheel drive.

"What's that?" she asked.

"Nadine," said Ethan.

Stacy felt herself stiffen involuntarily. Here it came, on monster tires: the coup de grace. Not only did she have to be verbally humiliated, she was going to get her heart skewered. Stomach clenched, she watched the Land Rover pull up in a cloud of dust.

The woman who alighted from the driver's seat surpassed even her worst expectations. She looked like something out of one of those Guess Who jean ads in the fashion magazines. She had on skintight black jeans over rolled-up socks and the requisite steel-tipped boots, which on her feet seemed anything but clumsy. Her button-down shirt was sexily undone to show a bit of cleavage, and a lot of sleek, tanned belly was visible where the shirt bottoms had been tied.

Adding insult to injury, she had flaming red hair—and very prominent cheekbones.

She sauntered toward them, Bette Davis-style, the thumb of one hand hooked through a belt loop, the other hand waving a greeting. "Hi, hon!" she called.

Stacy felt her already sinking stomach do a tiny flip. She would never in her life be the kind of woman to alight from a Land Rover in the middle of the desert, looking as though she'd just stepped out of the pages of *Vogue* and saying "Hi, hon!" like that.

She crossed her arms, trying to remember which facial muscles were best used to activate a smile as the woman strolled over, smiling. Stacy had to fight back an impulse to close her eyes as Nadine put out her arms—

And went right into Zachary Matthews's waiting embrace. The other archaeologist had come up beside Ethan, and Stacy hadn't even noticed. But now she felt her whole tensed body sag with relief as she watched Nadine, who was obviously Mrs. Matthews, give her husband a hug, squeeze and peck on the cheek. When she stepped away, her eyes alighted on Stacy with a look of delighted surprise.

"Who's this?" she cried.

"Stacy Morrison, Nadine McGuane Matthews," Ethan said, expressionless. He was back to playing wooden Indian.

"Hi," Nadine said, shaking Stacy's hand with genuine warmth. "It's certainly nice to see another female face among all these Neanderthals."

"Go on, you love being surrounded by men," Zachary said, chuckling.

"Dream away, Matthews," she said. "Where'd you blow in from, Stacy? Is that your Volvo back in the lot?"

"Yes, that's my rented heap," Stacy said, taking as much of an instant liking to this outspoken redhead as she'd been prepared to dislike her moments ago.

"Brody didn't tell us you were coming," she said, shooting Ethan a curious glance. "Holding out on us, eh?"

Ethan shrugged. "Stacy's an unexpected guest."

"Well, I'm glad you made it," Nadine said. "These guys can really give a girl a hard time. Now maybe we can even out the balance a bit." She smiled at Stacy again. "I hope you're not a vegetarian."

"Me? No," Stacy said, puzzled.

"Good. Because I've got plenty of meat and potatoes in the Jeep. Hey, Collins! Pierce!" She put her fingers to her lips and made an earsplitting whistle. "Drop those toy shovels of yours and unload the Rover, will you?"

The site was already abuzz with activity. Stacy realized she'd come upon the archaeologists at the very end of their working day. "Look, why don't you, ah . . . hang out for a bit?" Ethan said. "Make yourself comfortable. I have to finish up some things with Zack here."

"Fine," Stacy said. "I don't want to be in anybody's way."

For a moment his eyes met hers again. "You're not," he muttered, and walked off to confer with his colleague.

Stacy supposed, given the circumstance, that she should consider this a high compliment. But she wondered, as she watched Ethan and Zack already deep in conversation, if she wouldn't have been better off driving her heap right back to San Diego before nightfall.

"ROTTEN LUCK," Ethan said.

Zack laughed, then furrowed his brow in his best Humphrey Bogart imitation. "Of all the archaeological sites in all the deserts of the world, she walks into mine, huh?"

"Exactly," Ethan said. "We've been getting some good work done, right? Having a grand old time, a coupla beers with the guys around the camp fire, and now..."

"I know. Now there's no telling what'll happen." Zack nodded, gathering up the map of the site they'd been examining on a rock some way from camp. "But you'll probably sleep more soundly."

"What?" Ethan looked at his friend's smile in true indignation. "No, no, you've got this whole setup wrong. I'm not going near that woman. Not after what she's done."

"So she called you a few names," Zack said mildly.

"Behind my back, in front of three million readers," Ethan corrected him. "While making a complete fool of me, hiring photographers to dog my every footstep—"

"Ethan, old man, you've told me," Zack protested. "And I agreed it was bad form, to say the least."

"Bad form? She was lying to me the entire time we were together," Ethan said, scowling. "Pretending she didn't know how all that publicity was being generated."

"Well, there's gotta be more to it," Zack said. "Why else would she show up here?"

"I don't know." Ethan studied the healing of a minor cut on the base of his thumb. "She says she came to apologize."

"No woman I've ever met flies three thousand miles just to say, 'I'm sorry,'" Zack said.

"I've been a hard man to get ahold of," Ethan said.

"Still," Zack persisted. "You know what this means."

"No," Ethan said, staring at his friend. "I do not know what this means. Maybe you'd like to enlighten me, good buddy."

Zack laughed. "Oh, I'm sure you'll be enlightened soon enough, pal," he said, and gave Ethan a friendly swat on the shoulder. "I'm going to help Charlie file his panels. You want to get that map back to Collins?"

"Sure," Ethan muttered, watching Zack stomp off, whistling. Sure. He could whistle. With a woman like Nadine at his side, he had his whole life figured out and together. He didn't have to contend with a complicated situation like this one.

Sighing, Ethan carefully folded up the map. Here he thought he'd really gotten away from it all, and that the whole sorry mess of New York was already behind him. He'd thrown himself into helping out on Zack's little expedition with a zeal that was almost manic, as Zack himself had noted.

Well, there'd been a lot of work to do. They'd discovered three or four caves full of petroglyphs before he'd shown up, and Zack had been happy to have an extra hand along to stake out the sites and catalog his findings. And Ethan had relished being back in the scrubland again, a man among men, with tools in his hands he could relate to and tasks he enjoyed performing.

Now in a matter of minutes he was right back where he'd started. New York had followed him, tracking him down to this remote edge of civilization. And what was he supposed to do about it?

Face it, Brody, he told himself. He'd brought New York with him, even before Stacy showed up. He'd been half a nervous wreck when he'd come out here, and the sleep he hadn't been getting, as Zack had mentioned, hadn't helped his general equilibrium.

At first he hadn't regretted pulling up his stakes in Manhattan as abruptly and decisively as he had done. But even as he was wending his way west on the flight to San Diego, the very night his exhibit had been opening at the museum, he'd begun having second thoughts. Shouldn't he have stayed to really tell Stacy Morrison what he thought of her? Or couldn't he at least have gone through the charade of playing host at the opening, and shown her what an absolute glacier of a guy he could be?

His first day here on the site, once the initial thrill of being up in the newly discovered caves had worn off a bit, the other stuff had started filtering in—that damned emotional stuff he hadn't wanted to feel or deal with. He'd missed Stacy Morrison. He missed the life he'd only just begun imagining might be possible for the two of them.

And as he'd nursed his wounds, he'd begun to entertain the slight, fanciful possibility that he had acted too hastily, that maybe he should have stuck around long enough to hear what she might have to say. That thought really annoyed him. It made him feel even more the sap. What, was he that dumb, that he'd let her wrap him around her finger again with a few well-chosen excuses?

Shaking his head, Ethan made a wide circle of the site, seeing Stacy and Nadine busily unwrapping foodstuffs as if they'd been old friends for years. Typical, that instant female bonding. Who knew what kinds of intimacies they'd be exchanging about their respective men? They were probably having a few more laughs at his expense even now.

"I think that's a final draft," Collins said, taking the map from him. "I put in those extra test units on the periphery in red pen there. You saw?"

Ethan nodded absently, not really listening as Zack's principal illustrator went on about the ink stencils he'd taken of the wall paintings. He couldn't help glancing back in the direction of the fire, already burning in anticipation of dinner.

There she was, looking as delightfully out of place as a purple orchid suddenly blooming among a patch of dandelion weeds. She looked great, damn it.

Wouldn't you know it? Just when he'd almost gotten himself convinced that he felt okay, that this wasn't going to be half as bad a case of withdrawal as the one he'd gotten post-Lucille, here she was. Just when he'd almost begun to believe he could accept the idea of never seeing her again.

Stacy must have felt his eyes on her. She looked in his direction, then shyly averted her face again. Ethan felt as if a little bolt of electricity had just leaped the dozen yards between them.

Much as he tried to fight the feeling, he was awfully happy to see her.

But he'd be damned if he'd let her know.

Chapter Eleven

"No, I usually wrap it up in a scarf," Nadine said, giving her hair a toss. "This sand and wind'll just ruin it, believe me."

Stacy nodded, taking another bite of the chili that had been warming on the small Coleman stove kit at their feet. Nadine was great. She'd already put Stacy at ease, seemingly without any effort or feigned friendliness. She was just naturally a warm person, and Stacy was grateful for her company. She couldn't imagine what it might've been like if she'd joined this expedition as the only female. "Do you always go on these digs? With Zack?"

Nadine shrugged. "Every other one, usually. We have a kind of home base in Belize. Zack still does most of his work down there, when he's not teaching back in L.A."

"Did you go to school together?"

Nadine laughed. "Lord, no. I was working in Hollywood, doing location scouting, and I got sent down to Central America to take photos of some places for a film that was being shot there. I met Zack in Belize. And it was hate at first sight."

"Really? You seem so perfect together."

"Oh, sure," Nadine said, leaning down for another helping of chili herself. "Worlds collided. I couldn't stand the sight of an unruly lug like him, and he didn't know what to do with a high-heeled Hollywooder tromping in on his sacred turf. It was really touch and go for a while there.''

Stacy looked over Nadine's shoulder to the camp fire, where the men were seated, plates and beers in hand. The dancing flames made their weathered faces look like something out of an old Western as they laughed uproariously at someone's anecdote. ''You think Guatemala was tough?'' she heard Zack's voice boom out through the darkness. ''You try dealing with the authorities in Chetumal, brother. You wouldn't last a day there, Pierce.''

''They'd eat Pierce for breakfast,'' Ethan said.

More laughter. ''I mean, listen to them,'' Nadine said ruefully. ''A bunch of little boys running around with machetes and shovels, playing treasure hunt all their lives. How was I supposed to take that seriously?''

Stacy nodded, remembering her first impressions of Ethan Brody. ''I know what you mean.''

''But then you find out that it's not just fun and games, and if you stick around long enough, you start to get the fever,'' Nadine went on. ''You learn some history and you start asking the kinds of questions they're always asking. Like how could there be a whole civilization somewhere, in some ways as advanced as we like to think we are, that just plain disappeared? Where did they go wrong? And what could we learn from that?''

''I see.''

''Except that's really not what hooked me,'' Nadine said, smiling. ''As you may well guess.''

''Ah.'' Stacy sipped at her soda. ''You mean, you found yourself considering some possibilities with Zack that you'd never thought you'd ever consider?''

''Precisely,'' Nadine said, and laughed. ''Something tells me you've gone through the same thing.''

"Well, I'm here, aren't I?" Stacy said ruefully. "Though I don't even know if I'll stay the night."

"Of course you will!" Nadine exclaimed. "If that man sends you packing, then he's the biggest fool I've ever met."

"It's not him necessarily, but me," Stacy said uneasily. "I mean, I don't know if I *want* to stay, if he's still so convinced I can't be trusted."

She'd told Nadine the basic outline of what was going on with Ethan and herself, since her new friend had asked, and there was something about her that inspired trading confidences. Nadine had been instantly sympathetic. "Look," she said now. "I don't know Ethan all that well, really, but I like him. And though I have no intention of getting caught in the middle of your personal problems, I don't mind offering you a suggestion, if you want to hear it."

"Of course I do," Stacy said, glad to have an ally.

"Don't let him throw you off course," Nadine said. "The man's feelings have been hurt, so he's liable to say anything, including a lot of stuff he doesn't mean. If you listen to what he says and not to what's underneath it, you'll get all fouled up."

Stacy nodded, remembering that look she'd glimpsed in his eyes. "But still, if he won't listen to me . . ."

"He'll listen," Nadine said. "Eventually. Unless you turn tail and run out. Which might mean he'd try to come after you. By which time you might be frustrated enough to make it difficult for him. And then . . ." She raised her palms. "You know that game. It can go on ad infinitum. Why not just hang tough now and have it all out, once and for all?"

"You're right," Stacy said, then sighed. "It sounds so simple when you say it like that. But . . ."

"I know," Nadine said. "Just hang in there."

Stacy kept that thought, as they returned to the camp fire for coffee, rejoining the men. Ethan still avoided looking at her directly, but didn't seem overtly hostile. Zack was perfectly friendly, and the other men apparently accepted her presence without comment.

These men, five in all and of different ages, were there to do a variety of jobs. Stacy listened carefully to the talk about tomorrow's work. It was basically a cleanup day, with the scaffolding being taken down and the last bits of research finished up. And once she had a sense of the evening's plans, she formulated one of her own. After a quick conference with Nadine, she was ready to put it into action.

When the men were gathering up their gear in preparation for the trek back to the cars and trucks, Ethan finally came over to her, hands in pockets, gazing off at the rock wall behind her as he spoke. "I suppose we can get a room for you over at the motel," he said. "That is, if you're planning on sticking around."

"Is that where you're staying?"

Ethan cleared his throat. "No, it's my turn to stay out here at the site," he said, indicating one of the two pup tents a few yards away. "Zack and I've been trading off. You know, some nights he plays guard, and sometimes I do. But since it's my turn..."

"That's fine with me," she said.

Ethan nodded, looking relieved. "Then you can get a ride back to your car with Nadine and Zack in the Rover."

Stacy shook her head. "That won't be necessary."

Ethan frowned. "You packing a flashlight? I don't see why you have to walk the desert at night, when there's—"

"But I'm not going anywhere," she said calmly. "I'm staying here with you."

Ethan's eyes blinked furiously behind his wire-rims. "Wait a second. Maybe you didn't understand. I'm bed-

ding down in one of those tents, in a sleeping bag. By myself.''

Stacy shrugged. ''There's another tent.''

''Well, yes, but it's full of artifact bags and tools. Besides, I've only got one sleeping bag.''

''Nadine said I could borrow hers.''

She couldn't help but feel a perverse pleasure at the look
on his face. He was stymied, poor fellow. Well, that's what
you get for not taking *me* seriously, she thought, as his
brow furrowed once more.

''Stacy, be reasonable. It's cold now and it's going to get
even colder. You're not dressed for this.''

He was looking for an out, was he? ''I packed a
sweater,'' she said pleasantly. ''I may be a New Yorker, but
I'm not entirely stupid. I do know that it gets cold at night
in the Sonoran desert.''

His eyes narrowed. ''You know that I'll be up at the
crack of dawn? And the rest of the crew'll be out here by
7:00 a.m.?''

''Sounds fine to me.''

''Wouldn't you rather be in a nice motel room, with hot
and cold running water and a shower?''

''I didn't come all the way out here to stay in a nice motel room,'' she said pointedly. ''I came to be with you.''

Stalemate. Ethan rubbed a hand through his hair. ''Your
choice,'' he muttered, and walked away. Stacy savored her
little victory with a smile. Sometimes a little stubbornness
could go a long way.

STACY HUDDLED by the fire in her oversize sweater. Cold
was one thing. Being frozen was another. Now that night
had fallen in earnest, she was amazed that only hours earlier she'd been wearing shorts and sweating in them. With
pants, long-sleeved shirt, sweater and jacket, she was still
shivering a bit, unless she sat right in front of the fire.

She looked over at Ethan's tent. She could vaguely make out his silhouette within, a shadow on the canvas cast by the Coleman lantern. She was doing her best not to get too annoyed, though she resented the feeling that she was being tested.

He'd explained that he had to write up his field notes, a nightly ritual that even her presence wasn't going to disturb. If she wanted to talk, they could talk afterward. All right then, she'd agreed. Which left her entirely alone out here in the utter darkness. True, the stars were beautiful. In fact, "beautiful" was far too inaccurate a word. She'd never seen so many.

She concentrated on admiring them so she wouldn't get cranky. He'd been in that tent for nearly a half hour now. And with everyone else gone from the site, she was finding the silence that surrounded her unnerving. She'd never heard this kind of quiet.

Stacy suddenly froze. Wrong. There was a noise and she wasn't alone. Something—some animal thing—was howling out there, and the sound of it made her blood run cold. What on earth...?

She looked back to Ethan's tent. Surely he'd come out, famous knife in hand. But no, the shadow stayed where it was, a man absorbed in his work. Fine, she thought, her heart pounding in her chest, this was fitting punishment. She'd be eaten by a wolf or something worse, while he calmly catalogued his rock collection in there.

A second howl joined the first, even closer, and she shot to her feet, staring wide-eyed at the periphery of the firelight. Two of them? What if there were even more? Was she about to be devoured by a pack of wild wolves, while Ethan Brody did nothing?

Forget all this stoicism, she decided, as the two howlers out there attempted some primitive bloodcurdling harmony. They sounded even closer.

How did one knock on a tent?

She stood there at the entrance, teeth chattering now more from fear than cold, and cleared her throat loudly. She waited two beats, then drew open the canvas flap. "Excuse me," she said.

Ethan looked up from his seated position on a rolled-up sleeping bag, notebook in lap. "Yes?"

"Sorry to bother you, but I was curious," she said, all nonchalance. "You said one of you always stayed out here at the site to guard it. Do you mind telling me . . . guard it from what?"

He seemed amused, damn him. "Well, from looters, actually. Not that there's anything of great monetary value that could be carried off from this particular site, but you never know. Some of the locals resent us coming onto their turf and removing artifacts they could sell themselves. So often enough there is a lot of thievery when a new site's discovered."

Stacy nodded. Behind her in the desert wilderness the Everly Brothers of the wolf kingdom hit another harmonized high note. "Looters," she repeated. "Anything else?"

Ethan listened for a moment. "If it's those coyotes you're worried about, you can relax. They won't come near a camp fire like ours."

"Oh," Stacy said, somewhat relieved. "Of course not. I knew that. Well, sorry to disturb you."

He nodded. "I'm almost done," he said.

"Take your time." The coyotes howled again, and she managed to force back an involuntary flinch. "I'll be...ah, around."

"Good," he said. "If you do happen to spot a mountain lion out there, though, give me a holler."

She paused in midturn. "A what?"

"Zack said he thought he saw a mountain lion nosing around up in the caves last week. I doubt he'd still be here, but you never know."

Stacy swallowed. "What...would a mountain lion look like?"

"Big," Ethan said. "You'd know it if you saw it." He gave her a little smile and returned to his work. Stacy let the flap fall and walked stiffly back to the camp fire, her eyes darting in all directions. Funny guy. Real cute. He knew how to make a girl feel at home, didn't he?

Mercifully the coyotes finished their brief concert, and all was quiet again. After a few minutes of that she wasn't sure which was worse. She had a sudden fierce longing for the familiar horn beeps, sirens and braking swerves that accompanied any given night in her apartment. Here each subtle rise in the wind made her imagine the stealthy feet of an approaching mountain lion.

There was a nice-sized piece of wood in the small pile nearby. Stacy hoisted it and dropped it into the diminished fire. In a shower of sparks it was soon aflame. Satisfied, she stood back.

"Good idea."

Ethan's voice startled her so that she jumped a few inches. Stacy hugged herself, turning from the firelight to face him. "It was getting kind of low," she said.

Ethan nodded. "Well, that piece ought to do for the rest of the night."

"You mean, we let it go out—later?" she asked.

Ethan smiled. "You'll be safe," he said.

"I wasn't worried," she insisted. They both watched the wood burn. "But just out of curiosity," she resumed after a moment, "what other kinds of, ah, creatures should I be aware of around here?"

"Snakes," he said promptly. "We see our share of rattlers this time of year. Occasionally a big diamondback.

You might come across a scorpion or two...some lizards, beetles. Nighttime, you have your occasional bat, owl, maybe a kangaroo rat.''

"Kangaroo rat?" she echoed, not even wanting to think about the other horrible animals that had headed his list. She'd gotten used to spotting the occasional mouse in New York City, but...

"Cute little guys, actually," Ethan said. "You see 'em bouncing around the dunes like furry Ping-Pong balls. They can leap two feet in the air."

"Great," she murmured. "You wouldn't be making this up, just so I'd be entertained and amused, would you?"

Ethan chuckled. "No, it's all true. Any hot water left?" He was ambling around the fire to the blackened kettle that was set on a rock inside the cooking stones.

"I think so." She watched him prepare a cup of Nestle's cocoa, thinking it an odd but logical choice on a night like this. "Enough for two?"

Ethan nodded. "I'll get you a cup."

"No, don't bother," she began, but he was already sauntering off into the darkness. She listened to him rummage around in his tent. It was a comforting sound, somehow. She realized this was the first moment she'd felt relaxed since her arrival. It was finally just the two of them, and they would have a chance to sort things out.

Momentary optimism buoyed her spirits and even gave her courage to move beyond the immediate periphery of the fire. She stood in the shadows, gazing up at the stars. It seemed as if not an inch of sky was empty. You could even see the Milky Way.

"Amazing, aren't they?" He was back, tin cup in hand. "Here, hold this napkin around it so your hand doesn't..."

"Thanks," she said, taking the cup of cocoa from him. She smiled at Ethan and was rewarded with a hint of a smile in return. Then he, too, looked away to regard the sky.

"In the city, there's so much reflection from the lights you can't see half of what's up there," he said. "Plus the pollution gets in the way."

"I guess that's one of the rewards of working in these kinds of places," she said.

Ethan nodded. "More stars to see, cleaner air, sure. It's a dividend."

They were both standing there gazing up at the panoply of distant planets and galaxies, with all of about a foot between them. It seemed simultaneously ludicrous and sad to her. Shouldn't he be holding her in his arms? Wouldn't it feel nicer, warmer, much more satisfying, even thrilling, to be looking up at this beautiful night together?

It was possible that Ethan had had the same thought, but his reaction was to move away. Stifling a sigh, Stacy followed his lead, moving back toward the fire with an air of studied nonchalance. "You must see some great sunrises out here," she ventured.

"The best."

So they were essentially talking about the weather. Stacy fought back a mounting surge of exasperation. Ethan was looking into the fire with a distracted expression, absently turning the cocoa cup in his hand. Clearly she would have to pave the way here.

"Are we not supposed to talk to each other?"

"We're talking," he said.

"About what's happened," she said. "Do I get a chance to explain now?"

He shrugged. "Explain away."

She bridled at the way he seemed so absolutely disinterested, but she did know better. "That magazine article." She hurried on before he had time to do much more than look her way. "The things I said in it, I never said to a reporter. I was on the phone talking to Eva. You remember my friend Eva?''

"Sure."

"And at the time I'd just met you, practically, and I had no intention of getting romantically involved with you or anyone, for that matter, so..."

She kept talking. But was he listening?

She talked on. Ethan stared into the fire, not saying anything, while she hurried on, explaining Christopher and the office politics. She talked about Richard's hiring the photographers without telling her. But through it all Ethan merely stood, as if listening to a story being told about a stranger.

"Ethan?"

Stacy drew closer. Ethan turned at last, focusing his eyes on some point to the left of her. "Yes?"

"Is any of this making sense? Am I getting through?"

He shrugged. "I understand why you did what you did," he said diffidently. "It doesn't mean I like it."

"I don't blame you," she said. "But if I'd known you better, if you and I had been closer, sooner..."

"You would've had Richard call off the photographers? Even if it meant jeopardizing your job?"

She stared at him. "I would have told *you*," she said. "And we could've avoided them together. Like we did that day at the museum."

"I thought we were close enough," he said grimly. "Even then. I was putting a lot of trust in you."

Stacy sighed. Why were men so difficult when it came to matters of pride? "Doesn't it mean anything to you that I'm apologizing *now*? That I've come all this way to see you?"

"You want to feel better about it," he said.

"Ethan!" Anger got the better of her, and the words were out of her mouth before she thought about them.

"Would you stop being such a thick-skinned dimwit and listen to me?"

Ethan's glower in the firelight was a scary shade of red. "Don't you mean addle-brained?"

"Well, you *are*!" she cried in frustration. "If you weren't being so pigheadedly defensive, maybe you'd understand what this is all about!"

"The only thing I don't understand," he said, "is why you slept with me so late in the game. I mean, you could've cinched things a lot sooner that way. Then I really would've been putty in your hands."

Her hand came up as if of its own volition. She delivered the slap across his cheek so hard and so fast that she was as shocked as he was. It probably hurt her equally, too, she reflected, judging by the way her palm smarted. The last thing she saw before her eyes filled with tears was the startled look on his face.

Then she turned away. There was no way he was going to get the satisfaction of seeing her cry. He was a mean-spirited ogre of a man, and she couldn't imagine why she'd ever thought he was worth this ridiculous effort she'd made. The thought of the time she was wasting in making a complete fool of herself brought the anger back up and that was enough, mercifully, to stop her from sobbing.

"Stacy..."

She could feel him standing behind her, so she moved away. "You're right," she said, wiping hurriedly at the corner of her eye with her still-stinging hand. "I never should've come out here to see you."

ETHAN STOOD a few yards outside the tent, staring at the flickering shadows on the canvas. Well done, he thought ruefully. Yes, he'd done an excellent job of screwing everything up, making the situation worse than it had been before.

As he watched, the light of Stacy's lantern went out. She was settled into her sleeping bag and he was out here, wishing he could have magically rewound this evening to an hour before. He hadn't meant things to go this way. But here they were, an angry, hurt woman in one tent, and himself pacing around the other, feeling as if he wanted to crawl into a hole.

Why hadn't he just listened to her apology, forgiven her and left it at that? Or more likely, ended up zipping their two sleeping bags together for a far more enjoyable end of a cold desert evening? He was a fool. All he really wanted was to take her into his arms again.

But wasn't that what had gotten him in trouble in the first place? He poked at the coal-like embers with a piece of kindling. He understood about Eva. He understood, too well, about Christopher. Even archaeologists could share war stories about the competition and laurel-snatching that went on in the field.

But the hired photographers, that still irked him, even though intellectually he comprehended her rationale. It wasn't so much the specific lie of it—that she knew and didn't say. It was that Stacy *could* be so duplicitous. How were you supposed to trust a woman like that?

He couldn't shake the feeling that she had to be doing all of this for some ulterior motive. He tried to remind himself that Stacy, unlike, say, Lucille, didn't have to forge her career out of Ethan Brody's contacts. But paranoid or not, he'd kept waiting for the other shoe to drop. Had she really come out all this way just to tell him she was sorry?

Ethan shook his head, exhaustion seeping into his already tired muscles. On a normal night he'd have been asleep by now. Chances were sleep wasn't about to come easily tonight, not when he was busy kicking himself.

But damn it, she'd asked for it, hadn't she? And what was he supposed to think? Stacy Morrison was an alien breed, he reminded himself. They had barely anything in common. If the truth were known, he'd only been protecting himself from further complication and heartache.

Because once he did forgive her, and stop beating himself up for having fallen so completely under her citified sirenlike spell, then he was in real trouble, wasn't he? He'd be wide open for the rest of it—the loving, the giving, the vulnerability—all the things he'd done with Lucille that had ended up making him such a miserable guy.

But Stacy was different, right?

Who knew? And the more he thought about New York City, that fast crowd she seemed to hang out with in clubs and galleries, the bewildering cosmopolitan environment that he couldn't imagine settling down in, the more it seemed that there was no way he'd stand a chance of having a serious relationship with a woman like her.

Bachelorhood. Celibacy. That was the answer.

These were the entirely unsoothing thoughts in his head as he unrolled his own sleeping bag and went through the motions of preparing for bed. In a matter of minutes he was flat on his back with his eyes staring at the darkness, absolutely awake.

Some plan had to be formed. Some decision had to be made. All right, he'd apologize for the words said in anger. He'd try to make peace between them. And then . . . ?

He'd convince her that once they felt okay about what had happened—if that was possible—she should be on her merry way. And if she resisted? Ethan rubbed his head, then smiled ruefully as the logical response occurred to him.

Why, all she had to do was spend a day on the site with him to realize this just wasn't where she belonged. Stacy Morrison, junior archaeologist? Come on! She'd hate it here. She'd see that this wasn't the life for her and would feel better about the two of them parting ways again, for good.

Then they'd both be better off.

Chapter Twelve

He hadn't been kidding about the crack of dawn.

It seemed barely light out when Stacy emerged from her tent to find Ethan cooking up breakfast over a freshly built fire. She'd slept in her clothes, so she changed quickly into a clean shirt, shivering in the morning chill. A glance in her compact mirror showed her a face that had clearly not had enough sleep. Stacy applied some fresh lipstick and eye makeup. Even if he didn't care, she was going to look her best.

She'd stepped out of her little desert sanctuary with some trepidation. But there he was, cheerfully humming as he cooked what smelled like eggs and bacon in a big black pan, looking fine, fit and even ... friendly?

"Hungry?" he called.

Stacy nodded uncertainly. She was ravenous. "A little," she admitted. The smell of fresh coffee made her nearly swoon in anticipation.

"I hope you like fried eggs," he said. "It's about all I know how to make."

"Sounds good," she said, still keeping her distance. Was Ethan Brody some kind of Jekyll and Hyde? Now he was holding his fingers up in a familiar V sign.

"Peace," he said.

"Peace?"

"I'm sorry if I hurt your feelings last night," he went on, while still expertly applying a spatula to the pan on the fire. "You know I didn't mean half of what I said."

"I do?" she asked. His look was almost plaintive. All right, she'd meet him halfway. "Oh. Yes, I guess so," she allowed.

"This emotional stuff. I'm not good at it," he muttered. "But I did want you to know I'm sorry. And I do believe, you know, that you're sorry, too. About that business in New York."

Too peculiar. She couldn't have written a better script for him herself, but even as she felt a wave of relief, she felt the beginnings of new anxiety. What was going on with this man? Was she ever going to be able to successfully decipher his inner psychology? Did she want to?

He looked absolutely smashing in brown corduroys and a red-and-black-checked lumberjack shirt, his hair unkempt and falling over his eyes. Of course she wanted to. Stacy stepped closer to the fire, thankful for the warmth. "When does it start heating up around here?" she asked.

"Within the next couple of hours," he said. "Coffee?"

"Thanks, I'll get it." She hurried over to take charge of the kettle. He was carefully transferring two perfect sunny-side-up eggs onto a paper plate. Some strips of bacon drained on a nearby paper towel.

"You must have slept really well," she said, nodding a thanks as he gave her the plate.

"Hmm?"

"I mean, you seem a lot happier this morning. About my being here. Did I miss something?"

"No," he said airily, putting some bacon onto his own plate. "I just had a chance to think things over, that's all. And I realized there was no reason to be bearing grudges. I mean, we're better putting the whole thing behind us, aren't we?"

Stacy nodded slowly. "I'm glad you feel that way."

"Although I'd understand it perfectly if you wanted to get back to the city this morning."

Aha. So was that his gambit—I'm sorry, you're sorry, shake hands and see you 'round? Not so fast, Professor. "I'm not in a major rush," she said.

"Well, whatever you want to do," he said, intent on spearing a piece of bacon with his fork.

Stacy watched him, once more trying to read his inscrutable visage. She'd had time to do some thinking of her own last night, lying sleepless in Nadine's bag and worrying about scorpions and hopping rats and all, let alone the situation with Ethan. And the conclusion that she'd reached was that the man was worth one more try.

She was here, wasn't she? And a deeply rooted intuition told her that if he could be as angry as he was, as hurt as he'd obviously been—then he obviously cared about her. So she wasn't about to let him scare her off that easily, not until she'd determined for sure whether or not they really had the basis for a relationship.

"I thought I'd stay the day at least," she said. "I've never seen real archaeologists at work. And Nadine was saying you'd been shorthanded, anyway."

Ethan looked at her, one eyebrow raised. "You mean you want to help out?"

"If there's anything a lay person like me can do, sure," she said, meeting that skeptical look of his with a defiant gaze of her own.

Ethan shrugged. "You're welcome to pitch in," he said amiably. "But..."

His eyes were lingering on her hands. Stacy looked down, wondering, then comprehended. Her nails. Well, she could stand a broken nail or two, if it came to that. "I'd love to pitch in," she said. "What do I do?"

"FLAGGING, tagging and bagging," said Pierce. "That's the main business."

Flagging what? she wondered, but merely nodded. Pierce was acting as site tour guide, and he'd been informative so far. She'd let him get to it. No reason to reveal the true depths of her ignorance, unless she absolutely had to. "Is that what's going on up there?" she asked him, pointing at the caves.

"No, they've been getting illustrations and photos of the petroglyphs," Pierce said. "Wall paintings. Ethan take you up there yet?" Stacy shook her head. "Well, you'll see 'em at some point. Meanwhile, let's see who needs a hand."

The rest of the crew had arrived around seven-thirty that morning. She and Ethan had neatly tap-danced their way around the edges of any real conversation until their arrival. Then the professor had turned her over to Pierce, before going up into the caves with Zack for a last inspection.

Pierce, she discovered, was Zack's equivalent of her Russell. An aspiring archaeologist, he was a graduate student from UCLA and this was on-the-job training for him. He was enjoying the opportunity to show off his knowledge as he guided Stacy around the site.

"That's Collins and Teller," he said, pointing at two men working some fifty yards from the base of the rocks. "Surveyors. They've been making maps of the site. Collins is the blond-haired guy with the notebook in his hand, looking through that transit. And Teller's the one with the stadia rod in his hand."

Teller was calling out numbers as Collins looked up from the tripod-mounted instrument that glinted in the sun, jotting them down on a spiral pad. The area they were measuring was a shallow pit carefully roped off. Teller had been holding up a metal rod at one edge of the area. He now bent down to adjust the wooden stake next to it.

"We try to be precise," Pierce explained. "Zack wasn't happy with the map they did, so they're double-checking their original calculations."

"What was in that thing?" she asked.

"Spirit sticks," Pierce said. "Pieces of wood that look like deer antlers."

"What were they used for?"

Pierce shrugged and grinned. "We're not exactly sure," he admitted. "But you find them in most of these areas where the Kuneyaay Indians were. The caves Zack found were probably religious centers of some sort. So in addition to the usual stone tools and pottery you find in these artifact scatters, things like spirit sticks turn up. Possibly symbolic implements, psychic divining rods, I guess."

"Are they valuable?"

"Not monetarily, really, no," Pierce said as they walked on. "But we've uncovered a lot of intact ollas—water jugs—some nice asphalt-covered baskets, bundles of arrow shafts, some knives. And the cave paintings are in excellent condition. So it's a worthwhile excavation, and one the S.B.I. people will have to take into consideration."

"S.B.I.?"

"This whole expedition came about because Professor Matthews was hired by a consortium interested in developing the area for a resort," Pierce explained. "As principal investigator, it's his job to determine whether there's any sites on the property of historical value that might make development problematic or even prohibitive. When the dig's over, his report—it'll be a survey of the area's cultural resources—will determine what exact areas S.B.I. might be asked to leave intact."

"Such as these caves."

"Right. There's plenty of Kuneyaay sites in the area, but Aida's in particularly good shape."

"Aida? Is that an Indian name?"

Pierce chuckled. "No, it's just that the professor's wife was singing in the cave to test out its echo when they first went in. So he named the site Aida after her, as a joke."

Nadine was up there now with her camera. Stacy had only had time for a brief conversation with her new friend before the professor's wife was climbing up the scaffold for some last shots of the cave. She envied the easygoing camaraderie she had with Zack, and couldn't help fantasizing a time when she and Ethan might share that kind of closeness.

At the moment she didn't even know where Ethan was. "Tell you what," Pierce was saying. "Why don't we put you to work on that telephone booth over there?"

Stacy squinted at the cactus-surrounded area he was pointing to, puzzled. There wasn't any phone in sight, just one of the other archaeologists digging a hole. "It's the nickname for a test unit," Pierce explained, seeing her perplexed look. "An excavation that's about one meter by one meter. Sandy's over there, bagging the last bits of a surface scatter we found yesterday."

"Okay," she said doubtfully. "But what do I do?"

"Simple," said Pierce. "You take a good hard look at a pile of dirt."

STACY WIPED the sweat from her brow as the late-morning sun beat down inexorably on her weary shoulders. The mesh screen in her hands seemed to weigh a lot more now than it had a few hours back. For a while there, sifting through ten centimeters of dirt had been almost fun, but by now it was definitely Work with a capital *W*.

She wasn't going to complain. She had in her mind a list of things she *could* complain about, including two broken nails, calluses developing on her palms, a few splinters and cuts, the itchiness of her sweat-soaked shirt sticking to her back, and the aching muscles in her arms. But she refused to say one word about any of it. She'd show him she could take it, come hell or high water. Not that there was much water for miles around. Hell, on the other hand . . .

A strangely shaped piece of rock caught her eye. Sandy was still digging nearby, and he'd given her very precise instructions as to what to look for. He'd been helpful but short on conversation. She had a sense that the stocky graduate student didn't understand what a woman like her was doing in a place like this and wasn't sure if he liked it. So after the first few questions, she'd tried to forge ahead on her own.

Stacy put down the screen. She'd been picking bits of rock and what turned out to be flint arrowheads and potsherds out of the dirt he'd dug, carefully sifting through each half inch of soil. She'd flagged—identified the location of—a number of such things, then tagged it—having Sandy add it to his notes and sketch of the unit—before bagging it: putting the ancient bit of stone into a plastic artifact bag.

These apparently were the nuts and bolts of archaeology. Kind of a bore after a while. Somewhere in New York, a condo was probably going up for grabs. Decisions were being made about film festivals. And here she was, mesh screen in hand, her nose stuck in a pile of dirt.

For what? To prove a point to someone who wasn't even looking. Had she entirely lost her mind?

"Lunchtime!" Nadine was striding toward them, a couple of gleaming soda cans under her arm.

"I like the sound of that," Stacy said with a sigh, wiping her hands on what had once been a nice pair of Banana Republic pleated khaki pants. "Thanks," she added, taking the can of soda and noting that Nadine had given them both Diet Cokes and Sandy a regular.

"What've you got there?" Nadine asked, pointing at the stone in Stacy's other hand.

"I believe it's a broken arrow shaft from the post-Mayan era," Stacy said dryly, examining the dark stone. "Either that or a worthless rock."

Nadine laughed, taking it from her. "Right you are," she pronounced. "Flint arrow shaft. Hey, Sandy, is she a quick study or what?"

Sandy grunted a grudging assent, seemingly more interested in drinking an entire can of Coke in one long swallow. "What's for lunch?" Stacy asked.

"Sandwiches. Ham, salami, cheese. Fruit. More soda. Come on over. You can pick out your personal preference."

Grateful for the reprieve, she left the "phone booth" and walked back to the camp fire area near the scaffolding, where other crew members were already munching on sandwiches. She picked out a ham and cheese and dug in, suddenly realizing how starved she was.

The food and drink were fast transforming her back into a human being, as opposed to a dirt-burrowing machine. "Where's Ethan?" she asked, looking around.

"He went thataway," Nadine said, pointing down at the other end of the sloping rock formation. "There's one small outcrop up there he wanted to double-check. Thinks Zack might've overlooked another possible cave site."

"Has he eaten?" Stacy asked. Nadine shook her head. "I'll bring him lunch," Stacy said.

"Good idea," Nadine responded, nodding approval. "Here, take one of these, and an apple and a tangerine."

Stacy hurried through the remains of her own sandwich, and then, paper bag filled with food and drink for Ethan, set off to find him. He was apparently climbing around the rocks at the other end of this hill of stone, and hadn't heard the call for lunch. He'd surely be pleased to see her. Wasn't this a friendly, caring, even domestic thing to do?

She trudged on, leaving the campsite behind. The base of the rock formation was lined with spiky cacti, a deep vivid green against the orange sandstone. There were giant fluffy white clouds scudding across a Technicolor-blue sky. Alone in the scrub, she enjoyed the sensation of being off on an adventure, the heroine of her own Western. Wasn't this the kind of country where John Ford had shot all those John Wayne pictures?

Here was the valiant frontier woman, lunch in hand for her hardworking cowboy. Stacy laughed aloud at the clichéd stereotype. Frontier woman from the Upper East Side, right. But she enjoyed the image, half expecting to see a horse-drawn covered wagon kicking up dust over the dunes.

"Ethan?" She was at the edge of the mesalike hill of rock now, and thought she could hear him rustling around above her head. "Ethan!"

Her voice echoed against the rock. After a moment he appeared, some thirty feet above her, peering down over the edge. "Hi!" he called down, looking surprised. "What brings you out here?"

She held up the paper bag. "Lunch," she called. "You want to come down? Or should I come up there?"

The smile he gave her made the morning's work seem worthwhile. "Hey, thanks," he said. "No, stay there, it's not an easy climb."

"I'll meet you halfway," she said, spying a cluster of rocks that formed a natural path of rising steps.

"Hey, you don't have to—"

"I'm on my way." She walked over, looking down at herself to make sure that all the requisite dirt smudges were easily visible. Yes, she was clearly a hardworking field hand, not at all a prissy city slicker. She was ready to talk arrowheads and—

What was that? She paused as she stepped onto the first rock, alerted by an odd sound that was a bit like chattering teeth, or... a rattle?

Stacy froze. She didn't have to look very far. She felt the color drain from her cheeks as she stared at the horrific-looking coiled reptile that was only a yard or two away on the next rock. She'd never been face-to-face with one before, but she surely knew a rattlesnake when she saw one.

And heard one. What a terrifying noise! Its tail was in the air, flicking back and forth as the snake's head rose, beady little eyes fixed on hers, spiky tongue inching out as it got ready to attack. Petrified, she could only stare in dread fascination, too frightened to run or heave the bag in her hand at the snake's ugly head.

They were fast, weren't they? Poisonous. Deadly? Stacy moved not a muscle, waiting for her life to start passing in front of her eyes. What a way to go. But she couldn't just stand there, could she? She had to move.

She put one foot back. Oh, no. The snake reared its head, the rattle seeming to grow even louder.

But it wasn't as loud as the gunshot. Even as she yelped, the snake was writhing in the air, then dropping back, a bloody mess where its awful head had been.

Stacy Morrison had never fainted in her life. But for a moment she felt a genuine swoon coming on. Only one thought kept her from giving into the sensation: Ethan Brody was watching.

For once, her knowledge of old movie heroines in Westerns really came in handy. She took a deep breath and steadied herself on her feet. In her best cool Barbara Stanwyck manner, she raised her eyes to meet Ethan's. He was standing on a rock ledge some twenty feet above, pistol in hand.

"Nice shot," she said, as if, well, he could've done better, and she'd seen better, but he'd done all right, for a guy.

Ethan stared down at her with a look that was priceless. He'd obviously expected her to scream for a week, or at least collapse. His face showed a range of emotions, from solicitous sympathy tinged with masculine indulgence at feminine weakness to bemused skepticism. "Are you all right?"

"Of course I'm all right," she said, giving her hair a flip. That was maybe a bit too much, but it was effective. Ethan's expression shifted into genuine appreciation. Emboldened, she continued acting the part. "That snake's coyote meat now, but I'm fine," she observed. "Are you coming down for lunch?"

Ethan opened his mouth, closed it, and merely nodded. Then he disappeared from sight as he began his descent. Now that he was gone, Stacy allowed herself a moment's relaxation. As soon as she untensed her muscles, she began shaking like a leaf.

The dead snake was only a few feet away, still twitching feebly as she dared a glance. The other impulse was to become violently ill, but she managed to fend off the nausea, stepping quickly past the rattler's corpse. Clutching Ethan's paper bag, she carefully made her way over the flat rocks, wanting to meet him halfway as she'd originally promised.

Impersonating a nerves-like-steel Western heroine did have other benefits. She actually felt calmer than she'd normally have felt, given the day's events. She'd almost stopped trembling, and was trying to think up cavalier jokes to crack about her brush with death as she came around the side of the sloping sandstone.

There he was, only a few yards above her head, climbing down the rock face, one plateau level up. She searched for a cool, calm and collected conversational gambit. "Is it hotter than yesterday or am I imagining it?" she asked. There you go—talk about the weather.

Ethan didn't glance over, intent on getting a firmer toehold on the rock. "You're just here earlier," he said, uttering a little grunt as he stretched out his leg. "It gets a lot hotter."

Stacy saw it before he did, but barely had time to react. The rock he'd just put his foot on had loosened under his weight. Before she could even cry out a warning, it had given way entirely. Right before her eyes Ethan was suddenly flailing in the air.

He fell to the ground before her with a sickening thud, twisting as he went. Amazingly, he landed on his feet, but the force of the fall made him lose his balance. Stacy dashed over to his crumpled form. "Ethan!"

He was lying on the rock, holding his leg. She knelt by him as he lay back, face briefly contorted. When he took his hand away from his shin she saw the blood. Again she had to stifle an impulse to give way to hysteria.

"I'm okay, I'm okay," he was muttering between clenched teeth. She knelt closer, reaching for the bottom of his trouser legs.

"Let's see that cut," she said.

"Sheer stupidity," he said. "I should've seen those rocks were too loose."

"If you had eyes in your feet, yes," she murmured, gingerly pushing up the pants leg. He'd cut his shin, probably in a scrape against the rock face while falling. She reached into her pocket for the bandanna she'd been using as a handkerchief. "Does it hurt a lot?"

Ethan shook his head. "No. Hey, you don't have to—"

"Quiet," she said, carefully dabbing at his bloodied skin. The cut didn't seem that bad, but it was enough of a gash to cause concern. "Can you move your foot?" she asked. "Try it."

Ethan wiggled his ankle, lips tight. "It's all right," he said. "Just a scratch."

"More than a scratch," she corrected him. "Though I don't think we're talking stitches. What about the rest of you?"

"Let's see," he said, and slowly sat up, Stacy grabbing his arm to help him.

"You seemed to land okay," she said nervously.

"I've never felt better," Ethan said, with a rueful smile. "Scraped my elbow, but nothing's broken, that's for sure. Hey, what are you doing?"

"You're going to bleed all over these nice macho boots of yours," she said, tying the bandanna tightly around his wound.

"Thanks," he muttered, then put a hand down, trying to stand up. Of course he was too proud to ask for help.

"Hold on," she said, annoyed. She came around his side and, kneeling, draped his arm over her shoulder. "Okay, now try it."

She hoisted him upright, nearly stumbling beneath his weight. Ethan grabbed hold of the rock face to steady them. "That's fine, thanks," he wheezed, and stepped away. But almost instantly he tottered on his feet. Stacy lunged to get his arm again. "Can't put weight on it," he said.

"Well, then lean on me," Stacy said.

Ethan looked at her, then glanced down the descending steps of rock. He shook his head. "No," he said. "You'd better go back over to Aida and get Matthews or one of the other guys."

"What for?"

He frowned. "No offense, but it's a bit of a ways down from here."

"Are you saying I won't be able to do it?" she asked.

"Well, it would be easier—"

"Come on," she said. "I can do it."

"Stacy..."

"Stop standing around dripping blood on these nice rocks, put your arm around my shoulder and let's go," she said defiantly.

Ethan hesitated, then thought better of arguing. He did as she'd told him, and Stacy began their descent. Ethan wasn't exactly deadweight, but the pressure of him around her shoulder and his slow one-legged progress did make it slow and difficult.

A number of times she nearly stumbled and lost her balance and scraped her palms raw, grabbing at rocks to steady them. But she was determined to get down without mishap. It was now a matter of principle.

Ethan, thankfully, made not a noise of complaint or apprehension as they made their slow way down from the rock formation. It seemed a lot longer going down than it had going up. They were both silent but for heaving breathing and the occasional grunt of effort.

He asked her twice if she wanted to rest, but Stacy shook her head. In truth, she was afraid that if she stopped, she wouldn't want to start again. But at last the green cacti and the sandy ground were within reach. On the final step they paused, Stacy helping Ethan to sit down, dangling his bad leg over the side of the rock face.

"Thank you," Ethan said.

"You're welcome," she said. "Would you like a not exactly ice-cold soda now?"

He'd kept a firm grip on the paper bag during their descent. With a smile he opened it now. "Share it with you," he offered.

Stacy shook her head. "I only drink Diet."

"You're out of your mind," he said.

"You're right," she agreed. "Give me a sip."

Chuckling, Ethan handed her the can. Stacy took a long gulp, reveling in the cold carbonation. She was soaked in sweat, she realized, her shirt feeling wet from collar to tail. "*Now* you can get someone," Ethan said.

"What do you mean?" She handed back the can.

"I mean I appreciate your superhuman efforts in getting me down that rock," he said. "But now why don't you go back to the site and get one of the guys? I'm not going to be able to walk back on my own."

"I *am* one of the guys," she said, drawing herself up in self-righteous indignation.

"Stacy Morrison," he began.

"Professor Ethan Brody," she interrupted. "I am simply not going to leave you out here in the middle of the desert with snakes and scorpions to contend with while I go running back to get someone else to do a job I'm perfectly capable of doing, as you should know by now."

Ethan sighed. "Have you always been this stubborn?"

"You bring it out in me," she said. "Would you like to eat your lunch now, or save it for when we make our dramatic return to the site?"

"I'll save it," he said. "Are you sure you want to do this?"

As an answer, Stacy jumped down from the rock and looked up at him expectantly. "Come on," she said. "Kind of slide yourself down into position."

Ethan did as he was told. She got an arm around him as he draped his arm over her shoulder, and they began the slow trek back to Aida. Again, she hadn't realized how far she'd walked earlier. Now, at this slow pace, it seemed as if they'd walked a mile when they'd only gone some fifty yards. And it seemed they still had a mile to go.

"It's a wonderful life, isn't it?" Ethan said as they trudged along. "These desert digs."

"I haven't had this much fun in ages," she told him. She was conscious that he, too, was soaked in sweat, and the odd thing was, she didn't mind the scent of his perspiration. In fact, she rather liked it. Heat, fatigue, the weight of him, the long stretch of sand ahead—none of that diminished the strangely buoyant feeling that swelled up in her as they struggled onward. She really was glad to be here, helping him. This meant she was clearly in love, because that kind of thinking otherwise was pure insanity.

"Well, it seems to have brought us a lot closer," he quipped.

Stacy laughed. "Yes, it has."

"You seem to have a lot of muscle for a city girl," he noted.

"I work out," she informed him. "At a gym. Twice a week when I can."

"It's paid off," he said. "Am I hurting your shoulder?"

"Absolutely not," she said, though she did feel as if his arm was slowly wearing a soft groove into it.

He was silent for a while as they continued. Then, under his breath, more to himself than to her, it seemed, she heard him say, "All right, Morrison. I owe you one."

That in itself, she decided, had made this entire trip worthwhile.

HE MUST HAVE dozed off, Ethan realized. He sat up with a start within the tent. From the light he saw through the open flap he could tell it was already near sunset, and he could smell franks and beans on the fire. It wasn't like him to have taken a nap, but he imagined it was due to his having had so little sleep the night before.

Feeling disoriented, he looked around for the walking stick Zachary had given him to use as a makeshift crutch. He'd been dreaming about Stacy. This was not in itself unusual these days, but the content of the dream had been odd. They'd been together in New York again, only it seemed as if they were actually living in New York. And he'd been enjoying that fact.

Odd, indeed. Ethan looked at the small bandage around his ankle and tested putting weight on that foot. It was already easier. He smiled suddenly, remembering the look on everyone's face when he and Stacy had hobbled into camp together, and the way Stacy had shrugged off the whole incident as if dragging a man across a half mile of desert was all in a day's work.

Ethan got to his feet, wondering where she was now. He'd thanked her for her help, of course, but that wasn't all he wanted to do. He wanted to let her know...

What? Ethan paused, running a hand through his tousled hair. It seemed that he'd fallen asleep thinking about her, dreamed about her, and woken up thinking about her, as if his unconscious and conscious mind were conspiring together to force him toward an inescapable conclusion. He couldn't stay angry at her.

He didn't even want to anymore. It had finally sunk in that she wasn't here for any other reason than that she really did care about him. That thought gave him a wonderful feeling, one he wouldn't venture analyzing, but he certainly liked it a lot better than the emotional torment he'd been feeling before.

The surprising thing was—but then, what was Stacy, if not consistently surprising?—that she had somehow overcome all of his prejudices in such a short time. He could've sworn she wouldn't last a minute working on a dig like this. He would've predicted she'd get the point that she didn't belong in this world, and that she'd have high-tailed it out of here hours and hours ago.

But there she was, looking impossibly radiant for someone who'd survived the long day she'd been through, sitting by the fire with Nadine and Zack, a paper plate in her hand. She hadn't noticed him yet as he emerged from the tent, so he had a chance to observe her.

She still looked a little like a transplanted Manhattanite, with her sneakers, her fashionable khaki pants and that shirt, which probably had a famous designer's name on the collar. But she also looked perfectly at ease with the rest of the crew. She was laughing at something Nadine had said as she caught Zack's eye, and then almost instantly was on her feet.

"Hey, it's the walking wounded!"

"Don't get up," he said, waving her back down as he hobbled over with the walking stick. "What'd I miss?"

"Just a grueling cleanup," Zack said. "Nice move, getting incapacitated at a time like this. You didn't have to lift a finger." He gestured at the neat piles of metal piping that had been the scaffolding.

"Yeah, I planned it that way," Ethan said, taking a seat next to Stacy.

"Franks and beans?" Nadine asked.

"Sure." He leaned over to look at the various pots and pans on the fire. "Hey, Pierce, what are you cooking up there?"

"Something special," Pierce said, digging into his pot with a long fork. "And it's ready. Here, give me a few plates."

Nadine passed them along as Ethan quizzed Zack on the camp cleanup he'd slept through. Everything had gone smoothly. The site machinery was dismantled, the various caves and test units mapped and catalogued. Collins and one of the other grads were already loading up Zack's

Land Rover with some of the heavier equipment, ready to make a run to where the trucks were parked.

"What is this?" Stacy held up her first forkful of Pierce's stew, a small chunk of meat on its tines.

"You don't recognize it?" Pierce grinned, and some of the other crew members laughed.

Ethan looked down at the stew in his plate and suddenly understood. "Stacy," he said. "You might not want—"

"It's a local delicacy," Pierce said. "Go on, see if you like the taste."

She was about to put the fork to her mouth, but Ethan's hand stayed her arm. "Stacy," he repeated. "I don't think . . ."

"Why?" She looked at Pierce. "Come on, what kind of stew *is* this?"

"Rattlesnake," Nadine said. "Pierce went back and picked up that big fella that nearly attacked you."

"It's delicious," Pierce said.

Stacy blanched, involuntarily dropping the fork onto her plate, to the delighted chuckles of the men around the camp fire. Pierce shrugged, making a great show of spooning a healthy chunk onto his own plate and taking a bite. He chewed happily.

"A little tough," he announced. "But good."

"Not my favorite," Nadine said dryly.

Ethan was watching Stacy. She glanced at him briefly, then picked up her fork again. "Oh, what the hell," she said. "I'm game."

And this was the woman he'd thought wouldn't last a minute on a dig like this? Once more, Ethan's hand stopped her in midtrajectory. "All right," he said.

"All right what?" She looked at him, confused.

"All right, enough," he said. "You win."

"I win?"

Ethan got up, and pulled her up with him. "That Rover loaded?" he called to Collins.

"We're on our way," Collins called back, turning on the motor.

"Hold on," Ethan said. "We need a lift."

AS ACCOMMODATIONS WENT, this one in Jacumba wasn't much more than a glorified Motel 6. It did, however, have a nice bathroom with hot and cold running water, a shower, a real bed and air-conditioning. For these simple things Stacy was overwhelmingly grateful.

"You really didn't have to do this," she told Ethan, as he turned on the lamp by the bed.

"Shut up," he said pleasantly. "I've had enough of your arguing."

"Well, really," she said, bridling. "You didn't have to practically drag me away from the campsite. I was perfectly willing to spend another night—"

"Give me a break," he said, sitting down on the bed. "You were dying to get out of there."

"I was not!" she cried, indignant, though she was almost deliriously happy to be back in civilization. Ethan was patting the bed next to him. Stacy folded her arms. "I think you're being very presumptuous."

"Oh, am I?" With a smile, he reached out and pulled her over to him.

"Hey, hey, hands off, buster," she said, without much conviction. "What is this all about, anyway?"

"I think you know," he said. "We have a lot of talking to do."

"If it's talking you're interested in, sir," she said, with an affected haughtiness, "I suggest you remove your arm from around my waist."

Ethan shook his head. "No, I like it better this way," he said. "Stacy, I've been finding it hard not to put my arms around you."

"Me? The woman who used and betrayed you?" She stared down at him.

"Okay, okay, I've been an idiot," he said, grimacing. "I should've accepted your apology sooner. Are you willing to accept *my* apology?"

"That depends," she said, feeling her heartbeat increase as he lifted his other hand to stroke her hair, a tender look in his eyes.

"You've been driving me crazy," he said. "Do you know that?"

His fingers' light caress on the line of her cheek was sending a shiver through her. Stacy grabbed hold of his hand. "*I*'ve been going crazy," she said, enjoying the feel of his warm skin pulse against hers. "I thought you were really going to let this whole thing end. Just walk away."

"Maybe I would've," he said. "If you hadn't shown up here like this."

"I guess I'm the smarter one of us, then," she teased, her body vibrant with delicious tension as he pulled her closer.

"Fine," he muttered. "I can live with that." He pulled her to him and quickly she was wrapped in his arms. As his lips closed over hers, her whole body pulsed to new life, enveloped in the warm strength of him.

She could feel his heart beating as fast as her own against her breast, and then a welling up of happiness overpowered her. Her lips sought his with a desperate eagerness. Her hands seemed to slide up around his neck of their own accord as he pulled her closer, molding her body to his. His musky, masculine scent, the sweet-salty taste of of him, the taut muscles that held her in willing captivity—all of it combined to sweep thought and pain away.

In between fervent, frenzied kisses, as her hands stole over his shoulders, gliding through his tousled hair, he whispered her name. As their kisses deepened in intensity, Ethan's hands seemed to be touching her everywhere at once in a paroxysm of aroused excitement.

"Hey." With a shuddering breath she broke away, gazing down into the tawny-dark eyes that were hooded with passion. "I thought we were going to talk."

"This is a kind of talking," he said. "Doesn't it get the basic point across?" Leaning back in his arms she could only weakly nod, and his eyes glowed with amusement and affection as he gave a deep, throaty chuckle. "I'm still in love with you. Even more than I was, if such a thing is possible. Couldn't you feel that?"

"Don't you know I love you, too? You addled-brained idiot."

"I guess I should've guessed," he muttered, and he reached up to plant a deliciously scalding trail of wet kisses along the line of her neck. Stacy let out a long sigh of pleasure, eyes half closing again, moving sinuously against him as his lips began to nuzzle the hollow of her neck and shoulder.

Stacy sighed again. "I've been miserable, you know."

"I didn't know." He looked up at her, shaking his head. "I thought I didn't really make any difference."

"No way," she said, and he smiled, giving the tip of her nose a gentle peck.

"Look, here's the point," he said. "You and me ought to be together, period. I don't care what we have to do to work out the logistics, but seeing as how we're in love with each other, we just will, that's all."

"Even though we're so completely unsuited for each other?" she murmured, ruffling his hair.

"If this is unsuited..." He shook his head. "But along 'unsuited' lines, wouldn't you like to get out of your dirty clothes and into a warm shower? And then into a nice cool bed?''

"I'll think about it."

"Think about this," he said, taking hold of both her hands and holding them to his lips. "I've been offered a teaching fellowship at Columbia. Think it might give us a chance to get to know each other, if I were to be in New York for a while?"

She stared at him; it was as though she could feel the earth shifting beneath her feet. She knew him well enough now to read the seriousness beneath his seemingly casual words. She sensed how hard it must be for him to be laying himself on the line like this.

"But . . . that's fantastic," she said. "Then I don't have to contemplate moving to Los Angeles."

Ethan blinked, his features relaxing into a bemused smile. "You weren't really . . . ?"

"I *want* you, you big dummy," she said. "Ethan, honestly, the main thing is knowing that you want *me*. I'm open to all kinds of suggestions—if love is the given."

"Love," he said, nodding, and kissed her hands again. "Yes, that's what I want to give you. Look, life's pretty short, Stacy. Don't you think both of us are entitled to a feeling like this?"

"Yes," she said.

"Then let's work it out. Let's be together," he said.

"Oh, yes—let's," she whispered, and clung to him, kissing his chin, lips, cheeks, trying in the best way she knew to erase any of the pain she'd caused him. Ethan returned her kiss, melding his lips to hers with a searing force.

She felt the power of their passion already overwhelming the bitterness and remorse, and put all of herself into the kiss, joy welling up inside her as he responded, his mouth claiming hers with renewed intensity. Finally they broke apart, Ethan gazing at her with a smile on his lips.

"I know we seem to come from different places, but when I'm with you like this..." He shook his head. "Listen, if you're really open to all kinds of suggestions," he murmured, "maybe we could discuss the two of us performing a certain sacred ceremony, to make this commitment we've been talking about official?"

"A ceremony?" Stacy's eyes widened. "Pre-Columbian or post-?"

"It's a ritual that's native to every culture," he said, "involving much celebration, with music, dancing, and the exchanging of rings."

"That sounds familiar," she said, her heart swelling as he held her gaze. "And it's a very enticing suggestion."

He let out a deep breath. "It feels right, doesn't it? After all, what we've got—it's solid somehow."

Stacy nodded, smiling. "Solid as a rock," she said. "Now kiss me again, Professor. So I can feel how right it feels...."

Harlequin American Romance

COMING NEXT MONTH

#301 CHARMED CIRCLE by Robin Francis

One relaxing month by the sea was all Zoe Piper ever expected from her four-week stay at Gull Cottage, the luxurious East Hampton mansion, but it turned out to be a month that would change her life forever. And then there was Ethan Quinn, the skeptical Scorpio with the dreamer's eyes.... The first book of the GULL COTTAGE trilogy.

#302 THE MORNING AFTER by Dallas Schulze

The morning after Lacey's thirtieth-birthday bash, her head pounded, her eyes ached—and she awoke in a Vegas hotel room. When a man groaned beside her in the bed, she thought she knew the worst. But it was yet to come. She was married—to a man she had met at her party. Last night's revelry must have affected her groom's brain—because Cameron wouldn't admit they'd made a mistake.

#303 THE FOREVER CHOICE by Patricia Cox

Christine Donovan had run away from Detective Paul Cameron, the only man who had captured her heart. Now she was face-to-face with him again as they tried to find out who was embezzling money from her aunt's perfume company. They were both determined to play it cool, but what they hadn't counted on was a love destined to be, and a criminal in the family....

#304 TURNING TABLES by Judith Arnold

Amelia's outrageous sister had done it again. But to get herself out of jail this time she hired a lawyer determined to take her case to the Supreme Court. Before the incident became fodder for the tabloids, Amelia had to stop Patrick Levine. But Patrick had his own plan—and a passionate desire to see how straitlaced Amelia would react when pushed too far.

You'll flip . . . your pages won't!
Read paperbacks *hands-free* with

Book Mate · I

The perfect "mate" for all your romance paperbacks

**Traveling · Vacationing · At Work · In Bed · Studying
· Cooking · Eating**

Perfect size for
all standard
paperbacks,
this wonderful
invention
makes reading
a pure pleasure!
Ingenious
design holds
paperback
books OPEN
and FLAT so
even wind can't
ruffle pages—
leaves your
hands free to do
other things.
Reinforced,
wipe-clean vinyl-
covered holder flexes to let you
turn pages without undoing the
strap . . . supports paperbacks so
well, they have the strength of
hardcovers!

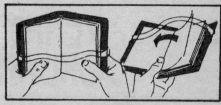

Pages turn WITHOUT
opening the strap

SEE-THROUGH STRAP

Reinforced back stays flat

Built in bookmark

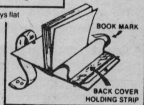

BOOK MARK

BACK COVER
HOLDING STRIP

10 x 7¼ , opened
Snaps closed for easy carrying, too

Available now. Send your name, address, and zip code, along with a check or
money order for just $5.95 + .75¢ for postage & handling (for a total of $6.70)
payable to Reader Service to:

> Reader Service
> Bookmate Offer
> 901 Fuhrmann Blvd.
> P.O. Box 1396
> Buffalo, N.Y. 14269-1396

Offer not available in Canada
* New York and Iowa residents add appropriate sales tax.

BM-G

Coming in June...

Harlequin Presents...

PENNY JORDAN

a reason for being

We invite you to join us in celebrating Harlequin's 40th Anniversary with this very special book we selected to publish worldwide.

While you read this story, millions of women in 100 countries will be reading it, too.

A Reason for Being by Penny Jordan is being published in June in the Presents series in 19 languages around the world. Join women around the world in helping us to celebrate 40 years of romance.

Penny Jordan's *A Reason for Being* is Presents June title #1180. Look for it wherever paperbacks are sold.

PENNY-1